SHADOW TOUCHED

SHADOW TOUCHED

A TOUCH OF VAMPIRE

BECKY MOYNIHAN

BROKEN
BOOKS

Published by Broken Books
www.beckymoynihan.com

ISBN-13: 978-1-7327330-6-0

Cover design by Becky Moynihan
Cover model by Ravven
www.depositphotos.com

To those who crave connection:
May you find what you're looking for
within the pages of a book.

PROLOGUE

He watched through the tinted windshield as she started up her silver Honda.

"She saw me in my true form," he said the second his drothen answered the call. "Don't worry, I took care of it. And I think you're right—she knows nothing, not even what she is. But I want to test her alone before we get the others involved."

Kade reacted strongly to the news, his shock through the phone clear.

"Yes, I know it's against protocol," he interrupted, unwavering in his decision, "but we can't fail this time. She's our last chance. Just give me a few weeks."

The Honda's lights flashed as she pulled into traffic. Ending the call, he unhurriedly pressed the ignition of his Lexus. At this hour, he knew she was headed home, having carefully studied her routine for the past four weeks.

When the tail lights faded, he adjusted his gloves and turned the steering wheel to follow her.

CHAPTER 1

Freaking fates, this place belonged in a slasher film.

The large curtainless windows were giving off "I can see you" vibes, and the ghostly blobs dotting the dark interior were excellent hiding spots for would-be axe murderers. The blobs were only white sheets draped over the furniture, but hey, they seriously made the space look creepy.

I pulled out my phone. Cue unreliable cell reception for added effect. I tapped on my social media accounts only to see the dreaded "couldn't refresh feed." Well, that sucked. There went the few friends I had.

"It's a fixer-upper, but you know how I like my projects," my aunt said cheerily for my benefit. "And, look, free furniture." She flicked on the entrance hall light—and nothing happened. With a long-suffering sigh, she fished out her phone and stepped onto the front porch, muttering, "Be right back. Gotta see if I can get an electrician out here this late."

I shrugged like it was no big deal. "I'll just be inside—" She walked off before I could finish, so I mumbled lamely to myself, "—looking for ghosts and serial killers."

Only two months and sixteen days left of this pretending, I reminded myself reassuringly. I could play my aunt's twisted game that much longer.

Pressing the flashlight icon on my phone, I began the preliminary exploration of our new home. We'd arrived sometime after midnight, having been on the road since before dawn. Aunt Tess had practically moved us across the country this time, from South Carolina to Rosewood, a small coastal town in Maine. Usually, we only hopped a state or two, picking a spot at random. But this time felt different.

Planned.

She hadn't even used a GPS to find this ramshackle house butted up against the woods. I had questions, as always, but knew better than to ask—especially this time. For once, I was pretty sure I knew what had spurred my aunt into moving again, and I wasn't about to stir the pot by demanding answers.

She was spooked, and a spooked Aunt Tess meant another move.

The sooner we could settle into this place without me making a fuss, the better. I was *done* moving against my will. Being underage sucked. It forced me to follow my aunt across the country as she uprooted me again and again, making meaningful relationships impossible. I barely tried to make new friends now. What would the point be? I would just have to leave them behind in a few months.

At nearly eighteen years of age, I no longer doubted that Aunt Tess was keeping secrets from me. Always moving for my "safety" wasn't normal. That, or she suffered from extreme paranoia. Either way, confronting her about it was pointless. She'd only become suspicious and ask if I'd seen anything weird lately.

I mean, yeah, I'd seen weird stuff. But was that really a good reason to move? This house was weird, this *move* was weird. What I saw or thought I'd seen shouldn't send my aunt into a packing frenzy.

Our new digs was a lot bigger than our last one though, set back on a private gravel drive. Too bad the white, two-story house smelled of mothballs and abandonment. Shivering in my jean shorts, I pulled my red hoodie over my thick hair, tucking the long, chestnut brown tresses behind my ears. The temperature in Maine was far colder than what we'd left behind. It was barely autumn but felt like a southern winter. I sure hoped this dump had a heating unit.

After exploring the outdated kitchen, complete with white laminate countertops and blue floral wallpaper, I opened the door leading down to a spooky basement. Listening to my morbid curiosity instead of common sense, I carefully descended the creaky wooden stairs. That typical earthy, mildew basement smell hit me and I wrinkled my nose.

At the bottom, something brushed against my hoodie and I choked back a surprised squeak. Expecting cobwebs, I blindly batted at the air and struck a solid object instead. I whipped my phone up, and the flashlight's beam revealed a swaying string. And attached to the string, dangling inches from my face, was a . . .

"Holy fates!" I jerked back and sat down hard on a dusty stair. Was that a *chicken's* foot? Okay, whoever lived here last had a sick sense of humor. "So creepy." I decided to save this part of my self tour until *after* the electricity was restored. Who knew what other surprises I'd find down here.

Hurrying back up the steps, I continued to the second floor where the bedrooms were. When I stepped into the last one with a window seat that overlooked the woods, goosebumps prickled my arms—as if my body was trying to tell me something. Yeah, that it was freaking *cold* up here. I already missed southern weather.

"Found my room, Aunt Tess!" I called, turning from the window to pull the white sheets off the furniture. Cool armoire. It had that vintage, shabby chic thing going on. When my words were met with silence, I headed downstairs again in search of my aunt.

She was pacing the driveway beside my old silver Honda, her

bright auburn hair catching the moonlight. "I didn't know what else to do," I heard her say over the phone, so I retreated inside again. Respect for privacy was rule number one in our house. But it wasn't until a couple of years ago that I'd demanded the rule go both ways.

I decided to busy myself with removing sheets, making sure no masked killers were hiding underneath them. I'd reached the dining room when something beyond the sliding doors moved. I whipped my gaze toward the backyard, heart jolting at the thought of someone watching me.

But it was only a deer.

Two of them actually, a doe and fawn, by the looks of it. The mother was too busy grazing on the overgrown lawn to notice me, so I oh-so-carefully unlocked the slider and nudged it open. The hinges soundlessly rolled back—which was unexpected, considering the state of this place—and I was able to slip outside undetected.

Turning off the flashlight, I raised my phone to snap a photo. The quality would be grainy, but I didn't often get to see wildlife this close. Our last several moves had been to small apartments in the suburbs.

As I tapped the button, the night lit up. Crap! I'd left the flash on. Startled, the mama and baby deer took off, leaping into the woods.

"Shoot." I clicked on my photos, hoping I at least got the shot. I smiled when two deer greeted me. Too bad their eyes were glowing from the flash, but . . .

Wait.

There were *three* sets of eyes. One pair was farther back in the woods. But it wasn't yellow like the others. More like a bright ruby . . .

Red.

A warning tickled my senses, followed by a memory. I quickly shoved the memory aside. There was a perfectly good explanation for this. Probably some trick of the light. I double-tapped the screen and squinted at the dark shape. Then squinted harder, willing the shape to transform into a deer. But the more I stared, the clearer it became.

There was a human in the woods.

A cold awareness skated across my skin, one I'd felt not too long ago. I fumbled to press the flashlight icon again and dropped my phone. I froze, suddenly realizing how isolated this place was. If there were houses nearby, I couldn't see them. Which meant that if I screamed . . .

Shoot. *Shoot!*

I snatched up my phone without taking my eyes off the woods. The memory came back to taunt me again, and I couldn't shake it this time. Freaking out, I whirled and dove headfirst into the house. Air whooshed from my lungs as I crashed to the floor, but I was up again in a flash, slamming the slider shut with a *thwack*.

"Kenna?" Aunt Tess's feet pounded the wood floor as she barreled into the house. "What's wrong? What happened?" Her wild gaze searched every nook and cranny as she approached.

Needing a moment to compose myself, I turned and carefully locked the door. If I told her what I saw—or what I *thought* I saw— we'd be halfway across the country by morning. And despite the creep factor of this house, something about it felt . . . right. I didn't know why, but I didn't want to leave this place yet.

So I turned and adopted an embarrassed expression before saying, "Nothing happened. I just wanted to explore outside and the door jammed."

She fixed me with one her deep, probing stares to see if I'd break, but I wouldn't. Not this time. Eventually, she sighed and let me off the hook. "Do me a favor and stay out of those woods, okay?"

"What?" I glanced out the window, pretending to notice them for the first time. "Why, are there bears in there or something?"

"Or something. Just promise me, McKenna. I'm trying to keep you safe here."

Feelings of resentment sprang up at that thinly-veiled guilt trip, as if the moves were *my* fault. I reached down and pinched my thigh *hard* to keep from saying anything I'd later regret. "Fine," I quickly muttered and looked away.

We stood in tense silence for a few moments, long enough for me to feel guilty. Argh! She had a knack for doing that to me. She released another sigh, saying, "Come on. There's no electricity or hot water, so we're gonna stay at a hotel for tonight. Hopefully everything will look brighter in the morning."

"Okay," I agreed, because there was no way I could fall asleep tonight in this house. Not without curtains on every single window.

Thankfully, after a visit from the local plumber and electrician, the house was live-in ready two days later—except we *still* didn't have curtains. Our storage container hadn't arrived yet, but we'd mastered the art of living out of suitcases for extended periods.

The one thing I hadn't quite mastered was the first day at a new school. Rosewood High would be my third school this year, but I'd purposefully lost count of how many I'd actually attended over the years. It was too depressing to think about.

I turned right on the road that led to Rosewood's small but picturesque downtown, following the directions Aunt Tess had written down for me before I left. With all the pine trees near our house, cell reception was still poor, including the GPS. I wondered if it would make her job difficult, since she often worked remotely as an interior design consultant. At least her car was arriving any day now, so she could work from a shop in town if need be.

I eyed the quaint and colorful stores along Maine Street, wondering if any of them had side jobs available that paid in cash. It was the only way I could save a little money since Aunt Tess wouldn't let me get a job. The only thing she'd finally caved on was letting me have a car earlier this year.

But I needed more money. That way, I'd be ready to strike out on my own the day I turned eighteen, the day I'd been counting down to for the last three years.

My trusty Honda traversed the windy roads with ease, allowing me to continue dwelling on my thoughts. Aunt Tess had been right. Things *had* looked brighter in the morning, and I'd put the red eyes in the woods incident behind me. I was determined to believe they belonged to a neighbor or hunter wandering the forest. Although, if they were attempting to shoot the doe, that was so not cool.

Besides that, everything else had been normal. The locals were direct yet friendly, which was refreshing. The town itself had less than six thousand people, which should put my aunt at ease. She hated cities—or crowds of any sort, really.

I would miss my morning runs to Starbucks though. The closest one was fifty miles away in Bangor. Guess I'd have to make do with Aunt Tess's poor attempts at coffee-making. The woman had amazing design skills, but she could barely toast bread. One thing she excelled at though was spoiling me on my first day at a new school. It was like her way of apologizing for uprooting me yet again.

Not only had she showered me with baked goods this morning—that she didn't make—but she'd bought me a brand new outfit. Thin beige crop-top sweater, ripped stonewashed jeans, and new ankle boots. Large hoop earrings completed the outfit, plus the silver charm bracelet that I never took off. I didn't usually get all dolled up for school, but I was a sucker for first impressions—even if my relationships didn't last long.

When I spotted the school five minutes later, first day jitters kicked in—although it was technically a month into the fall semester, which sucked. Rosewood High was a typical flat-topped, red brick building with a few newer wings branching off to the sides. But what made the jitters do backflips in my stomach was the fact that a *grave-yard* resided next door.

I was getting some serious bad omen vibes.

So distracted by the sight, I took the turn into the school parking lot a little too fast. A tall figure was suddenly there, standing right in my path. "Fates!" I slammed on the brakes, tires squealing. *Stop, stop, stop!* Squeezing my eyes shut, I braced for impact. The seatbelt dug into my sternum as the car jerked to a stop, and my head snapped back to hit the headrest.

Dazed, I stared at the dashboard for an undetermined length of time, then unbuckled my seatbelt. Pushing the door open, I stumbled out, expecting to see blood and innards splattered over the road. I registered distant shouting and pounding feet, but all I could focus on was the patch of road in front of my car.

The *empty* patch of road.

There was nothing there. Absolutely nothing.

"Are you okay?" Someone touched my sleeve and I immediately pulled away, blinking several times to orient myself. Unfamiliar faces crowded around, some concerned and others confused.

"Y-yeah, I'm fine. I just . . ." I pinched my thigh as hard as I could. "I don't really know what happened actually." So much for first impressions. This had to be my worst one yet.

"McKenna Belmont?" A short, curvy girl with skin a couple shades lighter than my olive-toned complexion elbowed her way inside the growing circle. Her mouth formed an O as she took me in from top to bottom. "Why, hello there. You McKenna?"

"Uh, yeah. Or just Kenna." Did she just check me out? Her wide, dark blue eyes were still openly roving without shame.

She stuck out her hand, flashing pink nail polish that matched the dyed tips of her blonde shaggy bob. "Isla Andrews. I'm part of the Welcoming Committee at Rosewood High. Looks like you've already met some people, good for you. If you'll just park over there, I'll show you to the administration office."

Her handshake was firm and confident, which made me like her immediately. This girl was the real deal, not an ounce of fakeness about her. I did as instructed and maneuvered my car to a parking spot at a snail's pace, which saved me from further embarrassment. The other students started to disperse, although a few leaned on cars and continued to watch me from afar. I supposed in a town this small, a new student was cause for gossip—especially one who had a freakout in the school parking lot.

"So where'd you move from?" Isla asked the second I emerged from my car.

Um, everywhere. "South Carolina."

"Oh, is that why you're so tan? I'm jealous."

A laugh snorted out of me. She was so candid. "No, I don't spend much time in the sun. Must be my Mediterranean roots."

"So it's natural? Double jealous. And your eyes are like molten silver." She must have noticed my rising blush, quickly adding, "Sorry if I'm creeping you out. Most people just tell me to shut up when I get too personal. You don't have to tell me anything."

"No, I don't mind." I didn't mind at all, actually, which surprised me. It felt good to have someone so genuinely interested in getting to know me.

All before entering the school building, I learned that Isla was a senior like me, her dad was the county sheriff, she had an older brother named Noah, was born and raised in Rosewood, and had never left Maine.

"I'm seriously going stir crazy. There's nothing to do in this town," she moaned. I smiled but didn't comment. There were far worse things in life than boredom.

When we stepped inside, a locker-lined hallway accommodating a diverse crowd of teens and teachers greeted us. Several maroon and gold posters dotted the walls above the matching maroon lockers, sporting the school spirit and a growling cougar mascot. Curious eyes tracked our progress, making my skin feel tight and hot. It annoyed me. Not the staring—which was to be expected—but my reaction to it. I wasn't normally this self conscious.

The downside to switching schools a month into the semester was catching up with what I'd missed. Every school had a different curriculum, and if I didn't adapt quickly, I'd start to fall behind. I couldn't let that happen, not if I wanted to earn scholarships for college—which I would desperately need since I doubted Aunt Tess would financially support me if I left her once I became a legal adult. Thankfully, I was used to the process by now. The school also had an art program, so I was good to go.

In the administration office, I was given a large stack of books and my class schedule. "Lemme see," Isla said, snatching it out of my hand, then promptly scowled. "Ugh, we don't have anything together until after lunch. Come on, I'll show you to your locker, then your English Lit class."

The scowl was there and gone again in a blink. Now it was *my* turn to be jealous. Despite my easy-going outward appearance, I was a sulker to the core. I accepted my schedule back and tucked it away so I could grab the large stack of textbooks.

"Here, I can help." Isla reached for the stack, but I shook my head.

"How about you get the door? I've got this."

"Deal. I didn't want to chip my fresh nail polish anyway." She grinned cheekily, opening the door with a flourish.

I smiled in return and nodded my thanks. Stepping through, I was promptly knocked sideways by a heavy hit to the shoulder. My books toppled to the floor and so did I. Except hands grasped my waist at the last second, keeping me from breaking my nose on the vinyl. I was lifted up and set back on my feet with ease, acutely aware of large fingers warming the strip of bare skin above my jeans.

"I'm so sorry," a male voice rushed to say.

I turned and he immediately released his grip. The warmth from his touch continued to seep into my skin though. The feeling wasn't unpleasant, just weird. Tucking clumps of hair behind my ears, I laughed nervously to show I was unharmed. "It's okay. I really should watch where I'm going."

He didn't respond, so I looked up, only to see him studying his open hands with a frown. Okay, then. I cleared my throat awkwardly and bent to pick up the scattered books.

"Oh, no, let me do that." He quickly joined me on the floor, scooping up books in his large hands. I used the moment to peek at his profile, discovering light brown skin, a square jaw, and spiked dark brown hair. He caught me looking and flashed a megawatt grin, his golden hazel eyes crinkling at their upturned corners. Before I could flush with embarrassment, he stood with the majority of my books and said, "You must be the new girl. I'm Reid."

As I straightened to a stand, the warning bell rang.

"Oh, here's your books. I gotta go." When I held my arms out, I couldn't help but notice that he seemed determined not to touch me this time. With a quick wave, he took off, calling over his shoulder, "Nice to meet you and sorry again."

Isla came up beside me and whistled quietly, watching him jog up the stairs and out of sight. "I'm so jealous."

I snorted. "Of what? Of being plowed over like a stalk of corn?"

"Yes. And because he touched you, and talked to you, and smiled at you." She sighed dreamily.

"Who is he?"

"Only Reid Zimmerman, Rosewood High's best football quarterback in decades and the most popular guy in school," Isla crooned, then snickered. "Something tells me my life just got a whole lot more interesting now that you're in town."

I laughed with her, albeit uneasily. Because "interesting" in my world meant packed boxes and a moving truck.

CHAPTER 2

The one perk to starting at a new school on a Thursday?

Today was Friday, and thank the *fates* for that.

I had woken up to a fever this morning. Still, I was determined not to miss school. It was only my second day, after all. First impressions hadn't been all that great, but I could always make up for it today.

I opened the packet of Aleve I'd received from the school nurse's office and chugged down the pills with a bottle of water.

"Not feeling well today, Kenna?" Isla set down her juice to eye me with concern. She'd basically adopted me and made sure I sat with her during lunch period, introducing me to a couple of her friends. Hailey Bradley and Peyton Goodall were nice, but nowhere near as genuine as Isla. I didn't think anyone was. They stopped their conversation to watch me with interest.

"I might be coming down with something," I admitted, poking at my salad which now looked unappetizing. "I'll just take a nap after school. Probably still tired from the move."

Isla nodded sympathetically, then brightened. "If you're feeling better later, you should come out with us tonight. There's going to be music and a big bonfire at North Point Cove."

"Everyone will be there," Peyton chipped in, playing with a strand of her straight black hair. "Including Reid Zimmerman." Her dark eyes flicked a glance toward his table, and a faint blush rose to her flawless brown cheeks.

I snickered when Isla and Hailey sighed in unison. I could admit that he was charismatic and handsome, but I didn't know if he was my type. Truthfully though, I was still figuring out what that even meant. My love life had a big fat zero stamped across it. Not that guys weren't interested in me—or me in them, for that matter. But with all the moving, there simply hadn't been time for dating. And I definitely didn't want a long distance relationship.

"I'll have to make sure my aunt is okay with it, but count me in," I said, to a chorus of squeals. I wasn't going to hold my breath though. Aunt Tess usually said no.

Hailey clapped her hands, her strawberry blonde curls bobbing as she bounced in her seat. "Reid might even say hi to us if you're there," she said, completely oblivious to how her words sounded. I didn't mind, really, even if I was essentially being used. I didn't have a lot of experience with relationships of any kind, but I knew all about feeling alone. Maybe helping these girls find companionship would distract me from my own loneliness, no matter how briefly.

But when I got home from school, the fever had worsened and Aunt Tess wasn't there. Her car must have arrived while I was gone. I checked the dining room table and, sure enough, she'd left a note.

Kenna, I'm visiting with a friend. Leftovers are in the fridge. Make sure to lock the doors and don't wait up. -Aunt Tess

"A *friend?* What sorcery is this?" I muttered, flipping the note over to see if there was a "just kidding" on the back. She hardly ever made friends—or spent time with them, for that matter. And she most certainly never stayed out late.

I pulled out my phone and called her number, sinking onto a chair as chills swept through me. Straight to voicemail. Hanging up,

I tapped the table and debated what to do. I decided on leaving her a text:

Anyone I know?

That wasn't *too* confrontational.

I sat for a moment longer, tired at just the thought of climbing the stairs to my bedroom. But I eventually did, dropping my burgundy school bag and ankle boots along the way. Aunt Tess would have a fit, but she wasn't here. She was out being *secretive*.

I suddenly decided that no matter how awful I felt, I was going out tonight with my new friends.

It was half past nine when I finally found North Point Cove, a stretch of rocky beach surrounded by pine trees. The air was nippy so I'd brought a hooded sweatshirt, but I left it in the car. When I'd woken from my three hour nap, my skin had been hot to the touch. Even after a cold shower, I still ached with fever.

I had almost given in to my exhaustion and climbed back into bed, but my annoyance with Aunt Tess's obtuseness kept me going. She'd always been a private person, but how had she mysteriously found a friend after less than a week of being here? Something was definitely different about this move. I could feel it in my bones.

And if she wouldn't talk to me about it, then I wouldn't tell her about this party.

Hearing laughter and thumping music, I followed a narrow, sandy trail through the pine trees until a large bonfire became visible. Beyond the glowing fire, ocean waves crashed against the rocks, illuminated by a bright, waxing moon.

The party was in full swing, at least fifty teenagers occupying the secluded stretch of beach. Couples dotted the sand, most of them making out. A handful of guys were throwing around a football, and I recognized the tall, spikey-haired one. Reid caught my eye and gave a friendly wave before throwing the football. When I spotted Isla, Hailey, and Peyton talking with a few others, I straightened and plastered on a fake smile. I *hated* pretending, even if it was to cover up not feeling well.

Isla saw me and broke from the group to pull me over. "I'm so happy you made it, girl. I was beginning to worry!" Even in low-heeled ankle boots, I struggled to keep up. The sand definitely wasn't helping matters. She introduced me to a few senior year Rosewood High students—whose names I promptly forgot—then handed me a red plastic cup. "Do you drink?"

"Uh, depends what it is." I sniffed the contents and immediately recoiled. "Smells like dog pee."

Isla busted out laughing and bumped my shoulder. Liquid splashed over the cup's rim, soaking my wrist. "Cheap beer, actually. I can take it if you don't want it."

"Sure." I handed the cup over gingerly, watching as she swallowed a mouthful. "So your dad—you know, him being the sheriff and all— doesn't mind you drinking alcohol?"

"Oh, he minds, but everyone here drinks. Not much else to do, you know? And after the hard time my brother gave him as a teen, he's a bit more lenient with me. Besides, I'm the baby of the family." She winked and took another swig of the foul-smelling stuff, choking a bit.

I huffed a laugh and dropped the subject. "So what kind of stuff did your brother do?"

"Oh, girl. *Girl*. It's more like what *didn't* he do. He's all mature and teaching at an exclusive school now, but when Noah was our age, he used to street race."

My eyebrows inched upward.

"And participate in illegal street fights."

My mouth formed a large O.

"And date every girl in his class and then some."

"Wow. No wonder your dad doesn't get on you for drinking."

"Right? And Hailey drove me anyway. We live in the same neighborhood. I would never drive while—"

A sharp ringing in my ears suddenly cut off her words. I popped my jaw and tried to clear it. The sound only intensified, until noises from all around blasted through my ear canals. Talking, laughter, shuffling feet, the music—the volume increased tenfold. I cringed and covered my ears, squeezing my eyes shut.

Argh. Stop, stop, *stop*.

A hand landed on my shoulder and I squinted to see Isla's concerned face. "You okay?"

I waited a moment before cautiously lowering my hands. The sounds had dimmed somewhat, but were still louder than normal. I nodded anyway, then winced. "Actually, I've got a bit of a headache. I might find a quiet spot for a while until it goes away. Is there any water here?"

"Yeah, I'll get you a bottle. I'm so sorry you're still not feeling well." She gave me sad, puppy dog eyes before whirling to find me a drink. Seconds later, she was back, pressing a bottled water into my hands and pointing to the left. "There's a dark, quiet spot over there. I'll be here if you need me."

"Thanks, Isla." *You're a good friend*, I almost added, but bit my lip instead. I was already growing too attached to this girl.

Hailey and Peyton looked a bit put out that I was leaving their group so soon—probably because Reid hadn't mosied over yet—but

I simply waved and took off across the beach. Thinking, let alone talking, was starting to hurt my head, so I tried to avoid the scattered groups, walking along the treeline.

I had almost reached the fallen log Isla had pointed to when I heard someone yell, "Hey, new chick!" I ignored them, because turning my head would have taken too much effort. A couple yards later, I heard feet shuffling along the sand, then, "Hey, no need to be rude. We just wanted to ask if you'd like to join us for a little game."

Someone tugged on my hair and I whipped around with a glare. Crap, wrong move. Pain splintered my vision. I must have blacked out for a second, because when I blinked next, a muscular blond guy was supporting my weight. His piercing green eyes weren't on my face though, but wandering down the deep V of my white shirt.

Yuck.

I struggled to free myself. When he let go, I said, "No, thanks, I'm not feeling well. I might even be contagious." Which didn't faze him one bit.

"Let me carry you to your car then. Tell me where it is and I'll—"

Frustrated at his bullheaded persistence, I went with blunt honesty. "No, really. I'm not in the least bit interested and you can go now."

"Ah, c'mon, don't be like that. I'm only trying to help." And before I could stop him, he scooped me up.

Seriously, dude. *Wrong* move. My fever spiked, along with the temper I usually kept on a tight leash. "Let me go *now*, you neanderthal," I snarled, and slapped his chest.

Male laughter surrounded us, his buddies crowding in close to watch—as if *I* was the game. Humiliation burned through me, followed by a boiling rage. Without warning, I lashed out at Neanderthal's face, raking my nails down his cheek. He bellowed and threw me to the sand. I landed on my back with a loud *ooph*, and lay there stunned and struggling for air.

"What's going on here?" someone said over Neanderthal's swearing. Bodies shuffled aside to accomodate a new face, one I thankfully recognized. Reid crouched before me, clear worry in his hazel eyes. "What happened? You okay?"

Still unable to speak, I simply glared at Neanderthal. Reid stood up and approached the guy, surprising me by shoving him.

"Are you messing with a girl again, August? You know how I feel about that. Let's see what *Coach* thinks about it when I tell him. I bet he'll bench you next game for this little stunt."

"She attacked *me*, man," August whined, jabbing a finger at me. "The little vixen was playing coy, then raked her talons down my face without warning. Look!"

I ached to defend myself, to put this creaton in his place, but what little air was in my lungs deflated when I saw his cheek. Four long scratches had ripped open the skin and were leaking blood. I lifted my hand and gasped.

My nails were filed to sharp points.

When the freaking crap did that happen?

Horrified, I looked up to see Reid frowning, his gaze riveted on my nails. I scrambled backward a few feet, then picked myself up and stumbled back the way I came, tucking my hands out of sight.

"Kenna!" Isla called when I passed her and the others on my way to the parking lot. I didn't turn, too busy trying not to faceplant as I speed-walked across the sand. The party's sounds dimmed the farther I went down the trail leading to my car.

When I was completely alone, my thundering heartbeats began to slow. No one was in the parking lot, so I stopped and leaned against my Honda to catch my breath.

With trembling fingers, I lifted the water bottle to my lips and guzzled the whole thing. The fever was raging hotter than ever. Sweat beaded my brow and I was half tempted to remove my shirt. Actually . . .

Casting a quick look around me, I set the empty bottle on the car's hood and yanked my shirt off, leaving on the sheer white tank top underneath. I wiped my face and neck with the shirt, closing my eyes and sighing when cool air kissed my overheated skin.

Better.

A strong gust of wind suddenly whooshed past me, making strands of hair smack my face. Startled, I wrenched my eyes open, checking the sky for signs of a storm. All was still. Not even the trees rustled. The whoosh came again, this time to my right. I whipped my head that direction, still seeing nothing.

"Hello?"

Silence.

Despite my fever, icy goosebumps prickled my arms. An awareness of being watched shivered through me. My body tensed, senses going on high alert. I'd parked at the only available spot farthest from the trail, my car butted up against the treeline. Being alone out here suddenly seemed like a really bad idea.

I squinted into the nearly pitch-black gloom where I'd last heard the noise. One of the partygoers was probably trying to scare me. Maybe that douchebag August.

"I'm not interested in your games, August," I called, nervous but also annoyed at his bullheadedness. When no one replied, I fished out my car keys, wanting to avoid another Neanderthal encounter. Remembering my sharpened nails, I jerked my hand up too fast and dropped the keys. I bent, noting with relief that my nails were short and square as I snagged the keyring. The fever must have addled my brain earlier.

I was reaching for the driver's-side door when a flash of red from the woods caught my attention. I turned, and what I saw froze me solid. There, yards away and cloaked by darkness, were two red eyes. They were glowing, even without a reflective light source. And they were staring . . .

Directly at me.

Before I could so much as blink, they were gone.

CHAPTER 3

A man cast in shadow blocked my path.
Only his red eyes were visible as he watched me.
I couldn't look away, even when he silently stalked forward.
Predator, my mind screamed. Run!
But I didn't, even while he dipped down to breathe me in.

My eyes flew open and I sucked in a startled gasp, blinking up at my bedroom ceiling while I replayed the dream.

Ever since that night a week ago—the night my aunt went into another packing frenzy—I hadn't dreamed of the man with the red eyes. But now that I'd seen red eyes watching me from the woods—not once but *twice* since we'd moved here—my memory of him came flooding back.

Shadow Man, I'd immediately dubbed him—since his features were entirely obscured by shadows. He was black mist in human form. Only his vibrant, piercing eyes were clearly visible.

He'd only approached me one time, but I would never forget the encounter, no matter how hard I tried.

After leaning forward to smell me, he'd said, "You're not human," his voice deep and rolling like a crashing ocean wave. When I'd simply gaped at him, too dumbstruck by his appearance to speak, he'd reached out with a gloved hand and captured my chin. "Forget this conversation," he said, his red eyes penetrating mine. "Forget my face."

And then he'd vanished.

"Did you hear about what happened this weekend?" Isla said the moment I stepped through the school doors Monday morning. The hall was bustling with chatter, more so than usual.

"No," I replied, then quickly added, "Sorry for ditching you at the party on Friday. I couldn't shake that weird fever." Thankfully, it had petered out over the weekend.

She waved the apology away, clearly having forgiven me for my disappearing act. Peyton and Hailey joined us then, crowding in close as Isla spilled the news. "A linebacker on the football team, August Henderson, was attacked in the woods Friday night. He's in the hospital."

I paused with a hand on my locker as the name registered. "Is he blond-haired and kinda brutish, by any chance?"

"Yeah. Why, do you know him?"

The girls were staring at me curiously, but I schooled my expression, even as my heart sped up. "Not really. We just bumped into each other at the party. He was . . ."

"A jerkwad?" Hailey supplied, winding a strawberry curl around her finger. "What, you were all thinking it! He's been a misogynistic douche ever since he grew peach fuzz on his face."

Isla and Peyton mumbled their agreement.

"Anyway," Isla continued, "my dad said there was blood everywhere. Bite and scratch marks all over him. Must have been an animal attack."

My eyes flew to hers in alarm. "What kind of predators do you have here in Maine?"

"Black bears, lynx, bobcats, coyotes—they *rarely* attack humans though," she tried to assure me.

"Knowing August, he probably instigated it," Hailey grumbled. Her pale blue eyes flicked to me and she shrugged unapologetically. "I dated him for a couple weeks last year. Worst mistake of my life. I'm still salty."

I nodded my understanding. Even one minute with him had been too long. "Will the sheriff's department look for the animal?" I asked Isla.

"Animal control will, but it'll be like finding a needle in a haystack. We're surrounded by forest."

I shuddered, glad that I hadn't been around when the attack happened. Aunt Tess would have for sure freaked out if she'd known I'd been there. Something like that was cause for a move. Thankfully, she hadn't found out about the party—just another secret between us. She had come in a few hours after I had on Friday night, sneaking upstairs like a teenager breaking curfew. She'd poked her head into my room, but I'd feigned sleep, still annoyed with her.

I spent the whole weekend in my room, curled up on the window seat drawing nonsensical things on my sketchpad. A chicken's foot. My ornate armoire. A bonfire.

A pair of intense eyes surrounded by shadows.

I could hear my aunt banging around the house, putting stuff away now that our storage container had arrived. Despite the lingering aches and fever, I'd almost felt bad making her do it by herself. Then bitterness would well up again and I'd resume sketching. I could have asked her where she'd snuck off to with her mysterious *friend*, but I wasn't in the mood for her excuses and lies.

Loneliness had pressed on my chest and I'd fingered the bracelet that used to be my mom's, comforted by its familiarity. Glancing at the bedside table where a photo of my parents and a three-year-old me sat in a silver frame, I'd whispered, "Wish you guys were here," a habit of mine when dealing with Aunt Tess became too much.

If they'd never taken that vacation without me—if they'd never boarded that plane—I was certain my parents and I would have been close. They would have told me everything, never leaving me in the dark. We would have stayed in the same house for years, and I would have countless close friends. They would've allowed me to have a job. They would have been proud of my future dream to pursue a college art degree. We would have talked about meaningful stuff over dinner every evening, laughing at each other's jokes and sharing all our secrets.

But in reality, all I had was a picture. In reality, all I had were the memories Aunt Tess had given me of them, because I'd been too young to remember them on my own. The only living relative who had wanted me was Aunt Tess, and most days, I wondered if she couldn't wait to be rid of me.

Well, fine. I didn't want to be with her any longer than I legally had to anyway, so I had stubbornly remained in my room all weekend while she attempted to make the rickety old house look like a home.

The warning bell rang then, startling me from my glum thoughts. I waved to the girls and headed for my English Lit class. I knew my way around the school well enough on my own now, thanks to my astute observation skills learned from constantly moving. I was about to enter my classroom when I felt eyes on me, which was ridiculous since dozens of students were still in the hallway. Glancing over my shoulder, I searched for the source.

I'd almost given up when the crowd thinned, revealing not just one guy staring at me from across the hall, but two. I didn't recognize them, but I'd only been at the school a couple of days. Both were tall, one with wavy, caramel-colored hair and the other black. Even from here, I could feel the intensity of their gazes.

But it was the guy on the left—the slightly shorter one with a sleeker build and obsidian hair falling into his dark, hooded eyes—that captured my attention.

I couldn't help but notice everything about him, from his aloof almost bored expression, to his skin a shade darker than mine. From the effortless way he wore his slim dark jeans and black button-down shirt, to the tattoos snaking out of his rolled-up sleeves. I even noticed the thick leather watch on his left wrist and the large ruby ring on his pinky finger.

He pretty much had "bad boy" stamped all over him with a "do not disturb" sign around his neck.

Still, I continued to stare like a creeper. I should be thoroughly embarrassed but couldn't seem to look away. Besides, he started staring first.

He suddenly broke eye contact and pushed through the administration office door, snapping me out of my weird stupor. The other guy, the carmel-haired one who looked like a bodybuilder, winked at me and entered the office too. A throat cleared from behind me, and I became all too aware that I was *blocking* the entrance to my classroom.

Okay, *now* I was embarrassed.

I quickly filed into the room and took a seat somewhere in the middle. That way, I could observe a good portion of the students without being noticed as often by the teacher. I almost jumped out of my skin when someone tapped my shoulder.

The first period bell rang while I turned in my seat to see Reid Zimmerman directly behind me. More embarrassment flooded my cheeks at how rude I must have looked by sitting down without acknowledging him.

"Good morning, class," our English teacher said, way too chipperly for this time of day.

Meet me after class, Reid mouthed, and I nodded without thinking before facing forward again.

But now that I had, worry niggled at the back of my mind. Reid's expression had been somber, and although I'd only known him a short time, the look seemed odd for him. I couldn't help but remember the argument he had with August before I'd left the party. He'd even shoved him.

My eyes widened. What if . . .

What if *Reid* had attacked August in the woods Friday night, and was now making sure I hadn't seen it?

What would he do if I had? Would he . . . would he threaten me so I'd keep silent? And if he was the violent sort, there was no telling what he'd do.

Okay, I was officially freaked out now.

For the duration of class, I could barely concentrate, too busy feeling Reid's eyes on my back. I fingered and twisted my bracelet over and over. Maybe I was being paranoid, but I didn't think so. I was pretty good at knowing when someone was staring at me. It was like a sixth sense or something. When the bell rang, I shot out of my seat like a bullet and beelined for the exit.

"Kenna," Reid called as I reached the door. I pretended not to hear.

Next was my World History class. Crap! Reid was in that class too. Thinking fast, I pushed into the girl's bathroom, almost knocking someone over.

"Hey!"

"Sorry," I muttered to the flustered girl and ducked into a stall. Slamming the door shut, I leaned against it and breathed deeply to calm my racing heart.

Hopefully Reid would take the hint that I didn't want to talk with him. If not, at least I'd be last to arrive in class and could avoid sitting near him.

But now I looked panicked. Like I knew something.

Fates, I shouldn't have run.

Too late now.

I left the stall a few minutes after the warning bell rang and slowly washed my hands. I looked up and spotted my dilated pupils in the mirror, barely able to see the silver-gray of my irises. "Calm down," I whispered to my reflection and tucked wayward strands of chestnut hair behind my ears. "Nothing's going to happen to you."

Then why did I feel like the next few minutes of my life were going to change everything?

With one last look at my nervous expression, I smoothed a hand down my scarlet paisley dress and exited the bathroom. The hall was eerily empty while I swiftly crossed it to reach my next class, clutching my books tightly to my chest. My heeled ankle boots echoed loudly against the tiles, the sound raising the hair on my arms. I was practically jogging by the time I reached the room, arriving just after the bell rang.

The teacher—Mr. Davis, if I remembered right—looked over at me with a slightly irritated expression. "Nice of you to join us, Miss Belmont. Please take a seat so we can *promptly* get started."

Oh, he was one of *those* teachers.

I scanned the sea of students in pursuit of an empty chair far from Reid. Moments like this were the stuff of nightmares. The silence, staring, and anticipation of where I'd sit. At least I wasn't naked.

Horror of all horrors, there was an empty seat directly in front of Reid, as if he'd saved it for me. I avoided eye contact, desperately renewing my search. There! In the back left corner, second from the last row, was another empty seat. I strode toward it without hesitation, making it halfway down the aisle before my gaze caught on the person sitting behind my targeted chair.

I slammed to a halt.

It was the guy from earlier in the hallway, the one with black hair that fell messily yet artfully around his face. He was coolly watching me, his lids lowered to half mast. The caramel-haired guy who'd winked at me sat next to him.

"Sometime today, Miss Belmont," the teacher said, distinctly annoyed now. "We're wasting precious time."

My cheeks flamed hotter than the raging fever from this weekend. I fixed my gaze on my shoes while I forced both feet forward and slid into the seat. If dying from embarrassment were possible, then I was about to keel over.

From my peripheral, I saw Reid turn to look back at me. But his weren't the only eyes I could feel. The stares from the two guys behind me penetrated my overheated skin like laser beams. My instincts went haywire, screaming at me to protect my vulnerable back. But I couldn't. I was stuck here. And concentrating on anything else became impossible.

So when Mr. Davis said, "What do you think of that, Miss Belmont?"—putting me on the spot *again*—all I could do was blink stupidly as every single head in the classroom swiveled my way.

Yup. I was definitely dying from embarrassment.

"Um . . ." I managed, but my mind was blank.

Seconds that felt like years ticked by.

Heat pricked my eyes and I quickly pinched my thigh, staving off the tears. *Don't cry, don't you* dare *cry!*

"I think the people's intolerance and prejudice was what instigated the war," a deep, rumbly voice said from directly behind me. "If they had chosen to respect each other's differences instead of exploit them, bloodshed could have been spared." The words were spoken in a lazy drawl, flowing like molten molasses—practically slipping beneath my skin and warming my insides.

Holy fates.

I hadn't realized voices could be sexy, but that right there was proof. It took all of my willpower not to turn around and thank my rescuer, because rescuing me was exactly what he'd done, intentionally or not.

"That's an astute observation—Lochlan D'angelo, is it?" Mr. Davis said, finally taking his beady eyes off me. "But next time, please raise your hand before speaking."

When he continued on, directing his attention to the rest of the class, my erratic heartbeats finally began to slow. *Lochlan D'angelo,* I silently repeated. I bet the name sounded heavenly coming from that voice of his.

Something knocked against the leg of my chair and my spine snapped straight. Without turning my head, I looked down to see a long, jean-clad leg extend beside my seat. *Lochlan's* leg. As more heat flushed my skin, I forced my gaze upward. I needed to stick my head in the cafeteria's freezer after this.

I managed to pull a fast exit and avoid Reid for the rest of the morning, but I knew this cat and mouse game couldn't last forever. He cornered me in the lunch line, using his body as a wall so I couldn't retreat. Gripping my tray, I tried my best to ignore him.

"We need to talk," he said quietly in my ear, his breath teasing my hair.

I added a fruit salad to my plate.

"Kenna, I'm not playing around. This is serious."

My pulse spiked. I was right. He did it. He attacked August and wanted to shut me up. I was so screwed.

"Back off, Reid," I said, hating how breathless, how *scared* I sounded. Feeling like a trapped rabbit, I backed up with my tray, elbowing him so I could escape.

Before I could, his fingers dug into my upper arm through my leather jacket. "I'm sorry, but this can't be ignored. You need to come with me."

When he started to tow me away, panic leaked into my voice. "Let go, Reid. I don't want to go anywhere with you."

When he didn't listen, I debated making a scene. Maybe smash my tray into him. That would hopefully give me enough leverage to yank free of his hold before he dragged me somewhere quiet—where no one could hear me scream. I was just about to make my move when he jerked to a halt, almost overturning my tray.

Confused, I looked up to see a muscle thrumming in his rigid jaw. His grip on me tightened, and I winced, more from surprise than pain. A low growl reached my ears, but it wasn't Reid's.

Someone chuckled darkly, and the growling stopped. "I would let her go if I were you."

I peered around Reid, immediately understanding why he'd stopped. The two guys I'd sat in front of during history class were blocking his path. The caramel-haired one must have spoken, his broad mouth still twisted with wry amusement. The other guy, Lochlan, stood preternaturally still, his dark eyes fixed on something with laser focus.

I followed his gaze to where Reid still held my arm.

"Kade," was all he said.

The amusement fled the other guy's face, and he adopted a look nearly as menacing as Lochlan's. "Seriously, man, let her go now."

Reid's hand immediately dropped to his side, then balled into a fist. "You don't understand."

"Oh, we understand *perfectly*," the guy I assumed was Kade said, his amusement returning. "Now step away before the Lochness Monster comes out to play."

At that, Lochlan snapped out of his intense staredown and rolled his eyes, donning an I-don't-give-a-crap expression. I blinked, completely thrown off guard by the change. So busy gawking, I didn't notice Reid leave until he was storming through the exit.

An uncomfortable silence fell between the three of us. Well, uncomfortable for *me* anyway. I fidgeted with my tray, suddenly aware that we had an audience. Practically the entire cafeteria, actually. Fates, would this day of embarrassment never end?

I opened my mouth, uncertain if I should thank them or not. I wasn't even sure what had happened exactly. Before I could make up my mind, Lochlan turned for the side exit that led outside. "Wow. Okay, then," I muttered as he pushed through the door. He hadn't even looked at me—besides my arm anyway.

Kade chuckled again, and I met his eyes for the first time, which were a pretty sky blue. He winked at me, drawling, "It's nice to officially meet you, McKenna Belmont," before sauntering after his friend.

Um . . .

Somehow, I made my legs carry me to where Isla, Peyton, and Hailey sat gaping. At me. This should be interesting. Sure enough, the moment I sat down, their mouths fired off questions in rapid succession.

"What were you doing with Reid?"

"Who were those two guys? They're *hot!*"

"Girl, if you weren't so nice, I'd have to kill you."

"They look way too mature to be in highschool."

"Did you see how cut they were? And those *jawlines.*"

Isla suddenly raised her hands for quiet. "Hold it, hold it! What we *should* be asking is why they've arrived right after Kenna did."

"Wait, what?" I said, finally finding my voice. "They're new here too?"

"Totally. I know every face in this school." She shrugged. "Must be a sheriff's daughter thing."

I frowned in thought. "How often do you get new students at Rosewood High?"

"Besides the new freshman, about a handful each year. But three seniors transfering a month into the semester? Unheard of."

"It's almost like they *followed* you here, Kenna," Peyton said with rounded eyes, then she and Hailey laughed at the absurdity of her comment.

I laughed with them, but the sound was forced. Fake. Because a part of me thought that maybe she was right.

CHAPTER 4

Being stared at all week by three guys got old fast, even if they *were* smoking hot.

It wasn't the weighted silence that wore me down, but the probing, almost expectant looks, like they were waiting for me to do something. Although I was still wary about the timing of Lochlan and Kade's arrival, they made no effort to approach me. I did my best to ignore them completely, especially when Reid would glare at the other two and stalk off. At least he'd stopped trying to talk to me.

Isla, Peyton, and Hailey simply thought Reid had come on to me too strong and I'd turned him down, hence the frustrated looks. I didn't want them to know about his possible involvement with August's attack in case he went after them next. Still, I was acting exactly like Aunt Tess, keeping secrets and spinning stories. I hated myself for it. Lies tore people apart, and I wanted so badly to keep the few friends I now had.

For once, I'd let my guard down, my desire for companionship outweighing the need to protect my heart. I genuinely felt a kinship with these girls, which was why on Thursday, I said yes without a moment's hesitation when Hailey invited us to a slumber party at her parent's lakehouse. "They won't mind if we stay there after school tomorrow," she explained to me. "They're both on business trips, so we'll have the place to ourselves. Bring your bathing suit 'cause there's a hot tub!"

Now I just needed a plausible excuse to give Aunt Tess so she'd let me go.

Over our Chinese takeout dinner Thursday evening, I dove right into the conservation, ripping the proverbial band-aid off. "Mind if I stay at a friend's house tomorrow night? We have a big test on Monday to study for."

I doubted we'd be doing any studying, but I'd bring my textbooks anyway to back up the story.

Aunt Tess looked up from her plate of kungpow chicken and fried rice. "Which friend?"

"Isla Andrews. The sheriff's daughter," I added, for further credibility.

She tapped a nail on the walnut tabletop for a moment, and I tried hard not to squirm in my seat. Finally, she said, "Okay. Just text me when you arrive, and make sure to be back by noon on Saturday. This place still needs a lot of work and I could use a helping hand this weekend."

My mouth almost fell open in utter shock. She hardly ever let me do sleepovers, especially without meeting the parents first. "I . . . Thanks," I murmured, not knowing what else to say.

We ate in silence for a while, which was normal for us. Always keeping our thoughts—and secrets—to ourselves. I knew I should tell her about the party last Friday, plus the animal attack, Reid's behavior, and the two new guys at school, but I knew what would happen if I did.

She'd have our belongings packed up by morning.

So I didn't. I actually *liked* it here. I liked my friends, and despite the weird stuff that had happened last week, I almost felt like I belonged here. I'd never felt that way before. It was warm and

35

comforting. No way was I going to let Aunt Tess and her paranoia steal that away from me.

Without looking up from her plate, Aunt Tess quietly said, "It's going to be different this time, Kenna Joy." I blinked at her in surprise. She only spoke that way once in a blue moon when she felt like opening up to me.

She had my full attention now. I slowly lowered my fork and searched her downcast face. But she wouldn't meet my eyes. After another long moment, she simply said, "It's almost over. You'll see," then lapsed into silence again.

When the final bell rang Friday afternoon, I was almost giddy with excitement. I hadn't been to a slumber party in, well, ever.

"You ready?" Isla asked, bumping my hip with hers as we exited our science class.

I actually grinned, wide enough to flash my teeth. It felt good having something to smile about. "Totally. I just need to text my aunt real quick." Hailey had picked us and Peyton up this morning in her flashy red SUV so we didn't all have to drive—except I told Aunt Tess that Isla had picked me up.

The lakehouse was twenty-five minutes north of here, past where I lived but even more remote and covered in forest. We already had our overnight bags packed and in the car so we wouldn't waste daylight.

Hailey and Peyton met us in the hallway, clearly as excited as I was. We practically pranced out of the school, drawing stares from all sides. So *this* was what normalcy felt like. I'd never been good at making friends quickly, so this experience was foreign to me. Foreign and wonderful. If I wasn't careful though, this could all be taken away from me in the blink of an eye.

Aunt Tess couldn't find out about this trip.

We were almost to Hailey's SUV when I heard, "Where are you ladies off to?"

Turning, I barely suppressed a groan. "What do you want, Reid?" Yeah, I wasn't Miss Congeniality anymore where he was concerned, so sue me.

But the others were.

"Oh, we're just having a slumber party at my parent's—" Hailey began, all googly-eyed and stuff.

I quickly cut her off, fully intending to apologize later. "It's a girl-only thing. Sorry, Reid, you're not invited. I'm sure the two guys you've been glaring at all week would hang out with you if you asked nicely."

Speaking of, I could see them on the far side of the parking lot, leaning against a black, expensive-looking Lexus. Too far away to overhear our conversation, they were still watching us intently. Watching *me*, more likely. Argh, this really was getting old. Flipping my ponytail behind me, I gave them all the cold shoulder and rounded the SUV to the other side.

"Seriously, what's a girl gotta do to get some anonymity around here?" I grumbled. Before I could climb into the back seat, someone pushed the door shut again. "Wha—?"

Reid's hazel eyes suddenly filled my vision as he leaned forward, boxing me in with his hands splayed against the car. "Don't go on this trip with your friends if you value their safety, Kenna," he hurriedly whispered in my ear. "Your time is up. Come with me now or you'll be putting them all in danger."

I tried to shove him back, but he was built like a boulder. My heart skittered nervously, and I scowled at him. "Get away from me, Reid. If you don't, I'm going to scream."

He stared at me incredulously, then shook his head. "I'm not the bad guy here. I'm trying to *help* you. You're—"

One second, he was there in front of me, and the next, crashing to the asphalt several feet away. A car honked and swerved, narrowly missing him when he rolled into traffic.

I clutched my pounding chest, too shocked to join the people rushing over to help him. Recalling how he'd flown through the air like a ragdoll, I looked for the person who'd shoved him. *I* most definitely wasn't capable of doing that.

But the narrow space between the two cars was empty. I was alone.

"Kenna?"

Isla's worried voice reached me as she hurried around the SUV. I moved toward her and promptly smacked face first into a wall. When I stumbled back, hands grasped my shoulders to steady me, then quickly fell away.

"Crap," I muttered, cupping my nose. I looked up, startled to see Lochlan.

"I heard a struggle," he said by way of greeting. "Everything okay?" His gaze kept flicking to the hand covering my nose, then to the rest of me—as if checking for injury. Despite how annoyed I'd been with his silent staring act this week, my body warmed under his perusal.

Stupid body.

"I don't know," I managed to say, then dropped my hand. "Does my nose look broken? You have a hard chest."

A single dimple indented his left cheek, there and gone again in a blink. When he leaned forward to better see my nose, his scent

38

drifted to me, a heady mix of amber, sandalwood, and natural male musk. Instead of pulling away, I had the strangest urge to lean closer and breathe him in. My heart fluttered like a drunken butterfly, further addling my brain.

Seriously, body, get a grip!

His head tipped to the side and a lock of shiny, black hair fell across his eyes. My fingers itched to brush the hair aside, because his eyes were—

"What's wrong?" he said, a note of unease tainting his usually silken drawl.

Crap, had I been staring at him like a weirdo? "I . . . nothing. Your eyes are just . . ."

He blinked and averted his gaze with a frown. "What?"

"No, they're—"

"I need to go," he abruptly said, turning away. "Your nose looks fine."

And with that, he took off.

All I could do was shake my head at his swift departure. "Your exit strategy sucks," I muttered after him, even though he was long gone. Whiplash much?

Isla arrived then, her wide blue eyes ping-ponging from me, to where Lochlan had been standing, to Reid who was picking himself off the ground. "You okay?"

"Yeah," I said, and fumbled to open the car door. "Let's just get out of here."

The girls joined me soon after, casting me covert glances from their seats. Crap, time to do damage control.

"Sorry about that. Truly. I'm just having . . . boy troubles," I finished lamely.

"Ooo, like love triangle problems?" Peyton said, turning in the front passenger seat to waggle her eyebrows at me.

I made a face. "Ugh, no, definitely not. More like stalker problems."

The mood dramatically shifted to one of concern. Oops.

Isla bumped her knee against mine. "Should I call my dad? He could come talk some sense into them."

Hailey snorted from the driver's seat. "More like *scare* some sense into them."

"He's not *that* scary," Isla said, rolling her eyes.

He is, Hailey mouthed at me, and a small smile twitched my lips.

"I've got it handled, but thanks anyway, Isla. I really appreciate it." And I did, more than any of them realized. I'd never had friends who wanted to watch my back before.

"I can't believe Lochlan shoved Reid into oncoming traffic like that," Isla said, buckling her seatbelt as Hailey backed up the SUV.

I frowned. "He didn't. He was across the parking lot when it happened. He got there afterward."

Now it was Isla's turn to frown. "Then who did?"

I opened my mouth, then closed it. Because I didn't have an answer.

During the winding, scenic drive, the tension gradually left my shoulders, along with my confusion over Reid and Lochlan. I didn't want anything to ruin this mini retreat, especially boys. Twenty-five minutes later, a single story, glass-front lakehouse came into view.

"Absolutely gorgeous," I breathed as I stepped from the car. I'd traveled to quite a few places over the years, but the natural beauty surrounding us was on another level. Mixed among the deep green pines were oak trees in brilliant shades of yellow and orange, with the occasional pop of red. Behind the lakehouse, I could just make out the edges of a sparkling blue lake.

A plethora of birds chirped overhead, the only sound besides the rustling of leaves. No man-made noises but our own could be heard.

I closed my eyes and inhaled the crisp, spice-scented fall air. "Perfect."

"Didn't you just move into a house surrounded by woods?" Peyton asked with a laugh.

"Yeah," I admitted, opening my eyes so I could grab my things. "But it's kinda creepy sometimes." I *still* hadn't explored the basement.

"There's a lot of mystery behind that house," Isla said as she tugged a large duffle from the back. "I did a little research after you moved here and found out that it's been vacant for a long time. I couldn't find any information on the previous owners or why the house never sold, but I'll keep looking."

"Maybe they were murdered and their bodies were stashed in the basement freezer." We all turned to gape at Hailey. "What? I read a lot of murder mystery novels."

Except now I was thinking about axe murderers again. And was there a freezer in our basement? Great, I was *never* going down there.

"Maybe no one's bought the place because it's haunted," Peyton dramatically whispered. "You know, ghosts with unfinished business or something."

"That too. Hey, there's a full moon tonight. We should tell ghost stories around the campfire." Hailey pulled something from her bag with a flourish. "I've got marshmallows!"

"I'm more interested in that hot tub," Peyton said with a jig. "I want to wear my new bikini."

After we'd settled in and toured the house, we decided to do a little outdoor exploring before the sun set.

"You guys go on ahead and I'll catch up," I said as they started down a trail to the lake. "Forgot my phone in the car." I could never pass up an opportunity to snap nature shots.

Rounding the front of the house at a jog, I spotted a gray truck parked near the bend of the long, private gravel road. I skidded to a halt, my instincts immediately on high alert. That truck hadn't been there when we'd arrived. I inched forward, using Hailey's SUV to hide me from view as I debated what to do. I could race back to the others. Safety in numbers, after all. But maybe it was only a neighbor.

Or a serial killer, my mind helpfully supplied.

I didn't want to put my friends in danger if the person was up to no good. My phone was feet away in the back seat of the SUV. I could call the sheriff's department and—

"Kenna."

I whirled, unable to suppress a frightened squeak. When I saw who it was, annoyance replaced my fear. "*You*. How did you find me here?"

"Your friend Hailey talks a lot. Wasn't too hard," Reid said, shoving his hands into his pockets.

"Why are you stalking me, Reid Zimmerman?" My voice cracked through the air like a whip. I didn't care how nice he'd been to me when I'd first arrived. His recent behavior was seriously freaking me out. "If this is about the night of the bonfire, I haven't told anyone and don't plan to. So you can stop *bothering* me."

He shook his head, clearly frustrated—which was stupid since he was the one instigating this. "It doesn't work like that. Look, I'm sorry for what I did. It was an accident. But it's my responsibility to clean up the mess."

Ice shot up my spine and I took a step back. "*Mess?* You mean me, don't you. *I'm* the mess." I could tell by his expression that I was right. "Please don't hurt me," I said, unable to hide the slight tremble in my voice.

"What? Kenna, I'm not here to hurt you. I came to—" A phone rang and he groaned loudly. Pulling the phone from his pocket, he checked the screen and swore. He shot me a clear warning look not to run and took the call.

"Yes?" When someone shouted on the other end, Reid pulled the phone away from his ear with a grimace. "I know! I'm not exactly new at this. You don't have to tell me every time. I'll be there in twenty." More shouting. "Yeah, but she still doesn't know—"

I took a slow step back, but Reid's eyes tracked the movement. A growl rumbled in his throat and I froze. Freaking fates, he was going to kill me and stuff my body in a freezer. I could scream, but the only people who would hear were my friends, and I didn't want them to get hurt.

Reid ended the call and stepped toward me, his movements jerky and agitated. "You need to come with me *right* now, Kenna. I'll explain when we're—"

When he reached for my arm, I backpedaled, barking, "No! Don't you dare touch me."

A wild light entered his eyes, making the gold flecks brighten. He cursed and dropped his gaze, lowering his hand. "Kenna . . ."

"I'm not going anywhere with you," I said firmly, preparing to punch, scratch, and kick him if he came a step closer.

He clenched and unclenched his hands, which I noticed were shaking. Sweat beaded his brow, his breathing labored. With each passing moment, the urge to run intensified. He looked two seconds away from snapping, and I didn't want to be within striking range. I was just about to make a break for the lakehouse when he suddenly retreated a step, then another.

"Get far away from your friends before it's too late, Kenna," he said, his voice strained and guttural. "I . . . I have to—"

He abruptly turned and took off down the road at a sprint. Instead of climbing into his truck though, he raced around the bend and out of sight.

A hush fell over the clearing once again. Even the birds were more quiet as the sun crept below the treeline.

"He's insane," I whispered, rubbing at the goosebumps on my arms. Adrenaline buzzed beneath my skin, and I couldn't decide between screaming or laughing hysterically to dispel the awful energy. Choosing neither, I started to walk. I desperately needed to collect my thoughts and blow off some steam before rejoining the others, so I veered toward the woods where I'd spotted a faint trail earlier.

I maintained a steady pace, walking quickly enough to burn off the adrenaline but cautiously enough not to trip on the roots and felled branches littering the trail. It wasn't until a good half hour later, when dusk was slowly stealing my vision, that I remembered my phone.

Crap, I'd forgotten it again!

"Real smooth," I muttered, turning back. "Now I'm easy pickings for any would-be murderers." I should have brought sneakers. These flats were rubbing the skin off my heels. Shivering from the cold, I zipped my cropped leather jacket and hurried along the trail. How far had I gone? Two miles? Three?

Snap!

Every nerve ending sprang awake at the sound of a stick breaking. I paused to listen, but only heard the wind rustling through the trees. It could have been a deer, but my mind immediately conjured images of Reid attacking August in the woods. And now I was picturing Reid stalking *me* through the woods this very moment, axe in one hand and a body bag in the other.

So when I heard another snap, I bolted.

Trees whipped by, branches snagging my clothes and the end of my ponytail. The fear-filled adrenaline from earlier returned tenfold, and I flew down the trail at a reckless pace.

I rounded a sharp bend only to find the way blocked by a tall, dark figure. Startled, I shrieked and tried to stop, but there wasn't time. It was like hitting a brick wall when I smacked into the human barrier. The air whooshed from my lungs as I bounced back from the impact. Hands shot out to grip my arms, and I immediately put up a fight.

"Let go, Reid, let me go!" I struggled in vain, the hold on my upper arms ironclad. Still, I wouldn't let him kill me that easily. I kicked at his shins, but his legs were so hard that I probably hurt myself more than him.

I was aiming for a much more tender spot when a deep, velvety voice said, "McKenna."

Inches away from kneeing his groin, I froze. That voice wasn't Reid's. My eyes snapped up and met Lochlan D'angelo's.

CHAPTER 5

"What are you doing here?" I blurted, so relieved that he wasn't Reid, I almost hugged him.

"I could ask you the same thing," he replied and released me. "You're on my property, after all."

"Wait, what?" I scanned our surroundings, half expecting to find a sign with his name on it.

"The property about a mile southwest of here and the surrounding land belongs to me," he explained patiently.

"Oh," I said dumbly, wishing I could smack myself. "Sorry, I must have walked too far. I'm staying at a friend's."

When he simply stared at me in that unnerving, aloof way of his, I lowered my gaze and gnawed on my lip. Well, this was awkward. I noticed he was wearing all black then, from his boots and jeans, to his hooded leather jacket. Not abnormal for him. But the slim-fitting leather gloves gave me pause. Huh. Maybe his hands got cold easily.

He tucked his hands in his pockets then, as if he'd caught me staring. "So you thought I was Reid." Not a question.

"Yeah, um, can you pretend you didn't hear that?" Was I forever destined to feel embarrassed around him?

"Can't."

My eyes flew to his face again, just in time to watch that left dimple disappear. "What?"

"Can't," he repeated. "I want you to tell me why he's been bothering you. And why he frightens you."

"He doesn't—" Crap, there was no lying my way out of this. Lochlan was sporting a "I know more than you think, so fess up" look. I sighed, admitting, "He thinks I saw something he didn't want anyone to see. It's why he followed me here today and demanded I go with him somewhere."

Lochlan's nostrils flared, and I watched with fascination as his jaw practically hardened to granite. "What does he think you saw?"

I shrugged and avoided his probing gaze. "That's just it. I didn't see anything. But now he's telling me to stay away from my friends before it's too late. I don't know if that's a threat to keep me silent or what."

"Did he touch you?"

Okay, whoa, that came out of left field. My cheeks warmed. "I— no. I mean, yes. He grabbed my arm once. You saw him that day in the—"

"Skin-to-skin," Lochlan interjected, so forcefully that I could practically feel the words *touching* me.

I pinched my thigh hard enough to leave a bruise. "Once," I mumbled, wholly uncomfortable with the direction this conversation had taken. "He grabbed my bare waist about a week ago to keep me from falling. Why?"

When Lochlan didn't say anything, I peeked at his face.

What I saw made me suck in a surprised gasp.

He quickly turned away.

"Your eyes." I moved to see them again, but he continued to dodge me. I frowned. After years of being taught to respect privacy, I almost backed off and dropped the subject. But an unexpected determination stole through me as a need to know what he was hiding overroad everything else.

I reached out to touch his face, saying, "Lochlan, I just want to—"

Faster than I could track, he caught my hand.

"Don't." The word was most definitely a command, albeit spoken quietly. Goosebumps erupted over my arms and legs, my body's response to the word.

"Why?" I pushed, unable to let this go yet.

"Because there's nothing to see."

I stared at my fingers clasped firmly in his gloved hand, then shocked myself by saying, "They're beautiful."

He stiffened and dropped my hand, still refusing to look at me.

And because his penetrating stare wasn't on me, I had the courage to continue. "It's what I wanted to tell you earlier today. I thought your eyes were just black, but up close, they're the deepest of reds."

His shoulder moved in a dismissive shrug. "Just a trick of the light."

I frowned again. Seriously, why was he being so weird about his eyes? I opened my mouth to ask him, but before I could, a faint howl shivered through the trees.

Lochlan's spine snapped straight. "Get back to your friend's house," he abruptly said, flipping his hood up to further hide his features. "These woods aren't safe at night."

"Lochlan," I called after him when he took off, his form quickly engulfed by the encroaching darkness. But he didn't return, leaving me to face the long trek back alone.

"Yeah, just run off and leave the girl alone to get lost in the woods," I grumbled under my breath, then spent the next several minutes complaining to an absent Lochlan while I struggled to follow the trail. I really needed my phone's flashlight right about now. "Maybe if you're lucky, I'll get eaten by a bear. That'll stop me from giving you awkward compliments about your unusual eyes. Oh, but don't worry. I'll make sure not to get eaten on your property. Wouldn't want you to feel responsible for my untimely death."

Snap.

Fates, not again!

Before I could freak out and take off running, I heard a familiar female voice call my name.

"Peyton?"

"Kenna!" she said again, flashing a bright light in my face as she hurried over. "We were so worried. Why are you out here? Are you okay? There's a truck out front and we thought someone had kidnapped you, or maybe killed you and dumped your body in the woods."

I snickered and shielded my eyes from her phone's flashlight. "I was thinking the same thing earlier."

"This isn't funny, Kenna." Peyton lowered the light with a huff. "We were seriously worried."

I curbed my laughter, stepping closer to better see her face. "Sorry I worried you all. Where are the others?"

"We split up. It was Hailey's idea. She said there was too much ground to cover as a group, but . . ." Peyton pressed her trembling lips together, her brown eyes unmistakably filled with terror.

"What's wrong? Did something happen while I was gone?" Fates, did Reid go after one of them?

"No, I'm just . . . I'm . . . I'm afraid of the dark, okay?" She winced at her own raised voice and peered nervously into the darkness.

Ah crap, I felt really bad now. "Well, you're not alone anymore. It'll be all right." I awkwardly wrapped an arm around her, not used to hugs, let alone giving them. She buried her face in my neck and clung tightly for a moment, then pushed away, sniffling.

"Don't tell Hailey, okay? She thinks I got over my fear years ago."

I mimicked locking my lips shut with a key and she huffed a weak laugh. "It's okay to be afraid, you know," I said as she texted Isla and Hailey that I'd been found. "We're all afraid of something."

She looked up from her phone. "Oh? What are you afraid of?"

Being lied to. Moving again. Leaving my new friends behind. Never experiencing a deep, meaningful connection with someone.

But I wasn't ready to share those fears with her, or with anyone else. So I simply shrugged, replying, "Axe murderers. Getting stuffed into a basement freezer."

Her laugh was genuine this time, and I smiled at the sound. "Let's go," she said, tucking flyaway strands of black hair behind her ears. "There's a hot tub calling my name."

With the help of Peyton's flashlight, the trail was much easier to navigate. We spent the time talking about her four younger siblings, perpetually exhausted parents, and pet rabbit named Twitchy.

"Twitchy?"

"You know, because rabbit's noses always twitch? Hey, I named him when I was eleven."

My laughter abruptly ended when I heard another *snap*.

"Must be the girls," Peyton said, her earlier fear gone. "Over here!"

"No, wait," I hissed, grabbing her arm. She looked at me questioningly, but I didn't explain, too focused on listening to the quiet surrounding us. Something wasn't right. It was *too* quiet. Not even the crickets were chirping.

A low growl suddenly rumbled through the darkness, making every hair on my body stand on end.

My grip on Peyton tightened. "Run," I breathed.

"W-what?" she stammered, her voice shaking with fear again.

More twigs snapped, closer this time.

"Run!" I shouted, and took off at a sprint, yanking her after me.

She stumbled, but quickly regained her balance, following my lead. I let her go and flew down the trail, relying on my instincts more than the flashlight's chaotic beam.

Over our pounding feet and labored breaths, I could hear something chasing us, something far swifter than we were.

Fear-tainted adrenaline shot through my limbs, giving me an extra burst of speed. "Faster, Peyton!" My left shoe fell off, then the other. Rocks and pinecones dug into my bare feet, but I didn't slow, keeping my eyes glued to the path.

Then I heard a scream.

Peyton!

I looked back, and my foot caught on a protruding root. Lurching forward, I braced for the fall. Pain jarred my bones as I hit the ground. I rolled several feet before coming to a stop.

Another scream lit up the night.

"Peyton!" Ignoring my aching body, I frantically searched for her. My eyes caught on the bright, flailing beam from the phone still gripped in her hand. Beyond the light was Peyton's terrified face as something dragged her feet-first off the trail.

I couldn't see what that something was, but the dark shape was *huge*.

Warmth trickled down my scraped knees when I picked myself off the ground and stumbled toward Peyton. "Hey!" I shouted at the hunched form, hoping to startle it. "Let her go!" Only a bear would be strong enough to drag a human that fast, but the thing looked *grizzly*-sized.

When the animal didn't slow, I found a sizable stick and raced after it. I was a few yards away when the thing finally dropped Peyton, lifting its enormous head to pin me with a stare. Glowing yellow eyes flashed and it released a warning growl. I raised my stick and yelled loudly, refusing to leave Peyton.

Without warning, it charged toward me.

I swung the stick far too late.

A force like a battering ram slammed into me. I soared through the air, back, back, back. My head struck the tree first, then my spine. I crumpled to the ground.

Unable to move or draw air, I helplessly listened to Peyton scream again. *I'm sorry*, I wanted to say but couldn't. *I'm sorry for recklessly wandering off and putting you in danger.* Aunt Tess had told me not to go into the woods, had warned me that something was in them. And now that something was going to eat me and my friend.

No. *No.* I was going to get us out of this mess. If I could just get my body to move, to *breathe.*

Before I could do either, a sharp *whoosh*, followed by a pain-filled yelp, interrupted Peyton's screams.

Then I was moving. But instead of being dragged across the ground, my body was lifted by a pair of strong arms. Wind blasted me in a powerful rush, sucking the little air I had from my lungs. The arms tightened, pulling me closer to a hard chest. The world streaked by in a dizzying blur, and I squeezed my eyes shut, praying I wouldn't throw up.

Less than a minute later, we stopped.

The world tilted again, but at a much slower pace as my body was lowered onto something soft. I moaned, my skull throbbing in agony. When I tried to lift my head and clear my blurred vision, something cold and leathery touched my cheek.

"Don't move," said a deep voice curtly. I stilled, because there was something oddly familiar about his voice. A hand slid down my arm, then the other.

"Peyton," I managed to rasp. "Sh-she needs help."

No reply. The hands continued their course—searching for injury? When they reached my legs, my rescuer inhaled a sharp hiss. I squinted at the shadowy form hovering above me, the features completely cloaked in darkness. Except . . . *there*. A flash of red. Or maybe I imagined it. Either way, my heart sped up.

"You're bleeding," the dark stranger said, almost breathlessly. "Did you get scratched? Bitten?" Before I could answer, the grip on my thigh tightened. What felt like sharpened nails dug into my skin. Startled, I gasped.

In a blur of movement, the grip vanished. And so did he.

Still reeling from the blow to my head, I remained where I was, replaying the sound of his voice. He had almost sounded like . . .

Shadow Man.

I couldn't be sure—everything had happened so fast—but if it was, what did that mean?

It means he followed you all the way from South Carolina, idiot, I inwardly thought. Goosebumps erupted over my skin at the possibility, but I quickly dismissed the notion. If I started to believe it was him, then I'd get jumpy again and Aunt Tess would notice. I hated pretending, but I hated paranoia even more. It didn't make sense that a red-eyed man cloaked in shadows would follow me across the country.

Unless he's a stalker serial killer.

Freaking fates, my mind needed to shut up now.

By the time my hazy vision cleared, the mystery man was long gone. Groaning, I sat up, relieved to find myself on the lakehouse's front porch swing. I slowly stood, grabbing onto a swing chain when I swayed. I managed to make it halfway down the stairs when I heard a scuffling noise from the gravel road.

My body coiled with renewed fear. I flicked my eyes to the SUV, wondering if I could make it to my phone in time before—

The noise became pounding feet. "Kenna!"

Recognizing the voice, I sat down hard on the steps, faint with relief. The sight of Isla and Hailey almost brought tears to my eyes. They were unscathed, and by the looks of it, completely oblivious as to what had just happened. I held up a hand before they could start asking questions. "Did Peyton make it back?"

"I thought she was with you," Isla said, her smile slipping.

"She was." I rubbed my temples and swore. "I'd show you where I last saw her, but I hit my head pretty hard. I'd probably pass out halfway there. You need to call your dad, Isla."

"What?" she practically shrieked. "You do *not* want my dad here, unless it's absolutely necessary."

"It's necessary," I said, trying to stay calm. "Please call him."

She squeezed her eyes shut. After a moment, she heaved a sigh and tapped her phone screen. "What should I tell him?" she asked while the phone rang.

"Tell him a wild animal attacked us in the woods. And tell him that I think it still has Peyton."

Quiet until now, Hailey whimpered. She wrung her hands and looked off into the distance as if considering going after her friend.

"Don't, Hailey," I said firmly. "It flung me through the air like I was nothing. We need help."

Her gaze snapped to mine. "And how did you escape, exactly?" she said, her tone almost accusatory.

I blinked, wholly unprepared to answer that question. What could I say? A dark, mysterious stranger who might actually be my stalker rescued me? "I . . . I don't—"

She waved my words away. "I'm sorry, that wasn't fair. It's just . . ."

Her voice grew smaller, like a child's. "Peyton's my best friend."

My heart sank. This was all my fault. My desire for friendship and connection had endangered others. I should have listened to Aunt Tess. Even Reid. If I hadn't gone on this trip, none of this would have happened. Peyton would be sporting her new bikini at this very moment, safe and sound in the hot tub with her friends.

I wanted a normal life so badly, but maybe I wasn't a normal person.

Maybe there was something in my DNA that attracted danger.

And maybe, just maybe, a part of me was starting to understand my aunt's paranoia. Life was fragile, and I needed to start taking that truth more seriously.

We sat in tense silence until, about fifteen minutes later, a black and white SUV with "Knox County Sheriff" stamped across its side rolled up the drive. A burly blond man emerged from the vehicle— I assumed Isla's dad. As he approached, it was obvious why Hailey thought he was scary. He'd immediately pinned me in place with a piercing look, his stare and stride unwavering. The resoluteness of his expression was unnerving, to the say the least.

"You did the right thing by calling me," he said, briefly assessing his daughter before fixing his steely blue-gray eyes on me again. "I presume you're McKenna Belmont. Where did you see Peyton last?"

I gulped, then pointed toward the side trail. "About a mile down that trail. She has her phone with her."

He nodded curtly. "None of you move from this spot while we check things out. Let's go, Lancaster," he called to the brown-skinned woman with a severe bun who was exiting the vehicle's passenger side. Probably his deputy. They both unholstered their weapons and took off.

We didn't budge from the front steps for hours. The full moon was directly overhead when shoes finally crunched against the gravel. We shot upright and Isla ran to meet her dad and the deputy. Hailey helped me up, my injuries barking in protest as we moved to join them. When I caught sight of the sheriff's dour expression, cold dread filled me.

"Daddy?" Isla said weakly.

"We found signs of a scuffle and this," he said, holding up a plastic bag with a cracked cell phone inside. Peyton's phone.

Isla gasped, but he ignored the sound and fixed a hard stare on me.

"You sure it was an animal that attacked you two?"

"I-I, yes. I'm pretty sure. It growled and ran on all fours," I stammered, uncomfortable with the impromptu interrogation.

"And there was nothing else? Just the animal?"

Crap! I couldn't mention the man who'd rescued me. If I did, he'd probably tell my aunt. And if that happened, she'd freak. My small taste of normalcy would be over and Rosewood would soon be a distant memory. Still, I should tell him. Maybe the man was dangerous and had kidnapped Peyton. I opened my mouth to explain, but what came out was, "That's all I saw."

I was a terrible, *terrible* person.

Sheriff Andrews stared at me a moment more, and I could have sworn he knew I wasn't being honest. But he merely nodded, saying, "There's too much land for us to cover. We'll round up a search party and sweep this whole area at the crack of dawn. I suggest you girls head on home. There's nothing we can do right now."

Hailey burst into tears. Isla pulled her into a tight hug, whispering words of comfort. And I . . .

I stood silently by, guilt gnawing a hole through my chest.

CHAPTER 6

I went through the motions of cleaning the kitchen window, but my mind was focused on anything but.

I worried that Isla and Hailey would never speak to me again if they knew the whole story. I worried that Sheriff Andrews would figure out I lied and call me in for questioning. I worried that they'd find Peyton's mauled body in the woods.

But most of all, I worried that last night's omission was only the beginning, that I would say or do just about anything to protect myself, even at the expense of others. That my selfish need to have a normal life would turn me into someone I hated.

A liar. A deceiver. A *fake*.

All the things I loathed were now staring me in the face.

I should call the sheriff and confess. I had tried to several times over the past twelve hours, but made excuses each time. Like how I didn't know for certain who had rescued me. Or maybe I'd imagined him completely. And telling people about him wouldn't solve anything. I wouldn't even know how to describe what happened without sounding like a crazy person.

But I couldn't deny the truth. I was allowing fear to dictate my actions. I was a *coward*, plain and simple.

I swiped at the window, smearing my guilt-ridden reflection.

Isla had asked us to stay the night at her place, but I'd opted to return home. The guilt was eating me alive, and I couldn't face their questions and suspicion right now. She and Hailey had both joined the search party at dawn, but my sore body prevented me from doing so—or so I told myself.

Aunt Tess thought I'd come home early from Isla's house because of a wicked headache. Just one more lie. The sheriff hadn't called her, but if Peyton turned up dead, no amount of lying would protect me from another move.

If Peyton was dead, I wouldn't want to stay here anyway. The guilt would destroy any desire I had for human connection. Better to move where no one knew me.

I glanced at the oven clock for the umpteenth time. Noon. I pulled out my phone to check for messages again. Nothing. Still no word on Peyton's fate.

"You're quieter than usual," Aunt Tess said from the dining room where she was *finally* putting up curtains. A blue bandana was wrapped around her vibrant red curls, a sure sign that she was in "designer" mode. That was her thing. No matter how short our stay, she always insisted on decorating the place. I, on the other hand, barely unpacked the boxes in my bedroom, let alone painted the walls or added homey touches. I never understood the point.

I tucked away my phone and resumed cleaning. "Just tired. Isla and I didn't sleep at all while I was over there."

"Too busy talking about boys?"

I paused my cleaning, cloth suspended over the glass.

"I'm just curious, Kenna," she said with a laugh. "I knew you'd start dating eventually. It would explain why you've been so secretive lately."

Panic flooded me. What was that supposed to mean? I continued cleaning, hiding my inner turmoil. I knew she was fishing for information, but I wasn't going to give her anything this time. "Nope, still not dating anyone. What about you? You haven't told me about the mysterious *friend* you visited all night long last week."

Now it was her turn to pause halfway up the stepping stool. I could feel her eyes on me, but I held my breath and kept cleaning, hoping she'd finally open up to me. She sighed and said, "It was just a meeting, nothing more. A discussion about how best to keep you safe."

"Safe from *what?*" I blurted, pinning her with an exasperated look. Usually, I avoided this ongoing and fruitless conversation like the plague, but after last night, I was feeling a bit unhinged. "What do you know that you aren't telling me? I'm not a little kid anymore. I can handle whatever it is."

She stepped off the stool to stand in front of me, her brown eyes softening in an almost maternal way—not that I believed the look was genuine. "The world is a dangerous place, especially for girls like you. As your legal guardian, my only thought is to protect you. Certain people, certain *things,* want nothing more than to find and destroy you. I won't let that happen, and that's all you need to know."

When my lips pursed, she grasped my arms and squeezed them. "I know you hate moving and that I don't tell you everything, but this is what your *parents* would have wanted, Kenna Joy. They'd want you safe, no matter what, and that's what I'm making sure of."

Great. She had pulled out the parent card and made me feel guilty again.

With a final squeeze, she released me and resumed her task. In the past, I might have been appeased by her cryptic reply, but not anymore. Why was the world a dangerous place for girls like me? And *what* was out to find and destroy me?

Only two months and four days left of this paranoia.

An hour later, just as I was taking a water break, my phone buzzed.

Seeing Isla's name, my stomach twisted into knots and I quickly answered. "Any news?" I rushed to say, slipping outside through the slider door.

"She's completely fine, Kenna!" came Isla's excited voice, crackling a bit due to poor reception. "Not a single scratch on her."

My abject relief was quickly replaced with bewilderment. I closed the slider behind me with a little too much force. "What? But . . . but the animal. I saw—"

"She said it grabbed her shoe instead of her leg, which was why there were no bite marks on her. In all the chaos, she dropped her phone and couldn't really see the animal though. They're ruling it a black bear attack. Maybe a mama bear protecting her cubs."

I sank onto the wooden deck stairs. "So where was she all night?"

"When she ran from the bear, she got lost in the woods. But get this. Reid found her walking along the side of the road about an hour ago. That gray truck we saw yesterday was *his*. He just happened to be out hiking and camping in the woods nearby."

I stared at the treeline without seeing, my poor mind desperately trying to keep up.

Before I could utter a reply, Isla spoke again. "Anyway, I'm heading home to get some sleep. Peyton's pretty shaken up so probably won't answer any calls this weekend. Plus, she needs a new phone."

"Thank you for calling me, Isla. I'm so glad Peyton's all right."

"Me too, girl, me too."

I ended the call shortly after, assuring her that *I* was fine too. But I wasn't. Guilt was still chipping away at me. Sure, Peyton wasn't dead, but she'd spent the whole night alone in the woods. She must have been terrified.

And a *black* bear? I wasn't an animal expert, but the thing that dragged Peyton off the trail had been huge. *Much* bigger than a black bear.

Then there was Reid's mysterious appearance. I knew he'd been in the area yesterday, so he very well could have been out camping, but it felt like more than a coincidence that he'd found Peyton when he did.

I dropped my face into my hands and groaned. Maybe the best thing I could do was put this whole disastrous weekend behind me.

By Monday morning, my tired brain had begrudgingly accepted defeat. I couldn't explain everything that had happened, but at least Peyton was alive and well. The sheriff also hadn't called Aunt Tess, so I was cautiously optimistic about my chances of staying here.

I exited my Honda, still a bit sore as I crossed the school parking lot. Halfway to the building, I stopped dead in my tracks, nearly toppling over. There, not twenty feet away, was a familiar gray truck. And standing beside it were Reid and Peyton.

As if they'd heard my approach, both Reid and Peyton stopped talking and turned my way. They froze for a moment, then Peyton gave me a forced smile and headed toward the school at a fast clip. I stared after her, confused and a bit hurt. Not that I didn't deserve the cold shoulder. I just hadn't expected that reaction from her. Was she mad that I'd left her all alone in the woods? Maybe she'd seen who'd rescue me and knew I hadn't told anyone about him.

Crap.

But why was she hanging out with Reid? Yeah, he had been the one to find her, but she knew he'd been stalking me lately. Reid was bad news. He was up to something, I just knew it. Maybe he was planning on taking her wherever he wanted to take me Friday evening.

Nope. Not going to happen.

I screwed things up for Peyton this weekend, so the least I could do was protect her from Reid Zimmerman.

Shoving aside my nerves, I marched over to him and jabbed a finger at his chest. "Stay away from Peyton. Whatever beef you have with me, keep my friends out of it."

He grimaced, looking everywhere but at me. "It's too late for that. Look, I can't be seen near you anymore. Let's make a deal—stay away from me and I'll stay away from you. Sound good? It's what you wanted anyway."

Not waiting for a reply, he grabbed his backpack from the truck bed and edged around me. He made it several feet before I came to my senses.

I charged after him. "No freaking deal—not after what you pulled this weekend. If you're going to stalk someone, it's going to be me, not Peyton. It's my fault she's in this mess, and—"

He rounded on me, stopping so abruptly that I almost plowed into him. "You're right, it *is* your fault," he growled in my face. Stunned by his sudden outburst, I didn't react, even when he grew more agitated. "I didn't want this responsibility. I was finally getting the hang of things, then you showed up. If you had just stayed home, none of this would have—"

"You have three seconds to back away before I ram my fist down your throat, Zimmerman," a male voice said directly behind me. "Three . . . two . . ."

Barely glancing at the newcomer, Reid released a frustrated growl and stalked off.

I stared after his retreating back, still reeling from the angry way he'd spoken to me.

"Little Kenna," the newcomer crooned, all traces of seriousness from seconds ago gone. He sauntered around me and I blinked up at an amused Kade. The golden highlights in his caramel brown hair practically sparkled, and his white V-neck tee showed off a powerful-ly-built chest. He and Lochlan couldn't be more different, I realized. They were day and night, both in looks and personality. "You're trouble with a capital T, you know that? Always keeping us on our toes."

Without thinking, I glanced over my shoulder.

"He's not here today."

I turned back to Kade with a frown. "What?"

"You were looking for our boy Lochie," he explained with certainty. "Sorry to disappoint, but it's just me today. I'm not doing too bad of a job though, right?"

My face further wrinkled in confusion. "Huh?"

He chuckled, then walked backward toward the school. "I'm protecting you from the big bad world," he said, jerking his chin for me to follow.

I did, because I wanted him to keep talking. "I don't need protecting," I said, catching up to him.

"Oh, little Kenna, but you do, more than you know."

I rolled my eyes. "Okay, then what do I need protection from, Mr. Cryptic?"

His look turned gleeful. "I like you," he suddenly announced. "And it's not my place to say. Ask Loch."

At the mention of Lochlan, my stomach did a weird flutter. I shook my head, preceding him into the building when he opened the door. "I'm guessing he told you about our little encounter in the woods Friday evening?" When he didn't reply, I glanced over to see that his eyes had widened. "I was on his property," I explained. "He ditched me just as the sun went down."

Kade's expression immediately smoothed. "It's technically *our* property. I live there too. And of course he told me. We tell each other everything. If he ditched you, then it was for a very good reason."

I snorted, navigating the busy hallway as I aimed for my locker. He leaned against the locker next to mine while I spun the combination. "So are you two brothers or something?"

"Or something."

I gave him a peeved look and he laughed.

"Let's just say we're brothers in every sense of the word except for our birth parents."

I wrinkled my nose in confusion. "So you're adopted?"

"No, but close."

"You avoid questions exactly like my aunt," I muttered, shutting my locker. The warning bell rang and I headed for my English Lit class.

"I assure you," Kade said, his long legs easily keeping pace with mine, "I'm usually quite forthcoming. But you're Loch's business."

Annoyed, I snipped, "I'm not Loch's anything. Just because he stares at me like he hopes my clothes will miraculously disappear doesn't mean we're together."

Kade roared with laughter, not caring in the least that dozens of heads whipped our way. "I'm telling him you said that," he gasped out and wiped a tear from his eye.

"Go right ahead," I grumbled, pausing at my classroom door. Before we parted ways, I couldn't help but ask one more question. "Why did you two move here anyway? Why Rosewood?"

His smirk grew a mile wide. "Why Rosewood, indeed," he said with a mysterious wink, backing down the hall and out of sight.

CHAPTER 7

Lochlan wasn't in school the next day.

Or the next.

When Friday rolled around and he still hadn't shown up, I couldn't shake the irrational feeling that he was avoiding me. When I'd not-so-subtly asked Kade this morning where he was, his reply had been, "He's taking a mental health break."

Um, okay.

Not that I cared if he showed. I just wanted to ask him a few questions. At least, that's what I kept telling myself.

I knew for certain that Peyton was avoiding me though, and it sucked big time.

"You going to the football game tonight?" Isla asked me after the final bell rang. I was so busy thinking of ways to approach Peyton that I didn't hear the question.

I glanced at her sheepishly as we filed from the classroom. "Sorry, what did you say? My mind was elsewhere."

She gave me a knowing, sympathetic look. "There's a football game tonight here at the school. Usually we don't go, but with Peyton hanging out with Reid so much lately, and him being the quarterback and all . . ." She let the statement dangle between us, letting me figure out the rest.

Oh. *Oh.*

Maybe if I put some effort into repairing things with Reid, Peyton would come around and start talking to me again. A week had passed since the lakehouse, and she'd dodged my attempts at apologizing several times since then. She'd even started hanging out at Reid's table during lunch, which I knew hurt Isla and Hailey too. They hadn't blamed me, but there was an undercurrent of tension between us now.

I sighed, then nodded. "I'll be there." Isla shot me a relieved smile and slipped her arm through mine.

It wasn't hard to convince Aunt Tess to let me go. In fact, I didn't even have to lie. "You'll be with Isla?" she'd simply asked, then told me to be back by midnight. I was starting to get suspicious but wasn't going to look a gift horse in the mouth. As long as we didn't ask each other probing questions, I could continue living a normal life here in Rosewood.

I'd changed into maroon pants and a golden yellow V-neck to show my team spirit, parting my hair into two french braids tied with red ribbon. I pulled into the school parking lot just as the sun kissed the horizon, surprised at how packed it was. At least I'd worn canvas sneakers tonight, along with my cropped leather jacket.

I checked my phone to see that Isla had already arrived and was saving us seats, so I crossed the parking lot at a brisk pace, sticking to the well-lit sidewalks as I made for the field behind the school. When I spotted the metal, high-rise bleachers, Isla stood and waved wildly. I waved back with a smile.

Weaving through the crowd, I managed to avoid bumping into too many people. Aunt Tess would hate this—the bustling about and boisterous noises, the bright lights shining down from all angles—but I felt my muscles loosen after a tense-filled week. The marching band was playing a fast, staccato beat, and the cheerleaders dressed in short maroon-and-gold skirts were geering up on the sidelines. The stands were filled with people wearing their team's colors, waving "Go, Cougars!" flags and banners.

An invisible weight slipped off my shoulders as I breathed in the delectable smells of fresh popcorn, hot dogs, and nachos. My stomach growled loudly. I hadn't eaten dinner yet, saving my appetite for the game.

I had just grabbed the railing to climb the bleacher stairs when someone rammed into me from behind. My shoulder hit the metal guard with violent force, and I yelped. The person shoved past me without an apology, racing up the steps. Before they disappeared into the masses, I caught a glimpse of their maroon and gold varsity jacket with the number eleven stitched on the back.

"Great school spirit," I grumbled and carefully rotated my shoulder with a wince. Definitely bruised.

I finished the climb to Isla with a little less pep in my step, but decided not to crush her high spirits by mentioning the incident.

"Are Hailey and Peyton here?" I said instead, and she pointed toward the concession stand.

"Getting snacks!" she yelled over the trilling drums and blaring trumpets. Sure enough, they were loading up on all the good stuff, situating four drinks into a cup holder. I dug in my purse for some cash but Isla waved it away, saying, "I've got it covered. I kinda forced you to come anyway."

I shook my head good-naturally. "Are you kidding? I wanted to come."

"Oh yeah?" she challenged with a smirk. "When's the last time you went to a football game?"

"Um . . ."

She laughed. "See? But I'm glad you came. It means a lot."

I knew what she meant, and I smiled, not even caring that it wobbled a bit. "I'll do anything to fix this. I hate that your friendship with Peyton is strained because of me."

"Girl, don't blame yourself," she chided, nudging me with her elbow. "It was a freak accident. Didn't I tell you things would be more interesting with your arrival? I, for one, am loving all the drama."

I snorted, then fell into helpless laughter. She joined me, and before long, we were both clutching our sides. What would I do without this girl? She brightened my life in more ways than one. "Thanks for that, Isla," I gasped out, "but you need a hobby."

She sobered, smoothing her expression to one of mock seriousness. "I have one already. It's very rigorous and time-consuming. In fact, I might have to make it a full-time job."

Stifling my laughter, I sobered too. "Oh? And what's that?"

She leaned in close and stage-whispered in my ear, "I'm stalking your stalkers. Kinda like a private detective. You're welcome."

My mouth fell open and I glanced at her sharply. Did she know about the red-eyed man? Had she seen him somehow?

"Free of charge, of course," she added before I could speak. "You get the friend discount. Just call me Isla, PI. Has a nice ring to it, don't you think?"

I swallowed, fishing for the right thing to say. "Who are you stalking exactly?"

"See? You desperately need someone to watch your back. What if one of them asks you out and ends up being a douchebag? I'm especially suspicious of Reid since he made a pass at you and is all over Peyton now. I didn't think he was the player type, but I've been asking around and checking his social media.

"Lochlan and Kade are trickier though. No one hangs out with them and they don't have social media accounts. Believe me, I've scoured the internet. I can't even find out where they live!"

Um . . . I knew that one. But did I want to tell her and encourage this sleuthing? I didn't know what Lochlan and Kade's intentions toward me were, but I was still wary of Reid's. If she poked around too much, she could get hurt.

Deciding to nip this in the bud, I said, "Reid doesn't want anything to do with me anymore. And Lochlan and Kade definitely won't ask me out. Especially not Lochlan."

The grin she gave me could rival the Cheshire Cat's. "Why so adamant that the dark and mysterious Mr. Stares-A-Lot won't ask you out? I've seen the way he looks at you, like a starving man who found a triple-decker cheeseburger."

Heat flushed through me and I spluttered nonsensically, which only made her cackle like a hyena. Thankfully, Hailey and Peyton's arrival took my mind off Isla's creepy new scheming gig. Hailey smiled as she sat next to me, but Peyton ignored me completely. Ouch. I focused on the food and drinks being passed around so I wouldn't do something unacceptable—like cry.

Minutes later, our football team charged onto the field, led by Reid Zimmerman. We clapped and cheered, but the tension between us was thick. When the game began, I could see right away why Reid was quarterback. His tall frame packed with lean muscle kept him light on his feet. And his throws were *fast*. My eyes could barely track some of them.

At half-time, the score was ten to seven, Cougars in the lead. Peyton left to use the restroom, and after a moment of indecision, I followed. Confrontation wasn't my thing. I always ended up losing when I finally had the nerve to speak up. But I had to make things right with Peyton, even if I lost her in the process. I needed to take responsibility for my actions and be a *true* friend.

I can handle it, I reassured myself, dodging bodies in an attempt to catch up with her. The girl could *move*.

"Peyton," I called as a group of giggling girls blocked my path. She didn't turn, either not hearing or ignoring me completely. Probably the latter. I tried not to let it get to me, I really did. I skirted around the girls and broke into a jog. "Pey—"

Out of nowhere, something smacked into my bruised shoulder, pushing me sideways. Then, before I could orientate myself, a large drink filled with crushed ice flew toward me, drenching my chest and stomach. I gasped in shock from the freezing liquid.

"Whoops," said a male voice, sounding far from apologetic. "So we meet again, vixen. A little birdy told me you'd be here tonight and I couldn't resist."

Peering up from my ruined top—which was now cherry cola red—I met the wickedly amused gaze of August Henderson. I blanked at the sight of him. If it weren't for his bottle-green eyes and bleach blond hair, I wouldn't have recognized him. Several angry red marks—*claw* marks—cut across his face, clearly still in the early stages of healing. One had severed his left eyebrow clean in half. Even his neck was mangled.

But what held my attention was the gold number eleven on his varsity jacket.

"Getting your fill?" he leered, gesturing at his face. "This is *your* fault, you know. If you hadn't teased and then rejected me that night at the party, I wouldn't have entered the woods to blow off steam. I had to get one hundred and fifty-three stitches. You *ruined* my face. On top of that, I can't play football tonight. Coach benched me for the next two games."

I backed up a step, trying to remain calm despite the bald menace in his eyes. "That wasn't my fault. You wouldn't leave me alone.

Maybe next time you'll take no for an answer."

He laughed cruelly, raking his eyes down my wet front. "No isn't in my vocabulary."

Yeah, I wasn't going to win this confrontation, not against a pig-headed guy like August. I abruptly turned and pushed through the crowd, saving my talk with Peyton for another day. Veering toward the parking lot, I quickly texted Isla that I wasn't feeling well. Coming here had been a mistake anyway. The world seemed to be against me right now, and wallowing alone in my sorrows sounded like a good plan. Maybe I'd sneak a pint of cookie dough ice cream up to my bedroom—after soaking in the tub.

Rounding the side of the school building, I grimaced as a cold chunk of icecube slithered between my breasts. I paused to remove my leather jacket and unstick my shirt, then resumed my trek.

Halfway down the sidewalk, I heard shuffling feet and male laughter behind me. I glanced over my shoulder and spotted a handful of guys rounding the corner. Their eyes met mine and I quickly jerked my head forward again.

Crap, the one in the middle was August.

I sped up, hoping to reach the parking lot before he could enact any more dumb ideas, but the feet behind me sped up too. I lurched into a jog, and so did they. Fear-fueled adrenaline spiked through my limbs and I flat out ran.

Go, go, go!

Suddenly, the parking lot sounded like a death trap. I'd never pull out my keys and start my car in time. They'd catch up and drag me into one of their own vehicles. Inwardly panicking, I did the only thing I could think of.

I jumped off the sidewalk and bolted toward the property fence.

I squinted through the darkness, practically blind but already knowing what lay beyond that fence. I knew and charged forward anyway.

I hit the chain link fence at a run, dropping my jacket and purse as I grabbed the top and heaved myself upward. My feet scrambled for purchase, my bruised shoulder screaming at me, but I managed to roll over the fence and fall to the other side.

Pain stole my breath away when I awkwardly landed on my bad shoulder. Fates, I was an idiot. I struggled to breathe, to move. The guys drew nearer, a few of them laughing—like this was a freaking *game*. Gritting my teeth, I scrambled away from the fence.

And plunged into the graveyard.

CHAPTER 8

"Oh, vixeeen, come out and play," August singsonged, and his goons chortled.

I curled up against the headstone, knees pulled tightly to my chest. The guys had fanned out along the graveyard's edges, trapping me somewhere in the middle. Now I was cowering in the shadows of a dead person.

Stop thinking about it, stop thinking about it.

But I couldn't stop. Graveyards reminded me of my dead parents, of their bodies that had never been recovered. I'd only been three when their malfunctioning airplane had crashed into the Atlantic Ocean, but I grew up with nightmares of being trapped alive underwater or underground.

Stuck in the darkness forever.

Slap! Hands came down on the headstone behind me. I yelped and scrambled away from the grasping fingers. More hands joined in, yanking my braids so that I fell backward to the ground. August loomed over me and I kicked at him, catching his inner thigh. He grunted but dropped down to trap me between his knees.

When his thighs squeezed my hips, panic flooded me in torrents. I bucked and writhed, extending my fingers to scratch him, but he caught my wrist in a punishing grip.

"Nah-ah," he chided. "Scratch me once, shame on you. But you're not getting the drop on me again. Where *are* those wicked talons of yours anyway? Decide to cut them?"

I whipped my other hand up, throwing a little surprise in his face. He reared back, cursing as fine dirt struck his eyes. I aimed for his cheek and dragged my fingernails over the angry claw marks. He bellowed and grabbed my flailing hand before it could do more damage. Then squeezed.

I choked on a sob as he bent the delicate bones to the point of breaking.

"August, you're hurting her, man," one of his companions said nervously, but August only laughed.

"Have you *seen* my face? She deserves it. In fact—" He wrestled both arms above my head, pinning them down with one hand before fishing something out of his pocket with the other. Flicking his wrist, he pointed a switchblade at my face. "—I think I'll return the favor."

My breaths came in ragged gasps as he lowered the knife to my cheek. "Please," I whimpered. "Please don't."

He paused. For a split second, I let myself hope that he had a decent bone in his body after all. But then he cocked his head to the side and said, "I remember now. That's exactly what I said, right before I was *mauled* to an inch of my life."

The blade's tip shifted, sliding down my face to my neck without cutting.

"This was the first spot. A bite mark," he murmured, almost trancelike, then dug the blade into my neck just above the shoulder. The skin split and I squeezed my eyes shut, fighting back tears. "Next, I was slashed across the chest by claws."

He palmed the blade and grabbed my V-neck. A loud rip cleaved the air as he yanked on the material. I screamed.

Whoosh!

In a blur of movement, his weight vanished.

My eyes flew open and I swallowed another scream. Because there, towering over me, was the red-eyed man. Black shadows curled up his legs, torso, and arms, obscuring his face. All except for his eyes.

It was him. I was certain this time.

It was Shadow Man.

The temperature plummeted as I beheld his cold, furious countenance. But, for once, those piercing eyes weren't on me. They were focused on August, whose feet dangled inches from the ground, his neck caught in the man's viselike grip.

"Take care of the others," he said, his voice sharp like a whip.

I struggled to prop my weight on my elbows, flinching when a gust of air whooshed by me. The other guys must have taken off, leaving their friend behind.

"You should have listened," Shadow Man said to August, whose legs began to flail uselessly. "I won't spare you this time."

I cringed when desperate choking noises left August as the life was slowly squeezed out of him. I loathed the guy, but I didn't want him dead, especially not because of me.

"S-stop," I managed to say. "Please."

Those eyes—those blood-red eyes—lowered to fix on me.

Predator. Run! my instincts screamed.

But I remained glued to the spot, heart in my throat, unable to look away. I didn't know if it was fear, stupidity, or something else entirely that made me stay. "Please don't kill him," I said, louder this time.

He continued to silently stare, long enough for August's body to go limp. Then he dropped him. After a moment, August rolled over and heaved air into his starved lungs. He coughed and groaned, but he was alive. He started to crawl away, eyes wide with undiluted fear.

Shadow Man wasn't done with him yet though. He crouched, gripping August's shirt to bring them face-to-face. "Last warning. Never touch McKenna Belmont again. Nod that you understand." August nodded woodenly. "Give me your car keys." August obliged without comment, and the man casually chucked the keys behind him. "Now run, and forget my face."

August immediately picked himself up and bolted.

Silence settled over the graveyard.

Wait a freaking second. What if *Shadow Man* had attacked August the night of the bonfire party? Maybe Reid had nothing to do with it. Okay, mind officially blown.

"You know my name," I suddenly blurted. Then shivered, more from his lingering stare than the night's chill. Silence stretched between us again.

Then he moved.

His approach was soundless, slow and calculated. He crouched before me like a phantom. I should have shoved him away. I should have run screaming. I remained perfectly still.

He reached out with a gloved hand. Paused. Inhaled. His gaze flicked to my neck, to where the knife had split my skin. He stared for the longest time, raising goosebumps on my flesh, then resumed his course. Cool leather skated across my cheek. He grasped my chin and tilted my face up.

But before he could open his mouth, I said, "I won't forget."

He froze.

His scarlet eyes shuttered. With uncertainty? Fear? Impossible. He was darkness personified. What was more confident and fearsome than him? Still, he hesitated, so I forged ahead, ignoring the way my teeth chattered with nerves.

"You followed me here from South Carolina. I remember when you first approached me. I'd picked up my order from the diner and there you were, hiding in the alley's shadows. You told me I wasn't human. You told me to forget your face. But I never did, so don't bother telling me again. For whatever reason, you saved me tonight. You saved me last week too—at least, I think you did. And I don't want to forget that."

His fingers spasmed against my chin. What felt like long, sharpened nails pricked my skin through the leather gloves, and I flinched. Fates, they weren't *claws*, were they?

Black, icy mist continued to billow around him, hiding his features from me. All I could do was peer into his red eyes, waiting for him to say or do something, *anything*. Would he admit to stalking me? Or would he threaten to kill me like he had with August? When he didn't so much as blink, the tension became too much and I jerked my chin out of his grasp.

Quick as an adder, he snaked a hand behind my neck and yanked me close. I gasped as he dipped his head toward my neck and breathed deeply. Only his gloves touched me, but I felt his breath against my skin like a warm caress. Hints of amber, sandalwood, and musk teased my senses. The scent was familiar, and I struggled to place it.

"Why don't you fear me?" he breathed against my skin, and my heart fluttered like a hummingbird's wings.

"I do," I managed to croak, my throat constricting. There was no point denying it. He must know how startling his appearance was.

"No. You don't." His hold on my neck tightened, and I swallowed, waiting. Waiting for something to happen.

When seconds that felt like hours ticked by and nothing happened, I reached out with trembling fingers and touched his sleeve.

He sucked in a sharp hiss and I jerked my hand away. What was I *thinking?* "W-who are you?" I stammered before I lost my nerve—or before he decided that killing me would be best.

Silence.

Far too late, I became painfully aware of my vulnerable position. We were alone in a graveyard, for fate's sake! He'd almost *strangled* someone to death only a moment ago. And, as much as my mind wanted to deny it, I didn't think he was human. I shouldn't be asking him who, but *what.*

"That's more like it," his voice rumbled in my ear, sending shivers dancing along my skin. "You *should* fear me."

His words finally jarred some sense into me and I tried to pull away. When his hold remained ironclad, I gasped out, "If that's what you think, then why bother saving me?"

After a long, torturous pause, he said, "I'm not saving you," and pulled back so I could feel the full might of his gaze. "I just don't want you dead yet."

Then, in a blur of smoke and shadow, I was in his arms. He shot across the graveyard at an impossible speed, confirming that he wasn't human. Before I could even gasp, he set me on my feet again, right beside my dropped purse and jacket.

With a *whoosh*, he was gone.

Blood-red eyes.
Amber, sandalwood, and musk.
Black obsidian shadows.
Cold and leather gloves.
Reaching for me. Reaching.

So close to touching.

I jerked awake, desperately clinging to the dream. I knew it was important, that I needed to remember something. But it was slipping, slipping, slipping away.

And, *poof,* the dream vanished.

"Argh." I sat up in bed and checked my phone. Three in the morning. I shivered as cool air kissed my bare arms, then swung my legs over the side and stood. After a quick bathroom trip, I returned, only to feel cold fingers of awareness skate up my spine.

Someone was watching me.

I stiffened, listening for any sound. The feeling continued to creep across my skin, raising goosebumps. I spun and almost shrieked when I saw movement, but it was only my reflection in the dresser mirror. I stared at my wide, pale gray eyes for a moment, then rolled them.

I was just about to look away when something shifted in the mirror. I froze and searched the reflective surface, fear tightening my throat. There! A flash of red. I whirled toward the window, noticing that I hadn't closed the curtains all the way. My bare feet were silent on the cold floorboards as I cautiously approached.

Both French casement panels were cranked open, just enough to let in the night's chill. I *definitely* hadn't left them open. It was too cold outside. A splash of color above the window seat drew my gaze downward and I gawked at the unexpected sight.

Perched on the windowsill, illuminated by a sliver of moonlight, was a single red rose.

I blinked. What the—?

As if afraid the rose would lash out and bite me, I slowly reached for it. When I picked it up and nothing strange happened, I rolled the stem between my fingers and promptly pricked myself on a thorn.

"Ow." I dropped the rose and stuck the injured finger into my mouth. Another flash of red from outside caught my eye. Pressing my nose to the window pane, I peered into the darkness. For a moment, everything was pitch black. And then, just beyond the treeline, two glowing red eyes winked into existence. I flinched back, then looked again. For once, the eyes were still there. *He* was still there.

Like he wanted me to see him.

Had *he* left me the rose? I couldn't think of any other explanation. But why had he? And how? My room was on the second floor and there were no trees nearby to climb.

An emotion I couldn't define shivered through me. It should have been fear, but it was something else entirely. Something that didn't make sense.

I cranked the windows shut and drew the curtains closed with a *snap*. My heart thundered as I backed away. I spotted the rose but continued to retreat, letting it lay where it had fallen.

I just don't want you dead yet.

I couldn't get Shadow Man's last words out of my head. What did they mean exactly? Was he planning on killing me at some point? It was hard to feel afraid though when he left me a rose instead of sneaking inside my bedroom to kill me.

I scratched out the doodle I'd drawn in my notebook and started a fresh one. Instead of harsh lines, I softened my strokes, outlining the figure in dark, billowing smoke. Argh, why couldn't I stop thinking about him?

The bell rang and I closed my notebook, relieved that lunch

hour was next. Isla and Hailey's chatter should help distract me from thoughts of my mysterious stalker. If only I had someone to confide in. I'd always dreamed of having a close friend I could share all my secrets with, and I wanted that friend to be Isla. But her dad was the *sheriff*. One slip of the tongue and Aunt Tess would be notified. One slip and I'd lose my new friends.

No, keeping all the weirdness bottled up inside was safest. That way I wouldn't lose anyone.

But when I spotted Isla and Hailey in the cafeteria minutes later, my heart sank. They were sitting next to Peyton at Reid's table. After my botched attempt at fixing things Friday night, I hadn't spoken to them all weekend. Maybe they'd given up on me.

Maybe I'd already lost them.

My eyes smarted with tears and I furiously blinked them away. Crying wouldn't fix things. I used to cry every time Aunt Tess announced we were moving again. I used to beg her to let me stay. It never did me any good.

I hadn't truly cried in years. A few tears here and there, yes, but I'd learned that my vulnerable side could be used against me. People saw tears as weakness, as a sign that you couldn't handle the hard stuff. Well, I *could* handle it, and I wouldn't give anyone a reason to doubt that.

Clenching my teeth, I strode into the room. As I headed for the lunch line, I tried to ignore the mostly unfamiliar gazes that followed me. They continued to pummel my back while I grabbed food I had no appetite for, then tracked my progress to an empty table far from Reid's.

Maybe *I* was the problem here. I could have walked over to their table and sat down, but . . . I wasn't brave enough. What if they took one look at me and told me to leave?

Apparently I could only handle so much of their rejection.

Okay, I was sulking *big* time. Pathetic.

With my eyes glued to my tray, I didn't notice the person bee-lining for my table. They bumped into it *hard*. The round metal top lurched sideways and my tray skidded off before I could grab it. Out of nowhere, a hand snatched up the tray midair while the table settled with a loud clang. Not a single thing was out of place when the hand slid the tray in front of me.

I tipped my head back to thank my food rescuer and was startled to find Lochlan there. I hadn't seen him in nine days—not that I was counting. The sight of him now brought mixed feelings, the most prominent being a fluttering beneath my rib cage.

Whatever, body.

It was on the fritz these days. First Shadow Man, now this guy. I couldn't trust my weird reactions toward the two of them.

Lochlan didn't meet my gaze though. He was too busy glaring at something to my left. I swung my attention that way and stiffened.

August was looking over his shoulder at me with an ugly frown. Remembering the feel of his blade, I itched to cover the bandage on my neck. I assumed he must have been the one to bump my table. Despite Shadow Man's warning, I doubted he would leave me alone. He hadn't enacted his revenge yet.

He continued to stare at me until I heard Lochlan shift. A small movement, but August's eyes flew to his. Visibly paling, he averted his gaze and rushed from the cafeteria.

I blinked, gaping after him. What was that all about?

Behind me, I heard a familiar, darkly amused chuckle. "That guy has a death wish." Without asking, Kade slid into the chair next to mine and set down his lunch tray. I did a double-take at his plate, which only contained a heaping mound of fruit. "You look lonely, little Kenna," he said, startling me into looking up at him.

Before I could answer, Lochlan claimed the seat opposite me. A very unfortunate blush decided to make an appearance then. Which was probably why I spoke without thinking, muttering a quick, "Girl problems."

Kade choked on a piece of fruit, spluttering, "What kind of girl problems are we talking about here?"

I froze, my eyes widening in horror. "Not *that* kind. I mean girlfriend problems. As in—"

He wouldn't let me finish as he hooted with laughter and slapped the table.

"Okay, thanks so much. I'm gonna go die now," I said over his cackling and grabbed my tray to leave.

A hand shot across the table and gripped the tray before I could. My gaze focused on the deep crimson stone in Lochlan's ring, then the thorn-covered vines tattooed up his forearm, refusing to go higher. I was *that* mortified. "Stay," he said in that smooth, unflappable way of his. "Kade promises to behave from now on. Isn't that right, Kade?"

Kade snickered, but bobbed his head in consent. I glared at him, not trusting his sincerity. He crossed his heart and raised a hand. "Scout's honor."

"It's three fingers, not two," I said after a moment, letting go of the tray. Lochlan relaxed and settled back in his chair, stretching a long leg out beneath the table.

"I'm so sorry, girl!" gushed a female voice, bustling around me in a swirl of pink skirts and vanilla body spray. Did Kade just sniff her as she passed? "I was trying to talk some sense into Peyton before you arrived, but you snuck on by me." Isla set her tray down to my right and bent to give me an awkward, one-armed hug. "I really am sorry.

Hailey is too. I know that looked bad."

I gripped her shoulder to return the hug, clinging like a lost kitten. My eyes started to burn and I squeezed them shut. *Yeah, I'm a bit obsessed with her*, I admitted to myself. Which worried me. If I was forced to leave Rosewood before my eighteenth birthday, losing her would crush me. Still, I was willing to take that risk. Now that I'd tasted true companionship, I didn't realize how starved for it I'd been.

"It's okay," I murmured, relieved beyond measure that she was still my friend. When she pulled away to sit down, I quickly blinked the moisture from my eyes, then realized with a start that we had an audience.

Or more like *I* did.

I cast the barest of glances at Lochlan, confirming what I already knew. He was closely watching me—which was normal for him but felt different this time. He'd observed a vulnerable moment. He'd seen a chink in my armor, and I felt naked under his piercing gaze.

Flustered, I cleared my throat and shifted my attention to Kade. Fates! His wicked smirk was almost worse. My last hope was Isla, who was flicking glances between me and the guys. I straightened in my seat, saying, "Um, Isla, this is Lochlan D'angelo and Kade . . ."

"Carmichael," Kade supplied, extending his hand across the table. "Nice to meet you, Isla Andrews."

She arched an eyebrow before shaking his hand. "You know my last name."

"I make it my business to know anyone associated with Kenna," he said with a wink.

Her eyes narrowed. "As do I."

Uh, okay. I peeked at Lochlan under my lashes, who was studying the two in contemplative silence. As if he'd felt my gaze, his eyes snapped to mine. The blackened depths seemed to pull me in, seeking to unravel my every thought. My breath hitched, but I refused to look away. I swallowed and his eyes tracked the movement.

"So when did this happen?" Isla said, jolting me out of my trance.

Suddenly parched, I reached for my bottled water. "When did what happen?"

She gestured around the table. "This threesome thing."

I choked on my water.

Kade guffawed.

My face burst into flames.

"This isn't—" I wheezed, only to be interrupted by Kade.

"We can make it a foursome, if you want."

"Kade," Lochlan chastised. All eyes turned his way, but his attention remained fixed on me.

Kade clamped his jaw shut and threw me an apologetic look. After a beat though, he muttered, "Isla started it."

She harrumphed, clearly not finding him all that amusing. "I just don't like being left out of the loop, and there is definitely something going on here. I need details, lots of them. What do you guys want with Kenna? And don't blow me off. I *will* find out, one way or another. My dad is the sheriff, after all."

I gaped at her. Wow. Go, Isla.

Kade whistled softly, openly staring at her with new appreciation, then jerked his thumb at Lochlan. "Don't look at me. Ask him."

Isla flicked pink-tipped blonde hair out of her eyes and blinked expectantly at Lochlan. I propped my elbows on the table and grabbed a fry from my plate.

This should be interesting.

CHAPTER 9

"We're here on business," Lochlan finally said, taking his eyes off me to answer Isla's question.

"What kind of business?"

"Family business," he replied cryptically.

"Was it a coincidence that you arrived shortly after I did?" I broke in, asking the question that had been plaguing me for weeks.

His gaze fell to his untouched food. Clearly he didn't want to divulge why he was here, but now that my question was out, I wouldn't back down. I *needed* to know. Too many weird, unexplainable things had been happening lately, and my gut told me that Lochlan had answers to some of them.

Time crawled by as I waited for his reply. Nerves got the better of me and I grabbed my bracelet, twisting it round and round my wrist.

Eventually, he peered up at me through his dark lashes and said one word, a word that shot ice through my veins. "No."

Fates. My suspicions were right. They had followed me here.

I let go of my bracelet to pinch my thigh. Now *three* people were following me, if I included Shadow Man. What the crap was going on? Was I in danger from them? Had my aunt been right all this time, or was I becoming as paranoid as her? I pinched my thigh harder.

"Whoa, easy there," Kade murmured soothingly, raising his hands. "You don't need to be afraid of us." I jerked my gaze to him, startled at his intuitiveness. He gave me a reassuring smile, but I was too busy internally freaking out to listen.

He shot a look at Lochlan, whose dark eyebrows had slammed down over his eyes. *So not helping, guys!* My fingers trembled from pinching so hard.

When I winced from the pain, Lochlan said, "We're here to find a missing person." He leaned forward, as if readying to give chase in case I bolted. "That's what we do—follow cases. It's a family business, as I said."

I stared at him, not understanding. Missing person?

Isla came to my rescue. "And you think Kenna is that missing person?"

His silence was answer enough.

I shook my head, finally finding my voice. "But I'm not. I'm not missing. I've lived with my aunt for almost fifteen years."

"And how much do you actually know about your aunt?"

The way he said it twisted my stomach into knots. Several conflicting emotions rushed through me, the strongest being panic.

"I . . . Is this a *joke?* It's not funny." My chair scraped back as I jumped to my feet. Lochlan was up nearly as fast. "Look, I don't know why you're saying this, but my personal life is none of your business. So, please, stay out of it." I stepped away from the table and Lochlan mirrored the movement.

The panic intensified, surging through my limbs. I whirled toward the exit but forced myself to walk calmly. When I heard Lochlan close in behind me though, I nearly burst into a sprint.

"McKenna," he said, and from the corner of my eye, I saw him reach for me.

Before he could make contact though, Kade called out, "Let her go, Loch."

Lochlan's hand curled into a fist, right before I picked up speed and left them all behind.

I called in sick, skipping my afternoon classes to spend the time driving around Rosewood. I mindlessly wove from one end of town to the other, finally stopping at North Point Cove to burn off some nervous energy. Removing my ankle boots, I trudged through the sand, glad that I had the beach to myself.

The sky was overcast, its angry gray clouds threatening rain. Wind tugged at my hair, blowing the thick brown tresses across my face. I only half paid attention to my surroundings while I navigated the rocks that led down to the churning water. My brain was too busy debating if Aunt Tess had ulterior motives toward me or not.

Sure, she was secretive and paranoid, but she was my mother's *sister*. She looked nothing like me or the photo of my mom though. Her skin was much fairer, and she had curly red hair and brown eyes. Still, siblings didn't always look alike. She also knew things about my parents, personal stuff. And she'd been babysitting me when the accident happened.

But I'd only been three years old. Maybe she'd left out some important details. What if she had—

Ding.

I fished out my phone, my toes inches from the pounding surf.

Need me to call my dad? Isla's text message read.

No. Thanks anyway though, I quickly typed, but paused before hitting send. Maybe it was time to confide in someone. There were too many unknowns now, too many people in my life with secrets. What if I was actually in danger? But from whom? The list of possibilities was steadily growing.

I pressed send and tucked my phone away. If I told Isla everything and she then told her dad, who knew what Aunt Tess would do.

Maybe striking out on my own early was the best option. That way, I was the one in control of what happened next. I couldn't stay in Rosewood though. I'd essentially become a fugitive, a runaway. But I would miss my friends. And I would miss—

Chilly ocean water sprayed my feet, startling me out of my thoughts.

"Thank you, water," I muttered, bending to roll up my jeans. "You just saved me from thinking something *really* stupid."

Eventually, I talked myself off the ledge and returned home. When I arrived, the sky split open and dumped rain. It was almost like an omen. A bad one. *Argh, stop!* I scolded my overworked brain, holding my bag over my head as the rain came down in sheets.

I had just closed the door and removed my jacket when Aunt Tess appeared out of nowhere. I almost peed my pants, whipping around to face her. "Gah, you scared me."

Instead of apologizing, she crossed her arms over her chest and stared at me expectantly. Unease trickled through me. "Well?" she simply said.

My mouth opened, but nothing came out.

"The school called," she continued, narrowing her eyes. "They said you left during lunch period due to illness. So where have you been for the last five hours?"

Five hours? Crap, it hadn't felt that long.

"I . . . I went for a drive," I confessed, scuffing the toe of my boot. "I needed to clear my head. I've had a lot on my mind lately."

She released one of her long-suffering sighs, closing her eyes for a moment. "Like what, Kenna?"

When she fixed her gaze on me again, I inwardly recoiled from what I saw there. She was giving me the *look*, the one that said my next words would send her into a packing frenzy. A well of resentment and anger surged up, nearly choking me. "I'm sick of this."

She stiffened. "Sick of what?"

I threw my hands in the air. "Your paranoia about every little thing. Yes, I had a bad day, but that doesn't mean we need to move again! You said it was going to be *different* this time, but that was obviously a lie. I can't take the moving and the secrets anymore!"

She pursed her lips. "McKenna Joy Belmont, don't you dare shout at me. I'm your guardian and will be treated respectfully."

"*Are* you though?" I threw back before I could stop myself.

Her mouth formed a surprised O. We stared at each other, our expressions equally horrified.

After an impossibly long moment, she ever so quietly said, "What is that supposed to mean?"

"Nothing," I quickly replied, looking away.

"Kenna."

"Nothing!"

"Kenna, you will tell me. We are not leaving this spot until you— Kenna, don't you dare leave this house!"

But I was already ripping open the door and storming into the rain once more. I'd snatched my bag off the floor on the way out, but not my jacket. Within seconds, my thin white shirt was soaked through. I didn't care. I didn't care about anything except getting far away from here.

Only one month and twenty-five days left.

Or maybe sooner, depending on how the day ended.

Aunt Tess followed me outside, but I ran to my car, slipping inside and turning the ignition before she could reach me. In a spray of mud and gravel, I reversed down the drive to the main road, then slammed my foot on the gas. The car fishtailed on the slick pavement, but I quickly straightened and shot down the road.

I drove without direction, letting my instincts take over as I sped faster and faster. I had screwed up. *Big* time. I punched the dashboard and the car swerved, nearly wrenching the wheel from my grip. I immediately slowed, shaking from fear and anger. When my heart was no longer threatening to suffocate me, I sped up again, but at a more reasonable speed.

Instead of heading downtown, I'd driven the opposite direction, which I'd never done before. Somehow, the dense woods blurring past looked familiar though. It took me a few minutes, but I eventually figured out where I'd seen this area before. On our way to Hailey's lakehouse. Bittersweet memories—mostly bitter—smacked me upside the head.

I almost turned around, loath to remember how the trip went from sweet to sour. How the four of us were now split in two. But my thoughts snagged on another memory then, of meeting Lochlan in the woods. He and Kade lived out here.

A part of me never wanted to see them again. They had stared at me for *weeks* without saying a word. For some reason, that made me feel like an idiot. Neither of them had stared because they were interested in asking me out. They had stared because it was their job.

I was their freaking *job*.

Yeah, we'll see about that.

My resolve hardened, and I tightened my grip on the wheel.

Sooner than expected, I passed the private drive that led to Hailey's lakehouse. Beyond that was another stretch of empty road. A few miles later, I skidded to a stop, almost overshooting what I hoped was the right turnoff. The drive was nearly hidden behind the twisted branches of a gnarled oak tree. I was hesitant to drive under the branches, afraid they'd snap off and land on my Honda.

Making it safely through, I drove down a windy, gravel drive at least a mile long. My wipers thwacked against the windshield, desperately trying to clear the way. Finally, the watery shape of a house swam into view. *House* was a cheap word for the place though. Even with the rain and approaching dusk obscuring most of the details, I could still make out a three-story maple wood monstrosity. Gable-shaped windows dominated the front, and porches wrapped around the bottom two stories.

"This creepy family business stuff must pay well," I grumbled, killing the engine. Rain pelted the windshield and roof, loud enough to drown out my arrival. Maybe Lochlan and Kade weren't even home. I searched for the black Lexus I'd seen them leaning against in the school parking lot, but the drive was empty. This place probably had a garage though. In fact, I wouldn't be surprised if there was a helicopter pad, it was that huge.

I sat there for who knew how long, listening to the rain and wondering why on earth I was here. I wanted answers, I knew that much, but did I actually believe what Lochlan had said about me being a missing person? "No freaking way," I said firmly. Did I believe he was dangerous? I couldn't answer that one. But if he'd wished me harm, he could have done so already. I had to hope that wasn't the case.

Gathering my courage, I opened the car door and stepped out. Rain further saturated my shirt, fusing the material to my body. I stood a few paces from the car, suddenly feeling like a half-drowned, weirdo stalker. Now that I was here, my earlier anger seemed inconsequential. Who was I to storm over here and demand answers?

As if in agreement, lightning forked the sky, followed closely by a boom of thunder.

I turned to leave when a sudden gust of wind to my left startled me. Damp hair smacked my cheeks as I whipped that way. Nothing was there but an empty stretch of lush green lawn. Still, the feeling of being watched shivered up my spine. I squinted through the rain at the house, but the windows were dark.

The last of my courage melted away. I shouldn't have come here. What if this wasn't even their *house?*

Another gust whooshed close by and I whirled, still unable to see anything. My heart thundered as I quickly backed up toward my car. I spun and reached for the door, but a tall, dark form barred the way. I yelped and backpedaled too fast, tripping over my own feet. Before I could eat gravel, a pair of arms surrounded me, halting my descent.

Blinking against the rain pelting my face, I peered up into black eyes mere inches from mine. "Lochlan," I gasped, too shocked by his sudden appearance to do anything but stare.

I expected him to quickly release me like he had the past couple of times I'd bumped into him. When he didn't, I became fully aware of his hands supporting my head and lower back—but especially his thigh wedged between mine, inching dangerously close to the apex. Without permission, my body heated in response to his nearness. My own hands reached up to clutch his slick leather jacket.

"What are you doing here?" His deep, silken voice was like a caress against my skin, and I shivered. When he continued to hold me, almost as if he didn't realize it, my brain emptied.

Why was I here?

And were Lochlan's eyes growing brighter? That deep wine red had returned, wholly captivating me. I felt stripped bare under the intensity of his stare, like my every emotion was spread out before him. I couldn't decide whether to pull away or draw closer, to hide or expose myself further.

A sense of déjà vu washed over me then. There was something familiar about his hold. A memory pricked at my consciousness.

Just as the memory began to sharpen, Lochlan jerked upright

and stepped back, leaving me devoid of his touch and teetering on unsteady legs. I blinked, shaking my head to clear it. Holy fates, what was *that?* I barely knew the guy and he'd made my body light up like a firework. Never in my life had I felt anything so intense and intimate. I'd completely forgotten who I was for a second. Who *he* was—a stranger who very well might be dangerous, a serial killer even.

After a moment more of calming my racing heart, I looked up at him, only to find his gaze pinned to my chest. I glanced down, immediately noticing why. My wet shirt was proudly displaying two very alert nipples. Instead of feeling annoyed or embarrassed at the attention, I had the oddest desire to make him squirm. So I did, popping my hands onto my hips, effectively stretching the shirt taut over my breasts.

"I came here for answers," I said, infusing confidence into my voice. "I want to know why you think I'm a missing person, and why Kade thinks I need protection. Also, why is it such a big deal if Reid touches my skin?"

At the mention of skin, he swallowed and forced his eyes back to mine. I tried not to smirk as he struggled to don his usual blank expression. Faster than I'd hoped, though, he was back in control, saying, "You shouldn't be here, McKenna."

My confidence slipped at his brusque tone. "Why?"

"You just shouldn't," he said obtusely, and reached for my arm.

I avoided his touch, my earlier ire toward him reigniting. "I'm not leaving until I get some answers. Look, I'm starting to freak out here. Everyone's keeping secrets, including my aunt, and I don't know who to turn to. Actually, I don't know why I even came here. For all I know, you're a stalker killer who's going to stuff my mutilated body in a basement freezer. I bet there's a really big freezer in your house."

Crap! Why did I just say that?

94

Rain slid down a deep groove forming between his brows. "I won't kill you."

I snorted and crossed my arms over my chest. "How come I don't believe you?"

"Because you're smart."

My jaw dropped. Uh . . .

"Turn to your instincts," he continued. "If you don't know who to trust, then trust them. And if they're telling you to run right now, do it."

"But . . ." I shook my head, beyond flustered. "My instincts are telling me that you have answers, and I want them, even if I have to stand in the rain all night to get them." I flicked a pointed glance at his house, but he ignored the silent hint.

"Go home, McKenna," he said, more firmly this time. "You'll be safe there."

"But I—"

"If you want answers, start by searching that house of yours. It harbours many secrets."

"Lochlan." I stepped forward, but he moved back, glancing at his wristwatch.

His lips thinned and he turned, striding toward the side of his house. Clenching my teeth, I followed.

"*Loch.*"

Not even the use of his shortened name made him pause. He disappeared around the corner and I sped up. When I rounded the house seconds later though, he was nowhere to be found.

I spun in a circle, squinting through the downpour. "What the crap?" He'd truly vanished.

Trying to rationalize his disappearance, I searched for clues along the house. After a few minutes, I growled in frustration and almost turned to leave. There was nothing here but a bunch of red rosebushes.

I slammed to a halt.

Roses.

Red ones.

Goosebumps erupted over my skin as something clicked in my brain, a connection I'd been subconsciously trying to piece together for a while now.

Lochlan had been wearing black leather gloves again.

And now, combined with the red roses and his disappearing act, I couldn't help but finally make the connection.

Lochlan and my red-eyed stalker had these three things in common. No, they had a *lot* more in common than that. They had both followed me to Rosewood, for starters. They both kept coming to my rescue. And they both sparked an awareness in me unlike anything I'd ever felt before.

It all boiled down to one impossible yet undeniable realization.

Lochlan D'angelo and Shadow Man were one and the same.

CHAPTER 10

Sending the twentieth call to voicemail, I tossed my phone on the bed and went back to eating my cookie dough ice cream. I had *never* avoided my aunt before—I'd never had the courage. But after today's realizations, something inside me had shifted.

I didn't feel like walking on eggshells anymore just to soothe Aunt Tess's paranoia. If she wanted to move after our confrontation today, then she could move without me. I didn't know how I'd manage to stay in Rosewood, attend school, and financially support myself, but I'd cross that bridge when the time came.

All I knew was that my need for answers outweighed the risks. There was a big empty box in my head that needed filling, and I wouldn't rest until it was overflowing with information.

"So what do you want to watch next?" Isla asked. Grabbing the TV remote, she scrolled through the movie options.

When she landed on a teen fantasy, I said, "That one looks interesting."

"Wait." She peered at me from her sprawled position on the bed. "You've never watched this cult classic before?"

"My aunt is kind of anti-fantasy." I made a face around my mouthful of ice cream. "I've watched a few fantasy shows when she wasn't around, but I usually draw and read in my spare time."

She shook her head and rolled over to better see me. "Do you think she'll call the police if you don't go home soon?"

I paused, then scarfed down more ice cream. "Dunno. Maybe." But I was already in hot water with her, so I honestly didn't care right now. I'd face her when I was good and ready, which wasn't tonight.

After my realization at Lochlan's house, I'd driven aimlessly for an hour, loath to return home. Not knowing where else to go, I had arrived on Isla's doorstep, soaked and miserable. She'd taken one look at my lost expression and ushered me inside, showering me with empathy, warm clothes, and comfort food.

Shortly after, while snuggled up with a fuschia pink blanket on her bed, I'd finally done it. I told her everything, my whole life's story. From my parent's sudden deaths, to the constant moving, to Aunt Tess's paranoia, to the endless secrets and lies. I even told her about the strange things that had happened to me this past month, including my encounters with a red-eyed shadow man.

The only thing I left out was my newest theory that Lochlan and Shadow Man were the same person. I wasn't quite ready to verbally admit that truth yet, still reeling at the prospect of Lochlan being something other than human.

When I had finished, Isla merely hugged me and said a movie marathon was in order. No hysterics, no frantic phone calls to the police or her dad. No judgment. She'd taken it all in stride and accepted me and my words at face value. I didn't quite know how to deal with the abject relief and gratitude I was feeling. I only wished I'd had someone like her to confide in *years* ago.

"Well," Isla replied to my uncertainty, "you can stay here for as long as you want. My dad will be fine with it."

"How can you know for sure?" I never knew if my aunt would be fine with something.

She sighed and tucked a fuzzy pink pillow beneath her chin.

"Since we're all about raw honesty tonight, I'll be completely honest with you. The reason my dad rarely denies me anything isn't because I'm the baby of the family—or even that Noah was such a rebel. It's because my mom died four years ago."

I lowered my spoon to the nearly empty container. "Oh, Isla, I'm so sorry."

She hugged the pillow harder. "Thanks. Cancer got her, and I know it still tears my dad up inside. He saves people for a living, but he couldn't save her. To cope with her loss, he buries himself in work and spoils me rotten." She shrugged, adding, "I don't mind the spoiling part though."

I offered a weak smile. "I wish I could remember my parents, but I was too young. All I have of them is a family photo and this." I lifted the silver charm bracelet that encircled my left wrist. "It was my mom's."

She crawled forward to better see the bracelet, then grabbed my arm, practically shoving it in her face. "Your pendant. I've seen the design before."

"Oh?" I studied the key-shaped charm more closely. The two half moons etched on its surface were back-to-back, with a line bisecting them and a single dot at each end.

"Yeah. I don't remember what it means, but I've seen that symbol in a book my mom had. Now Noah has it. Ever since she passed, he's been big into sorcery. He thinks he's a warlock or something." She snorted and I chuckled, dropping my arm.

We stayed up way past our bedtime, swapping childhood stories and bingeing the first two movies in the fantasy series. The more I watched, the more contemplative I became. If Lochlan was Shadow Man, then he wasn't human. And if he wasn't human, what was he?

As the end credits rolled on the second movie, I drifted asleep thinking of supernatural beings.

Especially the fast ones whose eyes changed colors.

His familiar scent swirled around me.
One scent. Two bodies.
No. Only one body.
His gloved fingers slid down my cheek.
My eyes fluttered open to see his hovering form.
Cloaked in shadow, all except his red gaze.
The shadows suddenly thinned.
His lips parted, revealing two gleaming fangs.

I shot upright, choking back a scream. My eyes frantically searched the unfamiliar room. I could still remember the dream. I could still remember his *fangs*. Spotting Isla's sleeping form on the bed beside me, I relaxed and settled against the mattress.

No more watching supernatural shows before bed, I warned myself, pulling the blankets up to my chin.

When my heartbeats slowed, I waited for sleep to reclaim me. And waited. Something was poking at my brain though. Something to do with the dream.

I rolled off Isla's bed and tiptoed across the room. Reaching the window, I slowly pulled aside the curtain, then slapped a hand over my mouth.

A single red rose graced the windowsill.

Chills raced up my arms and I stepped away, shoving the curtain back in place. For several minutes, I stood and replayed the vivid dream in my head. I had smelled him. I had seen him. And I had . . .

I reached up and touched my cheek.

And I had *felt* him.

My eyes widened as reality sank in.

It hadn't been a dream.

"What is this sorcery?" I mumbled, already feeling a tiny jolt of much-needed energy.

"Good, isn't it?" Isla shut the door of her white Mini Cooper and took a healthy swig of her own drink. Staying up late on a school night had its consequences, and we'd both needed extra eye concealer this morning. Thank the fates for caffeine though. "Mama Jo's Cafe is a hidden gem here in Rosewood. They have the best coffee I've ever tasted."

I nodded my agreement, which surprised me. I didn't think anything could top Starbucks. Even this early, I was optimistic about the new day. With Isla by my side, I felt ready to tackle the hurdles ahead of me. I'd face my aunt later today, but right now, I needed to deal with whatever was behind those school doors.

Starting with Lochlan D'angelo.

Instead of throwing away the rose from last night, I'd stuffed it into my bag before leaving Isla's for whatever reason. I hadn't told her about the incident, worried that she'd freak out. I mean, Shadow Man—er, *Lochlan*—had broken into her house, for fate's sake.

But fangs? Were those real or imagined? I'd been watching a movie about *vampires*, after all.

Either way, I was going to confront him about the stalking thing. And the breaking and entering thing. And maybe the attacking August thing. Crap. If I mentioned any of those things, he'd know I was aware of his alter ego. I had no idea how he'd react to that.

"Two o'clock," Isla muttered under her breath as we entered the building.

Speak of the devil, there he was, leaning against a locker across the hall from mine, his cohort Kade beside him. Not surprisingly, both their gazes latched onto me the second I walked through the door. I waited to feel fear—the sane, *rational* emotion to have under the circumstances. Instead, a dangerous warmth surged through me. Dangerous, because my body was obviously suicidal.

When Lochlan's eyes skated down my front, landing on my bare legs, I blushed fiercely. Isla had let me borrow an outfit for the day, and since her pants didn't fit me, I'd selected a jean skirt. A *short* one, made all the shorter by my taller frame. Paired with ankle boots, my long legs were on full display, and Lochlan was eating them up.

"Good goddess," Isla breathed beside me. "He's totally screwing you with his eyes. I think I just got pregnant."

If I'd been drinking my coffee right then, I would have spewed it across the hall. "I can't believe you just said that," I whispered, mortified. She merely snickered. Okay, change of plans. I would *not* be confronting him right now.

When Isla headed for her locker, I veered toward mine, doing my best to ignore the eyes on my back. I opened my locker and a note fell out, fluttering to the floor. Before I could grab it, someone else did. I looked up to find Kade leaning against the locker next to mine, wearing a mischievous grin.

"Oh, little Kenna, the games you play," he crooned, waving the note in the air.

Nervous energy shot through me. Was he referring to my knowledge of Lochlan being Shadow Man? Or maybe I was simply reading into things like a paranoid freak. What if he didn't even know himself? Seemed unlikely since they lived together, but either way, I needed to tread carefully.

I tipped my chin up, adopting a bored expression—or tried to anyway. "I'm not playing any games. And that's mine, so if you please."

He tsked, but handed the note over. "Sure thing. I already read it anyway." At my glower, he feigned hurt. "Don't be mad at me. I'm just looking out for you."

"Well, don't," I said coolly to cover up my nerves, tucking the note inside my English Lit textbook. "In fact, I'd like it if you and your *friend* backed off."

At that, he instantly sobered, straightening to his full height. "Why, what changed?"

Uh oh. Maybe I should go back to being the girl who kept her mouth shut. I huffed as if annoyed with this conversation and slammed my locker closed, all while debating what to say. "What do you mean?"

"Yesterday evening, you came to see us. You wanted answers. So what's changed since then?"

I chuckled flippantly, but it sounded strained even to my ears. "Why don't you ask Lochlan? After all, he tells you *everything*."

Flicking my hair behind me, I stormed down the hallway. When he didn't follow, my knees weakened with relief. I actually liked Kade despite his teasing, but he was practically tied to Lochlan's hip. It was better that I keep my distance from him too.

Whatever Lochlan was up to, I was almost certain that Kade was in on it.

I sat in the front row of English class, hoping to focus on *school* rather than the dozens of things plaguing my mind. Halfway through the period though, I remembered the note from my locker. Slipping it out, I peeked inside while Miss Finch was busy reading aloud from our assigned book.

Letters in blocky capitals read:

Stay away from Lochlan and Kade. They're dangerous.

Well, crap. There was nothing like confirmation to get the heart pumping. But that wasn't all, I suddenly realized. Kade had read the note earlier.

Fates, I was so screwed.

Someone was watching me.

Not a casual bypasser look, but a deep penetrating stare. I walked faster, my low heels clipping smartly against the tiles. I rounded the corner and spotted my destination. I could make it. I could—

"Did you get my note?"

The low male voice in my ear made me jump, and I dropped a book. Cursing under my breath, I stopped to pick it up, but someone was already holding it out to me. Startled to discover the person was Reid, I hesitated, then accepted the book with a muttered, "Thanks."

"Keep walking," he whispered in reply, jerking his chin toward our next class.

I did, since I was pretty sure by now that I'd misjudged him. I still didn't trust him, but I didn't think he was trying to silence me for witnessing August's attack anymore. "I thought you weren't supposed to be near me," I whispered back, darting a quick look at his profile.

"I'm not. But I overheard your conversation at lunch yesterday."

Uh . . . That was impossible. He'd been sitting on the opposite side of the cafeteria. What if . . . No, I didn't want to think it. But I did anyway, wondering if Isla had broken my confidence and told Hailey and Peyton everything. I mean, they had known each other since grade school, but I'd hoped she was different. I'd hoped she would be that one person I could trust.

"I was wrong about you," Reid continued, interrupting my worried thoughts. "The first time I met you, I thought I'd accidentally—Well, never mind that part. It doesn't matter now. What matters is that, despite our differences, I don't want to see you get hurt.

"There's this story my dad told me when I was a kid. I thought it was just a fairy tale, but when Lochlan and Kade explained yesterday why they were here, I remembered that it was about these three dark princes who were cursed. And the only way they could break that curse was by finding a—"

Suddenly, Reid vanished. I glanced over in time to witness Lochlan slam him against the lockers. Several students gasped and scuttled out of the way. With a snarl, Reid shoved him off, only to be slammed back again. I froze, shocked and uncertain what to do. Lochlan pressed his forearm against Reid's throat and fiercely whispered something I couldn't hear.

Finally deciding to intervene, I stepped forward, only for an arm to settle over my shoulders and forcibly steer me away.

"Yeah, not a good idea, little Kenna. Not when the Lochness Monster has come out to play." In a single fluid move, Kade plucked the books out of my hands.

I craned my neck back to glare at him. "Didn't I just tell you to stay away from me?"

"Yes. And I decided to politely ignore your request," he had the audacity to say, leading me toward my next class.

I ground my teeth together. "Let me go, Kade."

"Not gonna happen."

Wrong thing to say. I grabbed his thumb that was dangling off my shoulder and bent it inward. Hissing sharply, he lurched away from me. I quickly whirled toward a still-fighting Lochlan and Reid, shoving past a few students to reach them. I had no idea what I would do, only that I wanted this stupidity to end.

"Stop!" I barked when Lochlan slammed Reid against the lockers once more. "Let him go, Lochlan. Reid can talk to me if—"

"Get off me, man," Reid growled, clearly not hearing me. He threw a punch, catching Lochlan square in the jaw.

At the sound of the impact, heat rushed through me, a startling fury that locked me in place. But as Reid cocked his arm back for another hit, I lunged at him without thought, snagging his shirt sleeve. When his fist plowed forward anyway, I grabbed his wrist with both hands and clung tightly. Even then, I could feel his superior strength. If he wanted to hit Lochlan again, I couldn't stop him.

But he didn't. He had frozen, his arm suspended midair.

And attached to his arm were my hands, still wrapped around his wrist. Before I could release him, warmth from his skin seeped into my palms. The longer I held on, the more uncomfortable the contact became. I was about to let go when a red light suddenly pulsed between my fingers.

Startled, I gasped, and so did Reid.

Out of nowhere, Lochlan swooped in and yanked me away. With an arm firmly locked around my waist, he stalked down the hall at a fast clip. If it weren't for his arm supporting most of my weight, I wouldn't have been able to keep up.

We passed Kade, whose wide eyes mirrored my own. Lochlan didn't slow, shooting right past our history classroom.

Nerves ricocheted in my stomach like bouncy balls.

"Lochlan, let me go or I'm going to scream."

"Don't," he said curtly, sounding so much like Shadow Man that my breath hitched. "I won't hurt you," he added, which didn't reassure me in the least.

He whipped around a corner as the second period bell rang, and I grew painfully aware of the hall's emptiness. Fates, this wasn't good. I tried dragging my feet and elbowing him to no avail. I might as well be a speck of dust for all he noticed. Remembering how Shadow Man—how *Lochlan* had picked August up off the ground with one hand—I finally opened my mouth to scream.

Quicker than I could blink, he pressed a hand over my mouth, muffling the sound. I reached for his arm, but in a dizzying whirl, he wrenched a door open and forced me inside. Before the door had finished closing, he managed to secure both my wrists while still covering my mouth.

It wasn't the door clicking shut and plunging us into darkness that freaked me out the most though.

It was the fact that during all the chaos, he'd somehow managed to slip on a pair of gloves.

CHAPTER 11

I screamed into the glove, thrashing against his grip.

His hold was unbreakable though. I was completely and utterly helpless.

He let me scream and struggle. Let me wear myself out.

And the whole time, he didn't say a word.

I couldn't stop a hot tear from falling. Then another.

I hated them. I hated *him*.

What was he going to do to me?

I just don't want you dead yet.

Fates, my time must be up. I was going to die!

Eventually, I had no choice but to sag against him, utterly spent. My chest heaved as I pulled in ragged breaths through my nose. He waited until I'd calmed. Waited with infinite patience.

If he didn't end up killing me soon, I was going to kill *him* for this.

"Promise not to scream and I'll let you go," his voice rumbled in my ear, deceptively smooth—as if to put me at ease. The thought ticked me off even more. He shifted his hold on my wrists while still keeping them firmly trussed together. "We could stay here all day if need be. The janitor probably won't open this closet until late this evening. All you have to do is nod."

Yeah, but they'd see your shadow self, I ached to shout at him.

Then what will you do? Kill them too? Another angry tear leaked from my eye.

When I refused to cooperate, he added, "Hate me all you want, but those are my terms."

At least he knew how I felt.

After another stubborn moment of silent rage, I nodded against his hand. Just like that, he released me. Before I could get any ideas about leaving though, he flicked on the overhead light and turned me to face him. His expression was inscrutable as he studied my face. I glared back with all the venom I could muster.

"How do you feel?"

I blinked, startled that he'd ask me such a thing. "How do I feel? I'm *livid*," I hissed, knocking his hand away when he tipped my chin up. "Stop. Touching. Me. You're a *monster*, Lochlan D'angelo."

His lips thinned, the only reaction I could get out of him. Ignoring my words, he gripped my face in his gloved hands and peered deep into my eyes. "How. Do. You. Feel?" he enunciated slowly and with force. I felt the question seep beneath my skin and burrow into my brain. It demanded an answer. I had no choice but to reply.

"Hurt," I snarled. The word was pried from my lips without permission, as if torn from a secret inner compartment. I bared my teeth as more words were forced from me. "I'm hurt that you're doing this to me. I'm hurt that you lied."

I heard him swallow. Felt his thumb wipe away a tear. "What did I lie about, McKenna?" he said quietly.

I clamped my lips shut, willing myself not to answer.

His eyes brightened to a wine red. "Tell me."

Words I wasn't prepared to share—ones that revealed how much I knew about him—pushed at my throat. They rose higher and higher, unfurling on my tongue. "Stop," I gasped out, shoving down the words again. "I feel *fine*. Is that what you want to hear? I'm completely fine."

If it stopped him from pulling words out of my mouth, I'd say just about anything.

A deep line formed between his brows. "How are you doing this?"

"Doing what?"

"Resisting. How are you resisting me?" His question tugged at me again, seeking to unravel my self control.

Desperation creeped in and I blurted the first thing I could think of. "I don't know. Maybe because you lack charm? Girls like that stuff, you know." Crap, *really?* To cover up my stupidity, I deflected. "Why do you wear gloves?"

His fingers stiffened against my cheeks. Bingo. Pressing my luck, I reached for his hands. Before I could make contact, he released me and stepped back. I'd seriously hit the jackpot. If I pushed a little harder, maybe he'd let me leave this closet.

"Is touching me that repulsive to you?" I said, slowly stepping toward him. "And *my* touch? Is that equally repulsive?" I raised a hand to his face. When he froze, letting me draw close, my bravado wavered. He was supposed to *retreat*, not actually let me touch him!

But I couldn't back out now, no matter how intimidated I was by his towering form in the small space. Fates, he wasn't even *human*, and I was trying to touch him. What did that say about my sanity?

My heart thundered, probably loud enough for him to hear. My fingers trembled as they inched closer. At the very last second though, he pulled away.

Relief weakened my knees, and I immediately dropped my arm. But there was something else too. A tiny stab of disappointment that refused to be ignored. Well, too bad. I was ignoring the feeling. Because it was *stupid*. I should not want to touch Lochlan D'angelo for so many reasons.

"I'm not repulsed," he replied a bit gruffly. Watching me closely, he removed his gloves, as if to prove his words. "But your skin can't touch mine for the same reasons it can't touch Reid Zimmerman's. Remember what happened last time?"

"Uh . . ."

"After Reid touched your skin last time, you fell ill with fever."

"What? How do you even—" Ah crap, of course he would know. He was *Shadow Man*. He'd been there the night of the bonfire party. He'd seen me strip off my shirt and mop my feverish brow. Not that I was embarrassed. Okay, maybe a little. Or a lot.

"Give me your phone," he suddenly said, and held out his hand.

"What?" Not caring that I sounded like a broken record, I gawked at his extended limb as if it were a striking snake. "N-no way. You stalk me enough as it is."

Without warning, he invaded my personal space, his body a breath away from mine. Before I could react, he slipped an arm around me and plucked the phone out of my back skirt pocket, all without touching me. He retreated just as quickly, saying, "This is so you can contact *me*. I promise not to call you unless it's an emergency."

Mouth slightly ajar, I stared at him while he typed in his number. The need to scream tightened my chest. The *audacity* of this guy. "Why on earth would I ever want to call you?"

He impassively met my steely gaze. "Let's hope it doesn't come to that. But if you feel unwell in the next twenty-four hours, call me. I'll explain only what you need to know." He handed my phone back, carefully avoiding my fingers, and reached behind him for the door handle.

"Wait," I said before he could leave. "That's it then? This whole man-handling me inside a closet charade was simply to give me your *number?* Un-freaking-believable. You know what? Screw you. I'm late for class."

I marched forward, deliberately knocking my shoulder into his on the way out—which freaking hurt, by the way. What was he made of? Skin-covered titanium?

So much for confronting him about his alter ego. I was too upset to get into that right now.

"The teacher won't notice your absence," he called after me, to which I snorted. Did he forget which teacher this was? I paused outside the classroom to school my expression, then sheepishly slipped inside. I waited for Mr. Davis to stop his lecture and embarrass me in front of the class again, but he didn't even look my way.

In fact, he didn't seem to notice me the entire rest of the hour.

"Okay, whoa, my brain just fried," Isla said, dropping her food tray onto a picnic table far from prying eyes and ears. She sank onto the bench and gaped at me.

I sighed and set down my own tray. "I know. I'm still having a hard time believing it." We had opted to eat lunch outside today so I could unburden to her once again without being overheard. I'd told her *everything* this time, from the roses on the windowsill to Lochlan being Shadow Man. "Sorry if this freaks you out. I just . . ."

"Girl, how are *you* not freaked out? If I'd been shoved into a closet by someone who transformed into an inhuman creature, I'd be curled up in the fetal position and balling my eyes out."

I snickered at the mental image. "No you wouldn't. You're much too strong for that."

"Hey, we all have our breaking points. Lochlan is way too intense for me. Now, if *Kade* shoved me in a closet . . ." She grinned impishly at my raised eyebrows, then smoothly changed the subject: "So tell me again what instigated the fight between Lochlan and Reid."

I shrugged, picking up my chicken wrap. "I'm not exactly sure. I mean, they've been glaring at each other from day one. There's obviously bad blood between them. But Reid warned me today that Lochlan and Kade are dangerous. Then he mentioned a story his dad used to tell him, something about three dark princes who were searching for a way to break a curse. And then—"

"Then your smoking hot stalker interrupted and started wailing on him?" Isla snorted at my head nod. "I know this is serious stuff, but I'm still jealous of all your boy drama troubles. At least I can live vicariously through you," she added, laughing when I rolled my eyes.

"I don't care *how* sexy Lochlan's voice is. What he did today was totally not okay. I'm super mad at him." Recalling how he'd rendered me immobile without breaking a sweat, I savagely bit into my wrap.

Isla shot me a sly look. "But you think he's sexy. That's gotta count for something."

I choked as a piece of chicken lodged in my windpipe. "That's not . . ." I spluttered, coughing to clear my throat. "I said his *voice* was sexy." When she merely snickered, I threw a fry at her. "Anyway, what if he's part of a gang or the mafia? It would explain why my aunt is so secretive and why we move all the time. Maybe she's running from someone. But that doesn't explain the weird stuff."

"Like the red eyes and shadow form?"

"Yeah. And how he can move so fast. And why I'm not supposed to touch him. And—"

"And why he's so hot?"

"Shut up." I threw another fry.

Her smirk suddenly vanished and she set down her fork. "Do you believe in supernatural stuff?"

"What, like demons and angels?"

"Yeah. But I'm thinking more earth-based, like witches and . . ." She paused to nervously chew on her bottom lip.

Oh no. So I wasn't the only one thinking it. That maybe, just maybe, we were dealing with . . . "Vampires?" I whispered for her, feeling dumb just for saying the word.

But she met my eyes and nodded soberly. Ah crap. "Well, you said Shadow—I mean, Lochlan—had fangs in that dream you thought was real, right?"

"Yeah, but we had just finished watching that vampire movie. I could have imagined it." I pinched my thigh, willing it to be true.

"But August was *bitten* and you said Shadow Man was there in the woods that night."

"I'm still not entirely convinced that wasn't an animal attack, Isla." I pinched harder.

"But there's something about that night I didn't mention," she whispered, panic creeping into her voice. "When they found August, he was almost completely *drained* of blood. The public report said his blood loss was from the bite and scratch wounds. But I overheard my dad saying to Deputy Lancaster that it was from something else entirely."

Oh. *Oh.*

I barely managed to swallow as bile raced up my throat.

"Freaking fates," I muttered.

"Lochlan D'angelo is a vampire."

The words drifted on the air and I waited for them to penetrate my brain.

No such luck.

"Lochlan D'angelo is a *vampire*."

Ugh. Still nothing.

Growing up in an anti-fantasy home made the concept beyond ludicrous. My mind wanted to explain away every single strange thing I'd seen, assure me that stuff like that only existed in books and movies. But the thought was there all the same, lingering under the surface like a tumor.

I killed the car engine and slumped forward in my seat, resting my forehead on the wheel. After the day I had, I was completely wiped of energy. Neither Lochlan, Kade, nor Reid had approached me after our disastrous morning encounter, but I'd still felt their eyes on me, more intensely than ever. And after seriously considering that Lochlan could be a vampire, every cell in my body had been on high alert.

Now, parked outside my ramshackle home, exhaustion consumed me.

I couldn't rest yet though. I had one more thing to face, something I was dreading with every fiber of my being.

So much for boldly confronting my demons today.

When I entered the house, the interior was as somber as a tomb. I warily searched for moving boxes, expecting half the house to be packed by now, but nothing had been touched. Still, I treaded carefully, uncertain of this encounter's outcome.

I found Aunt Tess sitting at the dining room table. As I approached, I noticed dark circles under her eyes and redness around the rims. She'd been crying. She *never* cried. Guilt twisted my stomach into knots. "You should have just dragged my butt out of school,"

I said lamely to break the layer of ice between us.

She folded her hands on the table, lowering her gaze to them. "I almost did."

I waited for her to demand where I'd been, to scold me, to order me to pack my things. The silence grew painful. "I'm sorry," I blurted, but only halfway meant the apology. I was sorry for running off and ignoring her calls, but not for speaking my mind.

She raised her tired eyes to mine. "I'm sorry too. I know this way of life hasn't been easy. I've tried my best to protect you, but . . . things will be changing soon."

My stomach churned anxiously. "What do you mean?"

With a weary sigh, she stood and crossed over to me. Picking up my hands, she squeezed softly, saying, "Don't worry, Kenna Joy. We won't be moving. Not this time."

CHAPTER 12

My shock and elation at knowing we weren't moving was cut short.

A headache had been pulsing behind my eyes all afternoon. It was now throbbing incessantly, pounding at my temples. Probably due to the little sleep I got last night.

I laid down for a nap, but my mind wouldn't rest. Eventually, I grabbed my phone and typed in a search for vampires. The internet lagged, eventually spitting out a slew of disturbing images and articles. Words like undead, evil, and demon caught my eye.

But Lochlan didn't seem evil—well, most of the time. He'd man-handled me earlier today and might have attacked August and drained his blood though. Gross. Okay, so he wasn't Prince Charming, that was for sure.

A terrible idea came to me then. An extremely dangerous one. I'd be stupid to ever consider doing such a thing, but apparently my need for answers still outweighed common sense.

Besides, what if I was wrong? What if Lochlan was nothing more than a human guy with a glove fetish?

There was only one way to find out.

The following morning dawned cold and bleak. I awoke with a groan, blaming the weather for my lingering headache. But it was the fevered flush to my cheeks that gave me pause. I couldn't pretend away Lochlan's warning from yesterday. He had seemed fairly certain that I would fall ill in the next twenty-four hours, and I had.

I took a cold shower and did my best to conceal the dark smudges under my eyes. If I didn't want answers so badly, I would have skipped school and stayed in bed all day. But the not knowing was driving me batty, so I pushed aside my weariness and headed downstairs.

"Aren't you going to eat breakfast?" Aunt Tess called chipperly from the kitchen, her voice expertly masking any strain between us.

"Sorry, I'm running late. Bye!" I replied back with equally fake cheeriness before exiting the front door. I wasn't hungry anyway, especially not for burnt toast and overcooked eggs. I also didn't want her probing eyes to notice how unwell I felt.

Getting through the school day was a whole lot harder than I thought it would be. I was pretty sure Lochlan noticed the signs of fever right away, but I kept my gaze carefully averted every time we crossed paths. By the time the final bell rang, the fever had spiked and I wanted nothing more than to rip my clothes off. Absently waving to Isla as we parted ways, I headed for the girl's bathroom.

I waited in a stall until the last girl left, then waited some more. If I wasn't currently half-delirious with fever, I might have abandoned my plan. I was being reckless and a touch crazy, but I also couldn't stop thinking about it. About *him*. I had to know what he was before this became a full-blown obsession.

When the bustling sounds outside the bathroom dimmed, I emerged from the stall and walked to the exit. Then shoved a wooden wedge beneath the door, essentially locking it.

The small action sent a wave of heat through me. I felt like a roasted marshmallow. Sweat slid down my spine and I grimaced, wrangling off my jacket and long-sleeved shirt. It was a struggle to leave my tank top on, I was *that* hot. I turned on the faucet and splashed cool water over my face and neck.

Letting the water run, I stared at my reflection for a beat. "Just get it over with," I muttered to myself. "Nothing's going to happen to you." Except the last time I'd said that, two mysterious guys invaded my world and I'd been struggling to cope ever since. Hardening my resolve, I reached for the paper towel dispenser and aligned my wrist with its sharp metal edge. I breathed in and out a few times, preparing myself for the pain.

Then dragged my skin along the edge.

I choked back a scream as fire burned up my arm, hotter than the fever. After another second of cutting, I withdrew my arm and hazily blinked at the damage. Bright red blood was seeping from a two inch gash on my right wrist. I briefly wondered if I'd need a tetanus shot after this, but the thought vanished as another wave of feverish heat barreled through me.

With a gasp, I doubled over, clutching the sink. I paused a moment to catch my breath, then placed my wrist under the water. Only for a moment though. Just long enough to wash away some of the blood. I turned off the faucet and picked up my jacket, slowly pulling it back on with a moan. I hated the thought of blood staining the sleeve, but it was a small price to pay for answers.

Unless I was wrong. Unless—

The door burst open, and the wooden wedge I'd placed beneath it ricocheted off the wall like a useless toothpick. I turned from the sink, equal parts startled and pretending to be as Lochlan's frame filled the doorway. He swept his dark gaze over my body, nostrils flaring. My heart pumped triple time.

Gulping, I managed to say somewhat calmly, "Do you mind?" and twisted the faucet as if to wash my hands. I glanced down, noting the way my fingers trembled. Not from the fever or even the pain, but from having *him* at my exposed back.

My plan had worked, but I almost wished it hadn't. I couldn't run from the truth now. There could only be one reason why Lochlan had barged in here like this.

He could smell my blood.

I had planned for this moment, but I hadn't thought of what would happen next. I silently cursed myself for not coming up with an *escape* plan. I mean, I hadn't believed it possible. That Lochlan could be a—

"Are you injured?"

I yelped and whirled to find him inches away. Backpedaling, I stumbled against the counter behind me. He reached out to steady me, then froze with a hand midair. His eyes locked on my right jacket sleeve. The blood hadn't seeped through yet, so I knew, just *knew* that he was scenting it right this very moment.

"I'm fine," I squeaked. *Real smooth.* I slowly tucked my arm behind me, and he tracked the movement. My breath hitched and I inched sideways, the need for space overwhelming. He gripped the counter's edge, cutting off my escape.

I couldn't tell if it was panic or the fever that made my head spin, but my escape attempt ground to a pathetic halt as I sagged weakly against the counter.

"Kade," I heard Lochlan say over the pounding in my ears. "I need supplies from the nurse's office. Now."

I squinted at the exit in time to see Kade backing away. He smirked, mouthing, *Trouble*, before slipping from view.

"Take your jacket off. I need to see your injury."

At Lochlan's words, true panic set in. My breathing came in short spurts, revealing my nervousness. "Um. N-no thanks," I stammered, blinking hard to clear my vision. "Stupid plan. Stupid, stupid plan."

"What plan?"

Crap, I hadn't meant to say that out loud. Another heatwave blasted through me and I couldn't hold back a small whimper. In the next instant, I was hoisted onto the counter. Shocked, I didn't react right away. When Lochlan's hands left my hips though, I realized how vulnerable my position was and shimmied toward the edge. Only for him to boldly wedge his body between my legs.

Freaking *fates!*

I wiggled backward until my shoulders struck the mirror, but he didn't take the hint. His hips continued to push against my inner thighs, trapping me in place. Never in my life had I been in a situation like this before. It was new and scary and overwhelming, but also thrilling and hot. So stupidly hot. The friction of his jeans against mine was seriously messing with my sanity. I had the dumbest urge to inch forward and—

"Look at me, McKenna," he said, using his sexy voice. *So* not cool.

Pursing my lips, I shook my head.

"You need medical attention. I only want to help."

Help? *Sure* he wanted to help. By sucking all the blood out of me.

At the mental image of him draining me dry, crazed laughter bubbled up my throat. Low at first, but quickly gaining volume. It was the unhinged, hysterical kind. The kind that, at any other time, would have embarrassed me. But I was way past petty embarrassment right now.

"Kade," he said over my helpless giggling. "We need to get this jacket off."

"What did you do to her?" Kade asked, his usual amusement replaced with concern. Which only made me laugh harder.

"*Nothing*," Lochlan said curtly.

"Everything," I said at the same time. My laughter suddenly died as more heat engulfed me. "I'm hot. *So*. Hot." I started to squirm out of my jacket, sighing when cool leather skated across my collarbone to aid in my efforts.

"Are you sure she won't—" Kade began.

"No, it's too soon. And the contact wasn't long enough."

"And when she touched me . . . "

"I don't think it was triggered."

"And you're absolutely certain we shouldn't—" The words abruptly cut off, as if Lochlan had silently told him to shut up.

When more cool leather slid over my skin, I sought out the hand's owner. Groaning loudly, I let my head fall back against the mirror. "Not you too, Kade."

A pause. Then, "What is she talking about?"

"No clue."

"I'm right here, guys," I grumbled. "So rude."

As the jacket fell away, a familiar hissing sound raised the hair on my arms. Shadow Man had made that noise—after discovering I was bleeding.

Oh crap.

I quickly glanced down at my exposed wrist covered in blood, then at Lochlan's face. The air fled my lungs. His eyes. They were glowing bright red.

"*Lochlan*," Kade barked, making me jump. In a dizzying flash, he was suddenly there in front of me, blocking my view of Lochlan. "Go. *Now*."

I didn't hear Lochlan leave, but the moment he did, the room felt . . . emptier.

"Sorry about that," Kade said, his usual amusement back as if nothing had happened. He lifted my arm with a gloved hand and whistled. "How did you get this cut?"

"Um . . . scraped it on the towel dispenser."

Chuckling, he placed a first aid kit between us. "I don't think it needs stitches. Luckily, you didn't cut yourself too deep." My eyes flicked to his, then away. Crap. He knew. His wide grin said everything. "So, little Kenna, what did you see earlier?"

He busied himself with pulling out supplies, letting the cryptic question dangle in the air. But I knew exactly what he was asking. I swallowed carefully before replying, "Nothing."

He eyed me knowingly, and my mouth dried. I squirmed under his steady gaze until he finally whispered, "Your secret is safe with me," and winked.

My brows inched upward. "But . . . why wouldn't you tell him that I know?"

"I have my reasons," he said mysteriously, obviously enjoying this turn of events.

"I thought you two told each other everything."

"Not *everything*. He's actually been rather secretive lately, so I consider this payback." Tying off the gauze wrapped around my wrist, he plucked a packet of pain meds from the kit and placed them in my hand. "Take these. Lochlan definitely won't let you leave until he's certain you're well enough to drive."

My stubborn streak reared up, and I almost denied myself relief simply because Lochlan wanted me better. Why did he even care? And I was still ticked off at him for a growing number of reasons. Sighing, I let the voice of reason win and accepted the bottled water Kade seemed to pull out of thin air.

Silence settled between us, but surprisingly, not the uncomfortable kind. Inhaling deeply to bolster my courage, I said, "If I ask you something, will you tell me?"

"Probably not. But you can ask anyway."

Despite the situation, I rolled my eyes. "What happens," I began haltingly, then plowed ahead. "What happens if I touch one of you for too long?"

"Caught that, did you?" He snapped the kit shut and leaned his hip against the counter. "Well, first of all, it depends on who you touch. Not all of us are the same. But, simply put, bad things will happen. You're not, shall we say, *compatible* with our kind."

Our kind.

"So you're a . . . You're one of them too?" *Vampire*, I wanted to say but couldn't. It was still too unreal.

Kade merely winked and pressed a finger to his lips.

Surprisingly, knowing Kade was a vampire didn't freak me out like knowing that Lochlan was. Maybe because he hadn't done anything *vampirish* yet. "How come you're not doing that eye thing on me? You know, to make me forget."

He choked on laughter, pounding his chest. "Unbelievable. Loch is *so* in for it with you." He shook his head, seemingly unconcerned that I knew about a trade secret of theirs. "The eye thing, as you so eloquently put it, is called thrall. As for making you forget, I believe you can be trusted with our secret. It's Loch who needs convincing."

I wrinkled my nose. "Is he like your boss or something?" He sure acted like one.

"Oh, he's much more than that." Straightening, he glanced at the door, then offered me a hand down. "We should probably head out before he gets suspicious. Remember, our little conversation doesn't leave this room."

I accepted his gloved hand and slid off the counter, pausing a beat to steady my legs. Before Kade could leave, I said, "I just have one more question." He side-eyed me warily, but I asked anyway. "Shad— I mean, Lochlan told me I wasn't human. So . . . what am I?"

He slowly expelled a breath, removing a glove to push his caramel hair back. "You might be our ruin," he replied after a thoughtful pause. "Or"—his lips suddenly curled into a devilish smile—"you might save us all. And I'm personally betting on the latter, McKenna Belmont."

CHAPTER 13

Yeah, this wasn't going to work.

I glowered at the half-finished drawing of Shadow Man, not liking how the addition of fangs looked. Snapping the sketchpad shut, I slid off the window seat to pace my room.

Four days had passed since the bathroom incident. Four days of keeping my distance from Lochlan and Kade. Four days of internally fighting with myself, of certainty one minute that vampires existed and utter denial the next.

I mean, neither of them had fangs, for starters. I'd carefully checked. But there was that realistic dream I'd had of Shadow Man with fangs. They both consumed regular food at school though, not blood. Then again, August had been attacked and nearly drained of his blood.

So equally torn between reality and fiction, I'd failed to tell Isla about my most recent brush with the unexplainable. Besides, after dropping the V bomb during our lunch conversation earlier this week, she'd seemed a bit shaken. Maybe she'd feel better if I had more facts—especially about the blood-sucking part.

Proof was my jam these days anyway. What could I say, I was a skeptic. A pessimist. A see-it-to-believe-it sort of gal. Probably a by-product of living nearly fifteen years with a paranoid, secretive aunt.

I paused in my pacing when I remembered Lochlan's eyes in

the bathroom, how they had glowed red when he'd seen my blood. Wasn't that proof enough? *No*, my doubting brain insisted. Argh, but hadn't Kade all but confessed to being one? He hadn't actually said the word though. *Vampire*. I needed to hear it out loud.

No, I needed to hear *Lochlan* say it.

After that, I'd demand he tell me what I was, including what Kade had meant by me being their ruin or savior, or whatever. He was probably just pulling my leg as usual, but these cryptic answers were leaving me wide awake at night, stewing for hours.

Diving for my bed, I snatched up my phone and scrolled to his number. Then stared at the digits until the screen went dark. Fates, why was it so hard to confront him about stuff? I checked the time. Ten o'clock. It was late, but not *too* late. What were the chances of him being at home on a Saturday night? Facing him in person wouldn't be any easier than calling him, but at least I could see his reaction to my questions.

Who was I kidding? I could hardly ever read his expressions.

Still, my mind was made up. I swiped a jacket from the armoire and carefully peered into the hall. Aunt Tess had always been an early riser, so she should either be in bed right now or getting ready to. A faint yellow glow shone on the hardwood beneath her bedroom door, but I went forward with my plan anyway, softly closing my door behind me. Knowing she'd never be okay with me going anywhere this late, sneaking out was my only option.

Besides the bonfire party, I'd never left without her knowledge. Now that she'd told me we weren't moving though, I wasn't so afraid to bend the rules a bit. Not that I was looking for trouble, but this was important.

The stairs creaked a few times on my way downstairs, and I winced each time, expecting her door to burst open. When I made it outside undetected, I sighed with relief, then cringed when I remembered the car. What if she heard the engine start up?

It was a risk I'd have to take. Now that I'd torn off the proverbial glue that had kept my mouth sealed shut, I wanted nothing more than to make Lochlan tell me point blank that he was a vampire. Quietly shutting my car door, I turned the key in the ignition. The Honda rumbled awake and I nervously bit my lip.

No turning back now.

I reversed with the headlights off until I reached the main road. I wouldn't be gone long. Maybe an hour tops. Still, a familiar sense of guilt pricked at my conscience for making my aunt's life more difficult. Ever since my disappearing act earlier this week, she'd been uncharacteristically subdued. The usual invasive questions and probing looks were missing, and when I did catch her staring at me, there was only resignation in her eyes.

I didn't mean to put that look on her face, but I needed more out of life than she was willing to give.

So, despite the nagging guilt, I continued down the road. When I reached the final dark stretch between Hailey's lakehouse and theirs, I kept my eyes peeled for deer. They loved streaking across unlit roads like this. Sure enough, something flashed in my peripheral and I flicked a glance out the passenger window. Nothing but inky black woods greeted me. I focused on the road again.

Only to find someone standing in the middle of it.

My heart practically leapt out of my chest. Slamming on the brakes, I made a split-second decision and wrenched the wheel to the right. The car veered off the road and plunged into a shallow ditch, coming to a jarring halt.

Gasping for breath, I fumbled to unbuckle my seatbelt, certain I had hit someone this time. Seriously though, why did this keep happening to me? I needed to call the police. I picked up my phone to dial. No, wait. I should see if the person was all right first.

The moment I stumbled from the car, my ankle boots sank into the damp earth. I fell onto my side, but managed to clamber up the slight embankment on my hands and knees. When my feet hit the road, I frantically searched for the person.

"Not again," I whimpered as my search came up empty. Maybe they'd rolled into the ditch on the opposite side. I crossed the road, cursing the darkness. Only a watery half moon lit the way. I needed a flashlight. Oh, right. My phone was still clutched in my hand.

"Hello?" I yelled into the ditch, attempting to press the flashlight icon with my trembling fingers. No response. The only sound was my thundering heartbeats.

Before I could shine a light on the area, something whooshed past me from behind, stirring my hair. I whirled with a yelp, but nothing was there. It happened again and I jerked around to face the dark woods. And that's when I saw them.

Two glowing red eyes.

Freaking *fates*. What game was Lochlan playing at? I was going to *kill* him for this. "That wasn't funny!" I shouted, still shaking from adrenaline. "One of us could have been seriously hurt."

When he didn't respond, when he didn't move from his spot in the woods, doubt nearly suffocated me. Lochlan had never endangered my life before. In fact, he'd come to my rescue whenever I was in need.

I still wondered if he planned to kill me someday, but I doubted it would be like this. Because *this*. This didn't feel right. This didn't feel like Lochlan at all. And I had a sinking suspicion that the eyes in the woods weren't his.

Before I could completely freak out, I managed to press the call button on my phone.

Maybe I was wrong. Maybe he'd pick up and I'd hear his voice in the woods. Maybe this was simply one big misunderstanding.

After two torturously long rings, he finally answered. "McKenna?"

Tendrils of fear wrapped around my throat.

When I failed to respond, his voice sharpened. "What's wrong?"

"It's," I whispered, "not you."

The red eyes blinked out and I choked back a scream.

"McKenna?" Lochlan's voice shot through the phone like a thunderclap. "Where are you?"

My numb legs shuffled backward toward the car. The car that was laying in a ditch. The car that was currently useless. "Down—" I tried to swallow and failed. "—the road."

"Don't hang up," he barked, sounding exactly like Shadow Man. "I'm coming."

"H-hurry," I breathed, listening for approaching footsteps. I'd never felt more exposed or helpless in my life.

Something tapped my shoulder and I whirled with a frightened squeak. At the sight that greeted me—a man with midnight skin, gleaming red eyes, and for-real freaking *fangs*—my limbs deadened. His black lips stretched into a wide, toothy grin. "Looking for me?"

I'd never felt such cold, terrifying fear. So cold that I couldn't move. Couldn't scream. Couldn't do a single thing but gape in silent horror.

"McKenna?" Clear alarm shivered through Lochlan's voice, but I was too petrified to respond. "McKenna, answer me!"

The man tipped his head in mild amusement. "Let's put the bloke out of his misery, eh?" In a flash, my phone went soaring out of my hand. It clattered onto the road several yards away. "Now," he said, leaning toward me, "I want you to run."

When I remained frozen, he frowned, then bent his head to breathe me in. A shiver of revulsion racked my body, but I otherwise stood perfectly still. Every instinct I possessed demanded I not expose my back to this man, and I was going to listen.

Even when he moaned and whispered, "Mint and freshly fallen snow," I refused to move. Even when he straightened to peer down at me with carnal lust in his eyes. "The rumors are true then. He's found another. What did he do, feed you his blood? Clever, but he shouldn't have left you alone. For decades, my greatest desire has been to taste the blood foretold to be more intoxicating than any other, and now, I finally have my chance. Nothing is going to stop me, not even you."

My brain was slow to register his words, but when he slid his tongue along a fang, I couldn't stay still a second longer. I spun and bolted. My car was a sitting deathtrap and the woods were too treacherous without a flashlight. I had no choice but to remain on the road. My boots pounded the asphalt, my frenzied breaths loud in my ears. So loud that I almost missed the whoosh.

A hand shoved me from behind and I went flying. With a pained grunt, I hit the ground and rolled several times, scraping my cheek. Before I could come to a stop, I was up in the air again, held aloft by my jacket. The man pulled me close, hissing through his teeth as he brought his face within inches of mine. He greedily eyed my cheek, the scraped one. I felt it then. Blood trickling over my jaw.

His head dipped and he flicked his tongue out as if to lick me.

Freaking fates, *no!*

I latched onto his shirt and drove my knee up, right into his groin. The satisfying groan of agony never came. Instead, sharp pain flared in my knee, bringing tears to my eyes.

He chuckled, wholly unfazed. "Naughty girl. You like to play rough, eh? I was going to make this slow and pleasurable for you, but rough is fine too. I can't promise you'll have a head when I'm finished though." He swung me around like a ragdoll and yanked my hair back, opening his mouth wide.

Before I could scream, before his fangs could descend, an unseen force whipped his head sideways with a violent *crack*. Then he was gone, jerked away in a rush of wind. I stumbled forward, falling onto my hands and knees. I looked up just in time to watch the man's head leave his body.

My throat worked, trying to expel a scream, but no sound left me. I simply stared while the headless body crumpled to the ground. Stared while a little flame sparked to life, then grew and grew as it consumed the body. But where was the head? That part seemed important. I needed to know where the head was. I glanced around me, expecting it to have rolled my way.

"McKenna."

I paused, blinking at my hands splayed on the road. That voice. I knew that voice. But where was the head? I couldn't find it, and that really creeped me out.

Someone crouched before me and I quickly rocked back on my heels, so fast that I landed hard on my butt. I looked up and immediately cringed away, whispering, "You're dead."

I had seen the man die. Seen and believed it.

A gloved hand reached for my face and I scooted back even more. "Not again. Please don't. Please."

"She's in shock, Lochie. Give her space," a voice said from behind me and I froze.

"I can't," the voice in front of me said, clearly distressed, which was weird. *I* should be the distressed one. But I wasn't. Everything was blurry and unreal and I couldn't understand why there were *two*

132

sets of red eyes staring at me now.

There had always been one.

I only *wanted* there to be one.

And then *he* had come, a demon of a man who had wanted to . . . to . . . Fates, he had wanted to drink my blood.

My stomach heaved and I slapped a hand over my mouth, fighting back the nausea.

"Yeah, this isn't good. Try taking the memory away."

"I *can't*," that voice repeated, the one I knew. "She resists me. I don't know how, but she's not like the others. And it doesn't . . . it doesn't feel right, making her forget."

A chuckle, then, "Did the Lochness Monster just use *feel* in a sentence? Miracles do happen."

I let my arm fall. "Where's the head?"

Silence.

"Did she just ask—?"

"Yes, she did." A dark form settled in front of me, blocking out all light. I flinched away, but a hand captured the back of my neck, firm yet gentle. Cool leather gripped my chin and tilted my face up. "McKenna, look at me."

I tried to shake my head, but couldn't.

"Careful, Loch, she's bleeding."

A thumb stretched along my jaw, wiping the blood away. "Look at me," the voice repeated, this time in rich, velvety tones that immediately slid beneath my skin. I closed my eyes and sighed, clinging to that voice. I didn't know why it affected me so much, only that it did.

My lashes fluttered open again and I saw red eyes mere inches away. I tensed, fear trickling back in.

"It's me. It's just me. You're safe."

Safe.

Why did I suddenly believe him?

Hesitantly at first, then with growing awareness, I let my gaze explore the face before me. It wasn't the strange man from earlier. Even with shadows curling around the edges, obscuring his features, I knew who he was.

"Lochlan."

He stiffened, his red eyes flaring brighter. I could feel the moment he started to pull away, preparing to vanish like he always did.

I gripped his leather jacket before he could. "Don't leave."

His gaze slid to my hand, but I didn't remove it. "You know who I am," he said after a lengthy pause.

"Yes." I swallowed, trying to find the courage to continue. "And I know that you're a . . ."

His eyes snapped to mine and I sucked in a breath. "I'm a what?"

Fates, he was going to make *me* say it. Everything had been turned around. I could no longer deny what he was though. What Kade was. What the man who'd attacked me was. I'd been given a front row seat to all the proof I needed and then some.

"A vampire," I blurted, almost hoping he wouldn't hear. Almost hoping he *would*, then laugh at me for being so ridiculous.

But I knew he had heard. And he wasn't laughing.

After a long moment, he quietly said, "Do you fear me?"

I raised an eyebrow at that, remembering our conversation in the graveyard. "I don't know. Should I?"

Someone close by snickered. "Told you."

Lochlan shot a glare at them. "Go make sure the roadkill is disposed of properly."

More awareness leaked in and I tipped my head back to see Kade. His face was dimly illuminated by the still-burning fire—rather, the still-burning *body*. Despite his pitch black skin and red eyes, his features were still the same, free of shadow. He grinned at me, revealing a bit of fang. Okay, crap, he really was a vampire.

"Don't go wigging out on us again, little Kenna," he said with a wink. "You're doing good." Then he flashed from view.

I lowered my gaze again, fixing it on the hand still gripping Lochlan's jacket. "A vampire just winked at me," I muttered, blinking rapidly. How was any of this possible?

"I won't hurt you," Lochlan said, drawing my eyes back to his. I frowned and shrewdly studied what little I could of his shadowed face.

"Then why did you say 'I just don't want you dead yet'?"

"You said *what?*" Kade shouted from several yards away, startling me. How had he heard that?

Lochlan huffed a clipped sigh and lapsed into silence again. His thumb absently traced the line of my jaw, his shadows caressing my bare skin like errant fingers. I couldn't decide whether to pull away or lean into the touch.

"Let's make a deal," he abruptly said and dropped his hold on me. My body chilled at the lost contact. Frowning at my bodily reaction, I released his jacket and stared at him expectantly. "You let me watch over you as I see fit, and I'll protect you from the things that go bump in the night."

"Like the vampire who just tried to snack on me?"

"Like that, yes. Do we have a deal?"

I cocked my head to the side, wondering what *he* would get out of this deal. An all-inclusive, permission-to-stare pass? I gulped, suddenly uncomfortable in my own skin. To make matters worse, my stupid mouth decided to open, blurting, "But who will protect me from *you?*"

Was it my imagination or did heat flare in his eyes?

Instead of answering, he rose and offered me a gloved hand. "You should go home. Kade and I need to comb these woods and make sure the threat's been eliminated."

I accepted his hand. "Uh, I kind of drove into a ditch, so—" As soon as my feet were under me, he vanished. My mouth popped open. Before I could get annoyed at his swift departure, he was back in a swirl of shadows. My hair blew back from his speedy return and I gasped, clutching at my chest. "How did you—?"

"We're faster than humans," he simply said. Well, *that* was an understatement. "You're all set to go," he continued, holding something out to me.

"My phone," I muttered dumbly, accepting it with numb fingers.

When he offered no further explanation, I started to walk and he quietly trailed me. I passed the charred body, focusing on Kade nearby so I wouldn't freak out. Beyond him was my car—which was miraculously on the road again. I stopped and gaped at it.

"We're also stronger," Lochlan supplied, an even bigger understatement. He'd just pulled a car out of a ditch at lightning speed, for fate's sake! When I slid into the driver's seat, making sure the engine was still working, he placed both hands on the roof and peered down at me. "It's imperative that humans don't know about our presence here."

I blinked up at him, catching the veiled order for my silence. "And what if they do?"

"We take care of it."

I gulped. "What, like kill them?"

His lips thinned. "Not unless we have to. Normally, a quick memory wipe does the trick. But if the whole world were to find out about us, war would ensue."

"Oh," I replied weakly, imagining him ripping the heads off the people I knew for uncovering his secret. What would he do to *me* if I betrayed his kind?

CHAPTER 14

A dark hand reached for me, curling around my neck.
I stared into the man's red eyes, unafraid.
Until his grip tightened. And tightened.
The shadows receded to reveal an unfamiliar face.
One filled with hunger.
He opened his mouth, exposing two fangs glistening with blood.
My blood.
In a flash, the fangs descended, biting into my neck.

"Kenna. Kenna, wake up!"

The screaming in my head abruptly stopped. My eyes flew open and I struggled to inhale. Something was still squeezing my neck! I glanced down, startled to see that it was my own hand. I quickly released my throat, blinking up at Aunt Tess's worried face.

"It was only a nightmare," she said, brushing damp strands of hair off my face. My throat was scratchy when I swallowed. Had I been screaming? After a long pause, Aunt Tess added, "Do you want to talk about it?"

Yeah, that would be a big fat no. Every time I *talked* about things that freaked me out, we ended up moving. Sometimes talking wasn't even necessary. She'd take one look at me and just *know*.

It's how we had ended up in Rosewood days after my encounter with Shadow Man—er, Lochlan.

I quickly shook my head, murmuring, "No, I'm okay." I wasn't, of course, but I still didn't want to move despite the danger I'd been in hours ago. Did that make me crazy?

Without comment, Aunt Tess stood. After a moment, I realized she was watching me nervously fiddle with my bracelet. I tucked my hands under the blankets. Her mouth silently worked, like she wanted to tell me something. Then, with a sigh, she merely whispered, "Goodnight, Kenna," and headed for the door.

Long after she left, I stared up at the ceiling and replayed the frightening dream. I'd felt so *helpless* tonight. I was no match for a vampire's superior strength and speed. If Lochlan hadn't stopped that man, I was certain I'd be dead right now.

And what the man had said about my blood continued to nag at me. Was there something different about it?

All I knew was that I'd somehow attracted the attention of vampires. And if more of them were out there looking for me, I needed to protect myself the only way I knew how. Picking up my phone, I scrolled to Lochlan's number and sent him a one-word text.

Deal.

They were waiting for me when I arrived at school Monday morning.

Not in the hallway this time, but in the freaking parking lot. Both were doing that leaning against the car thing, which was super hot for whatever reason. The second I left my Honda, they lazily peeled themselves off their car and sauntered my way. Even in jeans and shirts casually unbuttoned at the neck, they exuded a natural confidence most men twice their age couldn't pull off.

Under their watchful gazes, I tried not to do anything embarrassing, like trip and fall flat on my face. I was already stupidly blushing from the accidental eye contact I'd made with Lochlan. Why did he affect me so much? In the light of day, he looked completely normal, like a regular human. Scratch that. He could never be described as normal or regular, no matter what form he took. There was something about him that drew me in, like a moth to a flame. Argh, was he doing that eye thing—thrall, or whatever—on me again?

When he and Kade were a few steps away, I held up a hand and they stopped. "Yeah, um . . ." Great opening line. I cleared my throat and tried again. "So, what is this?" I circled a finger in the air to encompass all three of us. Okay, not much better.

"Loch got your text the other night," Kade spoke before Lochlan could, cracking a wicked grin. "You should have seen the way he—"

Lochlan shot him a clear warning look. Kade's returning smile was anything but apologetic. That cool dark gaze swung back to me. "Having second thoughts about our deal?"

Wait, hold up. It sounded like he *expected* me to break the deal. I crossed my arms and narrowed my eyes at him. "No, but I think we should discuss the terms some more. You know, set ground rules and stuff."

He carefully inspected my defensive posture. "Such as?"

I struggled not to squirm under his scrutiny. "Well, for starters, don't follow me around like two bodyguards. It looks suspicious, and . . ."

Lochlan and Kade raised their eyebrows, waiting.

Crap, I was so in over my head here.

"And it makes me uncomfortable," I rushed to say.

"What if we just followed you around like two friends?" Kade countered, clearly trying to suppress laughter.

140

I frowned. "But we're not."

Lochlan's jaw hardened.

"But we could be," Kade continued doggedly.

I huffed and glanced around, making sure no one was eavesdropping. "Look, I know that I'm just a job to you guys. I'm only agreeing to this deal because I can't defend myself against *you know what*. And that's another thing. I have questions that need answers. When I couldn't sleep last night, I wrote down a few things." I pulled out a slip of paper from my bag. "I'll write down more when I think of them."

Kade snatched the paper before Lochlan could, earning himself another look. He scanned the list, then howled with laughter. "Garlic? Holy water? *Sparkling skin?*" He continued to chortle while Lochlan read the list impassively.

I propped my hands on my hips. "Hey, the internet has lots of conflicting information. But if any more *you know what* come after me"—I awkwardly shrugged and stared at my shoes—"I need to be prepared."

The laughter stopped. A throat cleared.

Surprisingly, it was Lochlan who said, "I'll give you the tools necessary to protect yourself. As for the rest of your questions, it might be awhile before I can answer them fully."

I looked at him, trying and failing to read his expression. "I don't do well with secrets," I bluntly informed him.

"I know," he said without missing a beat. "But I can't tell you everything yet."

Yet. There he went using that word again. I was starting to hate that word.

Before I could argue, he tucked my list into his jeans pocket and headed for school.

Kade and I silently watched him go. The moment he entered the building though, I rounded on his sidekick. "What will it take to get some answers out of you?"

He tapped his chin and appeared deep in thought. "Hmm . . . bake me a triple-decker cheesecake and my lips might loosen."

"Are you serious? Don't you like"—I lowered my voice to a whisper—"drink blood?"

"Mmm, if you're offering. It would help wash the cheesecake down."

I pinched my lips together, not sure if I was going to be sick or burst into hysterical laughter. "Yeah, that's not going to happen," I muttered with a grimace. "Ever. So just get that fantasy out of your head."

He chuckled. "Too late. But if you really want answers," he said, walking backward toward the school, "come to our place directly after school. Lochlan will be out for a few hours, so we'll have the place to ourselves. That is," he added with a wink, "if you trust me not to eat you."

I snorted and followed after him. "I think I'll take my chances."

Hours later, as I slowly climbed the stairs to Lochlan and Kade's home, I regretted not telling Isla where I was going. I mean, if Kade *did* decide to go all vampire on me, no one would know where to look for my body.

"Right this way, Miss Belmont," he said with a slight bow, holding the massive oak door open for me to precede him. "That's the first myth I'd like to clear up. Vampires don't need permission to enter your home. If they're in the mood for a midnight snack, they can go right ahead."

I froze in the doorway to gape at him, doubting my decision to come here even more.

"Not that I make a habit of doing such a thing," he quickly added, as if to reassure me. When I continued to stare, he muttered, "Tough crowd. No one appreciates my jokes."

Finally managing to unglue my feet, I crossed the threshold, saying, "That's because it's hard to tell if you're being serious or not. So where did Lochlan go? Oh . . ."

I halted again, struck speechless by the home's interior. Warm, gleaming hardwoods swept over the floors and walls, climbing a massive staircase to adorn the ceiling three stories above. Banisters from the second and third floors allowed an unobstructed view through the gabled front windows.

"He went to get a fresh supply of bl—Uh, we needed groceries," Kade said with a cough and closed the door. "Lochlan doesn't like to shop local, so he went to Bangor."

"Hmm," I murmured, only half listening as I craned my neck back to better see the foyer's double-tiered, wrought iron chandelier. "So it's just you two in this huge house?" I wandered farther in, catching a breathtaking view of the lake through the living room's expansive rear windows.

"Yeah. For now."

"No parents?"

He chuckled. "No. We're both of legal age and enjoy our independence."

"Jealous." Turning in a circle, I surveyed the living room's stone fireplace, dark leather furniture, and ornate rug, the decor tastefully done in warm earth tones. Something about the place eased the tension in my shoulders. It was so *normal*-looking, not at all where I expected vampires to live.

"Want something to drink?" Kade said, following in my wake. "A slice of cheesecake, maybe?"

I glanced back at him with narrowed eyes. "You already have cheesecake?"

He shrugged, unsuccessfully hiding a grin. "Not a triple-decker one."

"Unbelievable," I muttered, following the open floor plan into the kitchen. More gleaming wood greeted me, along with a copper range and stone tile backsplash. The white quartz countertops sparkled, reminding me of a question I had. "So if your skin isn't made of diamonds, then how can you walk in sunlight without burning?" I bit my lip, expecting him to laugh at the question.

"Because I'm blood-bonded to a Venturi," he explained, like that made all the difference in the world. He moved to the stainless steel fridge and opened the door. "Thanks to my drothen bond, I received several perks that a Venturi is naturally born with—like near immunity to the sun and stronger abilities."

I blankly stared at him. Wow, there was a lot more to this vampire thing than I thought. "So what exactly is a Venturi? And what does that make you?"

"Venturi are born-vampires, the elites of our race. They are the rarest and most powerful vampire. Feltore are your typical made-vampires, the "bitten ones"—which is what I am. Without a drothen bond to a Venturi, we are slaves to the sun. Legend has it that Cain from the Bible, the firstborn son of Adam and Eve, birthed the vampire gene. God punished Cain for murdering his brother Abel by making him into a Feltore. The bloodlust and aversion to the sun forced him to leave his family and wander the earth alone in darkness.

"But he soon discovered the gene could be transmitted through his seed and blood. He mated with a human female, siring Enoch, the first Venturi. To build and protect their community, Cain and Enoch then turned many humans into vampires, creating Feltore. They appointed Enoch their ruler, revering him for his powerful abilities."

I struggled to digest this wildly unbelievable information. Venturi and Feltore? Cain from the *Bible?* "So . . . what happens to Feltore if they're exposed to the sun?"

He set a mostly-uneaten cheesecake on the kitchen island and gestured widely with his hands. "Poof! Their skin goes up in flames within seconds. I hear it's an excruciating way to go."

I gaped at the casual way he said it, but he was too busy unwrapping the cheesecake to notice. My next question came at the worst possible moment, right when he pulled a knife from the chopping block. "How can *you* be killed then?"

He paused to look at me, knife poised midair. The hair on my arms stood on end. Freaking fates, I should have kept my stupid mouth shut. I was alone with a *vampire*. A creature that was much faster and stronger than me. And I'd just asked how to kill him.

He suddenly vanished with a whoosh, and I choked back a scream. Before I could bolt for the exit, a voice whispered in my ear, "Why, do you want to kill me?" Every muscle locked in place, even with a predator at my back. The only thing I could manage was a weak head shake. "What about Loch?" Another head shake. "Good girl."

Just as suddenly, he reappeared behind the kitchen island and carefully cut into the cheesecake.

"Remember the vampire from the other night?" he said conversationally, as if he hadn't completely freaked me out seconds ago.

An affirming nod from me this time.

"That's how you kill us, Feltore and Venturi alike. Head

145

decapitation, followed by burning. You couldn't find the Feltore's head because Loch temporarily chucked it into the woods while he burned the body. Strawberries?"

I blinked at him dumbly. "Huh?"

He held up a plastic carton. "I like strawberries on my cheese-cake."

"Sure," I mumbled and shifted in place, my earlier zeal for answers nowhere to be found.

"You can also rip out our hearts and then burn us," Kade continued while dumping a small mountain of sliced strawberries on our cheesecakes. "Not really something a human can easily do—the ripping our hearts out part. But there's another way to incapacitate us." He smiled, like we were simply discussing the weather. "You're gonna have to discuss that one with Loch, though."

"Why?" Feeling my bravery return, I inched toward an island barstool.

"Because he said he'd give you the tools necessary to protect yourself," he replied, snickering. "Never thought I'd hear him say that. There's something special about you, McKenna Belmont. Now come here and eat this cheesecake before I do."

Confused by his words, I focused on the part that made sense. "Hey, back away from my slice." I made grabby hands for it and he relinquished the plate with a lopsided grin.

"If you want to know the way to my heart," he said, handing me a fork, "look no further. I practically live on this stuff."

He dug into his cheesecake and I debated bringing up the elephant in the room. You know, the choice of beverage part. Realizing what a mistake that would be while we were *eating*, I instead said, "What's the way to Lochlan's?"

Wait, why the *crap* did I just ask that?

146

Kade paused midchew and hiked his eyebrows.

I quickly focused on my mound of strawberries, jabbing a forkful of them a little too hard. "Forget I said that."

"Okay," he immediately replied, surprising me. "But," he added, pointing his fork at me, "you have to do something in return for my silence."

I eyed him warily for a moment, then popped a loaded fork of strawberries into my mouth. "And what's that?"

"Give Loch a chance."

Swallowing too fast, I choked on a wedge of strawberry and practically hacked up a lung. Kade did his speedy vampire thing, pressing a bottled water into my hand a second later. I guzzled it while he hovered nearby like he was considering doing the heimlich on me.

"Do you do that a lot?" he asked when it was obvious I could still breathe.

"What, choke? Or react strongly to shocking requests?"

"Both. I'm always surprised by how fragile non-vampires are."

"Nice one. You managed to avoid the word human there. You know, since I'm supposedly not one." I stared at him pointedly, then stuffed a rather large bite of cheesecake into my mouth.

His grin returned and he went back to eating his cheesecake. "You're good at deflection. I still need an answer though. Will you give Loch a chance or not?"

I frowned, more than a little afraid of where this was heading. "A chance to do what exactly?"

"Get to know you, vice versa. That's all he wants."

I continued to frown at Kade's earnest face, completely non-plussed. After a moment of consideration, the only thing I could think to say was, "But why? Why me?"

He set his fork down and leaned both hands on the countertop, all humor gone from his face. This was it, I realized with a start. Kade was going to tell me. I would finally find out why they were—

The heavy front door banged open and I almost tumbled off the barstool.

"Change of plans, Kade," called a voice from the foyer. A very familiar one that shot equal parts dread and excitement through me. "Everett is coming for a visit. He heard we were staying here, so we need to—" The voice abruptly cut off.

Kade's eyes widened. He opened his mouth to speak, but before he could, something whirled me around so fast, I almost flew off the stool. Righting myself, I gasped as Lochlan's face appeared within inches of mine. Used to his aloof expressions, I shrank back from the pure fury in his dark eyes.

"What. Is. She. Doing. Here?" he said in clipped tones, the usual smoothness nowhere to be found.

Although he was looking at me, the question was clearly for Kade. Which was a relief, since my tongue was currently plastered to the roof of my mouth. "We were only discussing the general history of our kind, Loch," Kade replied, his voice calm but with a wary edge. "She needs to know these things—"

"So you brought her *here?*" Lochlan snarled, making me recoil even more. The counter dug into my spine as I tried to create distance, but he only leaned closer, gripping the island on either side of me.

"You're scaring her, Lochlan," Kade warned.

"Good," Lochlan bit out, his nostrils flaring. "Maybe this'll teach her to stay away since nothing else has."

My body flushed hot, then cold. I was shocked, hurt, and *furious* that he would storm in here and treat me like this. Regardless of the consequences, I snapped, "My reply to your earlier request, Kade, is no. He doesn't deserve it. As for you, Lochlan, I'm breaking our deal. You want me to stay away? Well, listen carefully. Stay. Away. From. *Me*."

With an ear-splitting *crack*, the island counter severed in two.

"Lochlan, stop!" Kade roared. In a flurry of movement, I was suddenly alone in the kitchen. An explosion of sound came from the living room as Kade threw Lochlan against the fireplace. The mantle splintered. Pieces of wood shot through the air like missiles. "Kenna, get out of here!"

I didn't need to be told twice. I was up in a flash, then flinched at the sight of a wooden fragment protruding from Lochlan's back. I hesitated for a split second and his eyes found mine. When I saw that they were still cold and unyielding, I raised my chin defiantly and marched out the front door.

He didn't come after me.

And I was *never* coming back.

CHAPTER 15

"So *pigheaded*."

I stormed the length of my living and dining room, pacing back and forth in an attempt to cool my rage. Aunt Tess had left me another note on the table, saying she'd be out until late tonight, so the first thing I did was call Isla and ask her to come over for pizza. I seriously needed someone to vent to. Screw Lochlan and his warning not to tell anyone about his kind. Besides, Isla practically knew anyway.

"Oh, and let's not forget domineering. And arrogant. And cruel. And—" Tears sprung to my eyes and I furiously blinked them away. "What the crap! I will *not* cry." Especially not over *him*. He didn't deserve them. They were angry tears, I told myself. Perfectly justified. No one had ever treated me the way he had.

But no one had ever come to my rescue like he had either. Or had I only imagined that he cared about what happened to me? Had I been too ignorant to see that he didn't want me in his personal business?

"Whatever," I grumbled, whirling to stalk the length of my house once more. "I won't be going anywhere near him again." Not when he turned into a monster every time I did something he didn't approve of. I was *not* okay with that.

The doorbell rang, then. Still in a mood, I answered the door to greet Isla.

"What's wrong?" she asked the second she saw my face. I touched my cheek and my fingers came away wet.

"For fate's sake," I muttered, scrubbing my skin dry as I ushered her inside. "Sorry, Isla. It's been a stressful twenty-four hours for me. I don't usually cry. Like ever."

When I turned from shutting the door, she wrapped me in a tight hug. "Girl, tears are like Drano. They clear the emotions clogging your body. It's healthy to pour those suckers out once in a while."

I released a loud snort-sniffle. "I think I'm more of a verbal vomit girl."

"That works too. Just let it all out. Let it—"

"I was attacked by a vampire last night," I blurted. Isla jerked her head back to gape at me. "Also, Lochlan and Kade are vampires. Also also, Lochlan is a big jerk."

Isla's lips formed a large O.

I stepped back to pace again, fiddling with my bracelet. "Just in the last two days, Lochlan has ripped off a head, picked up my car, and split a quartz countertop in half."

Isla squeaked. "Are you okay? Is that why you have a scratch on your cheek and a bandage on your wrist?" The blood drained from her already pale face. "Did one of them bite you?"

I stopped pacing to reassure her. "No, I'm fine. Physically, anyway. Lochlan stopped the vampire from biting me. But the guy said something weird about my blood. And the other day, Kade said something weird about my touch. I was looking for answers today when Lochlan went all jerkwad on me. I'm seriously over his whiplash personality."

She sank onto a high-backed armchair. "So, the vampire thing aside, they followed you here for a reason. Something must have drawn them to you. We need to figure out what you are to them before someone decides to kidnap you or worse."

Now it was my turn to gape. "How are you staying so levelheaded about all of this?"

"Oh, I'll properly freak out about it later," she replied with a toss of her pink-tipped hair. "But I want to focus on *you* right now. We need to find out why vampires are interested in you before anything *really* bad happens. Have you told your aunt?"

"What do you think?" I deadpanned.

"Okay, dumb question. Have you searched her things?"

"What? No. Privacy is sacred to her."

She arched an eyebrow. "And why do you think that is?"

I huffed and resumed my pacing. "You're starting to sound like Lochlan. He told me to search this house if I wanted answers."

"And did you?"

I made a face. "No, but—"

Knock, knock, knock.

"Pizza's here." I hurried to open the door before remembering the tip. "Come on in. I'll just be a sec," I told the pizza guy, turning to find my wallet.

"That's okay. I'm fine out here," he said in an amused tone.

I found my school bag in the dining room and quickly rummaged inside for some cash. Returning, I held out the bills and accepted the ham and mushroom pizza. "Thanks."

"Have a nice evening, Miss Belmont," the guy said, his voice practically a purr. Surprised that he knew my name, I looked at him fully. In the waning sunlight, his handsome, albeit sharp angular face was cast in shadow, including his eyes. A baseball cap kept his jaw-length, inky black hair behind his ears.

He was maybe a couple years older than me, but I'd never seen him before. He could have picked up my name from when I'd ordered online, but it was still strange that he remembered.

"You too," I murmured so as not to appear rude. With a crooked smirk, he tipped his hat at me. When he turned to leave, a ring on his left pinky finger caught the light, flashing a dull red. Frowning, I watched him saunter to his car.

First off, why was a person with a car like *that* delivering pizzas? Must have been a graduation present from mommy and daddy dearest. And secondly, his gait was familiar, which didn't make any sense. How could the way someone walked be familiar?

I shook my head and closed the door. "That was weird," I said to Isla, but she was no longer sitting on the armchair. "Isla?"

A scream came from somewhere in the house and I almost dropped the pizza. Dashing toward the noise, I set the pizza box on the dining table and skidded around the corner.

"Isla?" I yelled, when I didn't find her in the kitchen.

"Down here," she yelled back. From the freaking *basement*. Great. I grimaced but descended the rickety stairs. When I was halfway down, she said, "Why is there a chicken's foot dangling from the ceiling? You guys trying to ward off evil spirits or something?"

"Uh . . . it was there when we moved in. Why on earth are you down here?"

"Searching your house for you," she called flippantly from somewhere inside the cavernous depths.

I inwardly groaned, grateful for her willingness to help but wishing she hadn't started with the creepy basement. At least there was electricity now.

"Check this out," she shouted from the far back corner. As I navigated the stacked moving boxes and piles of unused furniture, I kept my eyes peeled for a freezer. Isla was poking at some dusty old boxes when I found her. "See? Isla, PI is on the case. This is why you need me."

"Careful," I said, pointing near her feet. "Rodent droppings suggest there's a nest of mice or rats inside one of those boxes."

She stiffened, then threw me a glare over her shoulder. I smirked unapologetically. Dust puffed into the air when she opened one, sending us both into sneezing fits. These boxes definitely didn't belong to me or Aunt Tess. They hadn't been touched in several years.

I ended up bringing down the pizza and pulling over a scuffed coffee table so we could at least eat while Isla rifled through the junk. The first couple of boxes only had shoes and clothing in them. The third did too. I was about to call the search a bust when Isla sunk her hand to the bottom of the last box and released an excited whoop.

"Look what I found!" Cramming her pizza into her mouth, she pulled out an ornate mahogany and silver jewelry box. "It'th locked. Lemme thee if I can find a key," she mumbled around her food and handed me the box. She dove into the clothes again.

While she rummaged, I studied the jewelry box. It was less than a foot long, a handful of inches in height, and heavier than I expected. I stared at the keyhole for a moment, unconsciously turning it toward my charm bracelet.

Frowning, I set the box down on the coffee table and grabbed the charm, studying its key shape with new eyes. *Hmm, I wonder . . .*

I slid the key into the lock and twisted.

Click.

My heart skipped a beat. I withdrew the key and slowly lifted the lid.

Isla gasped and peered over my shoulder. "How did you do that?"

"My charm. It fit into the lock. Must have been a coincidence . . ." My voice died when I caught sight of the box's contents. There, right under my very nose, was a photo of my mom and dad.

"That is *definitely* not a coincidence," Isla said in hushed tones.

A shiver of dread ran up my spine, and I was half tempted to slam the lid shut. Instead, I swallowed with difficulty and picked up the photo. Underneath were a few more and I collected them all, staring in shock at one of my mom holding me as a baby. I'd never seen a baby photo of me before.

"Kenna," Isla whispered when I continued to stare for an undetermined length of time. "What if . . . what if your *parents* used to live in this house?"

I blinked, unable to fully grasp the ramifications if that were true. Instead of replying, I peered into the box again. An ornate, silver knife not much longer than a letter opener lay on top. I shuffled it aside and gaped anew when I spotted an exact replica of my bracelet, identical charm symbol and all.

"This is creepy," Isla breathed, and I couldn't agree more.

At the bottom was a rolled-up bit of parchment, yellowed with age. I carefully unrolled it, pressing it flat against the table.

"What does it say?" Isla crawled up beside me to better see. "It's like a poem or something. Ah, that's too bad. There must have been a water leak down here. The ink is smudged along the bottom half."

Squinting at the sharp cursive writing, I read the top half aloud:

"*Three dark princes, monsters were they.*
Cursed in their true forms, they must pay.
Bound to the night, along with their kingdom.
'Til the hundredth year, or a cure can free them.
Beyond that time, the curse remains.
But night becomes day, a monster to stay.
Only one can free all, before it's too late.
An elusive maiden, with a touch that slays."

After that, the ink was smeared and I could only make out the final three words: *for an eternity.*

But it was the first three words that had stolen my attention. I barely registered the rest, too busy wondering if this was *the* story Reid had been trying to tell me about before Lochlan had intervened.

"Are you seeing what I'm seeing?" Isla said in disbelief.

I nodded woodenly, whispering, "Three dark princes."

Out of everything we'd just discovered, this poem might be the most disturbing of them all.

Curled up on my room's window seat, I stared at the half-finished drawing of Shadow Man and flipped the page to a fresh one. I knew exactly what my fingers were itching to create. I shouldn't though, most *definitely* shouldn't. But the pencil I held began to move anyway, outlining the shape of his dark eyes.

While I drew, I couldn't stop thinking about my newest discovery. The urge to confront Aunt Tess about the jewelry box was still overwhelming, even hours later. In my imagination, she spilled her guts and told me everything. But in reality, I knew that pretending as if I'd never found the box was my only option. Thankfully, she wasn't home yet, or I might have given in anyway and finally had it out with her.

Those photos of me and my parents must mean that my aunt had been to this house before, right? Could Isla be right that my parents had once lived here? If so, why had my aunt moved us back here?

The questions burned on the tip of my tongue, but I didn't dare expel them. I'd have to be subtle about getting the answers I needed from her, which meant no snooping through her stuff, no matter *how* tempting. With my luck, she had her room boobytrapped for intruders anyway.

As soon as Isla had left though, I'd brought the jewelry box up to my room and hid it in the armoire. The box's contents felt like they belonged to me and I was loath to part with them.

Somewhere around midnight, while thinking about the story of the three dark princes, I dozed off. Startling awake at the sound of my sketchpad thumping to the floor, I set my pencil down and rubbed my gritty eyes. A cold awareness skated across my skin, and I stiffened, squinting into the darkness outside. With my bedroom light still on though, it was hard to see anything. At the thought of *Lochlan* out there, peering up at me, I reached for my curtains.

But before I could shut them, something red on the windowsill caught my eye.

I flinched back. "You've *got* to be kidding me," I muttered, scowling at the rose as if it had personally insulted me. Knowing that *Lochlan* had left it didn't bring me any comfort. In fact, I was more at ease with his alter ego than with him at the moment.

But a rose wasn't the only thing he'd left me this time. A note and a knife also adorned the windowsill. A freaking *knife*. Fates, he could have slit my throat while I slept and be done with me once and for all. As for how he got up here, I simply added flying to the list of things a vampire could do that humans couldn't.

Unfolding the note, I was both surprised and disappointed at its contents. In a rather elegant handwritten scrawl, the note said:

McKenna. I will honor my promise to provide you with a tool that can protect you. As for your question, anything silver will weaken us, causing immense pain. But a silver object lodged inside our hearts for too long will eventually kill us. I'm entrusting this silver dagger to you as a gesture of goodwill. —L

"Goodwill, my butt. How about an apology?" I grumbled. Despite the bitter words, my stupid heart fluttered like a tipsy bird, happy that he'd finally answered one of my questions. My heart was *way* too easily pacified.

I set down the note to pick up the dagger. It was slim, tucked inside a silver sheath engraved with vines and roses. Wait a minute. The jewelry box contained a silver dagger too. Coincidence? With my luck lately, I didn't think so. Chances were that the owner of the box knew about vampires. And if that was the case, either my parents had known about them or Aunt Tess did.

Freaking fates.

Maybe they *all* knew.

Finally. A stroke of luck.

The next day, Lochlan and Kade didn't show up for school, which meant I could speak to Reid without interference.

I need to talk to you, I mouthed at him while the first period bell rang.

He nervously glanced around the room as if he expected Lochlan or Kade to materialize at any moment. I actually felt sorry for the guy after what happened with Lochlan last week. He had been so relaxed and happy-go-lucky when I'd first met him. Now, a month later, he was unpredictable at best. So when he acknowledged me with a frown and quickly looked away, I was more disappointed than surprised.

Still, I pursued him into the hallway when class ended, not missing the irony of our swapped positions. "Reid," I hissed as he deliberately dodged me on his way to our history class. By the time I caught up with him, he was already seated inside the room.

Nice try, but he should have chosen a better spot. I boldly approached and plunked into the seat next to him. "I need to ask you a favor," I spoke to his profile, since he wouldn't look at me. Heaving a sigh, I continued anyway. "You don't have to speak to me, but could you just text me that story your dad told you? You know, about the three princes?"

When his eyes darted to the door, I felt a pang of guilt for causing him stress. Normally, I would back off, but this was too important. My gut told me that this story was the missing puzzle piece, that if I could read the full thing, I would understand why my life had been so weird lately. Why it had *always* been weird.

"I can't," he finally whispered, so low that I almost missed it.

"Why not? Because of *them?*" Frustration crept into my voice despite an attempt to suppress the emotion.

"I can't speak, text, or even write down words that pertain to certain things. I *literally* can't. Sorry, Kenna. I would if I could."

Understanding hit me, along with anger at those two meddlesome vampires. "Did they do that eye thing on you? Thrall?"

Alarmed, he finally looked at me. "You know about that?"

"Yup, among other things. So this story your dad told you—does he have it written down somewhere, by any chance? If so, are you allowed to give me a copy?"

He thought for a moment, fiddling with his pen. Then his hazel eyes brightened. "Yeah, I think I can. But I'll have to find it on my own. I can't even ask my dad."

Grinning victoriously, I quickly scribbled my phone number on a scrap of paper and handed it to him. "Text me as soon as you find the story."

"Sure," he said, sounding relieved now. Before I could face forward, he added, "You should know something about Peyton. She's not upset for the reasons you think. She's been through a lot this past month and wants someone to blame. That person ended up being you. I . . ." He cleared his throat and glanced away. "Just know that it wasn't your fault. It's mine."

I frowned, confused. "What—"

"Good morning, class," Mr. Davis promptly said as the bell rang.

I tried to focus on the lecture, but found it hard now that I had yet *another* mystery to solve. Peyton still wasn't talking to me, and to support her best friend, Hailey rarely hung out with me and Isla anymore. The separation stung, but I hadn't given up hope that Peyton would eventually forgive me. Now Reid was saying I wasn't to blame? Add that to the growing list of things I needed to figure out.

When I exited the building at the end of the school day, Isla as usual managed to distract my overworked mind with a few words. "So what are you going to be for Halloween next Friday?"

"Uh . . ."

She jabbed a finger at me. "Don't you dare say you're too old! The school throws a party every year. I'm pretty sure they do it just to keep us unruly teenagers off the streets though," she said with an eye roll, then batted her lashes at me. "We should coordinate outfits."

I smirked at her unrestrained excitement, but gave in. "Fine. You pick. But nothing too revealing, I mean it."

Her eyes filled with fake innocence. "Would *I* do something like that?"

I glanced pointedly at her short skirt and tight crop top, but she waved my judgy look away.

"I'll be good, I promise. Oh, this is going to be fun! You should come over after school that day so we can get ready together."

"Sounds like a plan," I said with a smile, genuinely looking forward to it thanks to Isla's contagious enthusiasm.

We parted ways and I was nearly to my Honda, fishing for my keys, when a shoulder rammed into mine. The impact shoved me against someone's car, smarting my hip bone. Grimacing at the ache, I straightened to face none other than August Henderson.

"You really should be more aware of your surroundings, vixen," he said with a condescending smirk and stepped into my personal space.

I quickly backed toward my car only for him to follow, reaching out to grab my arm. I twisted away, but he snagged a handful of my jacket and yanked me to him. "You really don't want to do this," I growled and jabbed my elbow into his gut.

He retaliated by seizing my bicep in a punishing grip. I sucked in a pained hiss. Before I could scream, he taunted, "Why? I don't see those boy toys of yours. It's just you and me, dealing with some unfinished business." I struggled to free myself but he only squeezed harder, forcing tears to my eyes. "I have a message for you. Everett says hi and that he'll see you soon. Oh, and he said don't bother trying to run. He'll track you down to the ends of the earth."

With that, he released me and sauntered off, leaving me bruised and shaken. Long after he left, I continued to stand in a daze, wondering what on earth had just happened.

When someone touched my shoulder though, I whirled, ready to put up a fight. "Get your hands off me," I spat before realizing it was Kade.

Oops.

All on their own, my eyes swept the area, searching for Lochlan. My heart sank when he was nowhere to be found. My body *seriously* needed a time out. It clearly had terrible taste in guys.

"What's wrong?" Kade said, seeing way more than I wanted him to.

"August," I let slip before I could think better of it.

"What did he do, Kenna?"

I bit into my bottom lip and avoided his probing look.

He swore. "I'm calling Loch."

"No!" I burst out, lunging for his phone. He jumped back before I could touch his bare hand. I dropped my arms with a grimace. "Sorry. I'll tell you, but . . . don't call Lochlan, okay?"

His eyes narrowed. "Why? Because of yesterday?"

"Yes and no. He threatened to kill August the next time he touched me, and I really think he meant it."

"He did," Kade said matter-of-factly, and I groaned.

"See? You can't tell him. Sure, August is a bully and has left a few bruises, but I don't want him killed."

Kade's brows slammed downward. "He hurt you? Then I'll take care of him myself."

He started to leave, no doubt planning to pummel August into the ground. Desperate, I blurted, "Who is Everett?"

Kade froze. He backtracked and was in front of me so fast that my mouth popped open. "Where did you hear that name?"

"I-I heard Lochlan mention him yesterday," I replied weakly in the face of an impassioned Kade. Thank the fates I had remembered in the nick of time. Mentioning what August had said would undoubtedly send him over the edge. As much as I loathed the blond-haired neanderthal, I didn't want him killed because of me.

At my words, the blue fire in Kade's eyes dimmed, and he shook his head with a resigned laugh. "You really do have excellent deflection skills. Fine, I won't harm the dirtbag. But I'm getting him expelled from the school."

"Deal. Now who's Everett?"

He sighed, scrubbing both hands down his face. "Everett is Lochlan's older brother. But the less you know about him, the better."

I crossed my arms and cocked a hip. "Why, is he even less charming than Lochlan?"

"Look, I know Loch messed up big time yesterday, but I promise he has redeeming qualities."

"Does he secretly save baby animals and help old ladies across the street?"

Kade gave me a somber look, clearly not amused. Neither was I.

"I know he's your friend and all, but he could seriously use a lesson in manners. Why are you here, anyway? You weren't in school today."

He shrugged carelessly, but his shoulders were rigid. "Loch just wanted to make sure you got home safely."

I blinked, caught off guard by his explanation. Then huffed and turned for my car. "You can remind your *master* that my safety is none of his business. Our deal is null and void." I slid into my car and started the engine. "Oh, and tell him thanks for the dagger, but stop leaving me roses."

He grabbed the door before I could shut it, demanding in a sharp voice, "What did you say?"

I frowned up at his penetrating stare. "Uh . . . about the deal? You heard me yesterday. I don't want Lochlan—"

"No. The very last thing you said. What was it?"

Okay, his intensity was starting to wig me out a little. "I don't want him leaving me roses anymore. Especially if he's not going to apologize for yesterday's behavior."

Kade continued to study me, disbelief now etched on his face. "He's been giving you roses?"

"Yes," I said slowly, my frown deepening. "He leaves them on the windowsill at night while I'm sleeping. Which is considered breaking and entering, by the way."

"Holy mother of Moses," Kade breathed, letting go of the door to shove both hands through his hair.

After a beat of watching him silently freak out about something, I sighed and snapped the door shut, taking off without another word. I needed a *long* soak in the tub after this strange, craptastic week.

CHAPTER 16

"I seriously can't believe you picked out *vampire* outfits," I said to Isla, mock-scowling at my reflection. I watched her adjust the high collar of my red-lined cape with a gleeful look on her face, clearly not sorry for her costume choice.

"They're 'sexy princess of darkness' costumes," she corrected, and handed me a dark red lipstick. "You don't have to wear the fangs."

"Good, 'cause you can't swallow your spit with those things in," I muttered, leaning forward to apply the lipstick.

Despite my protests, I actually liked the outfit she chose for me. The shiny black bodysuit fit me like a glove, and it wasn't *too* low. My boobs weren't about to fall out or anything. The only other skin left exposed were my hands, unlike Isla's costume, a lacy vintage top with flared sleeves and barely-there black shorts. She still looked vampirish though with her blood-red lipstick and high black collar. Paired with leather, thigh-high boots, she put the sexy in vampire.

If she was hoping these outfits would get a reaction out of Lochlan and Kade though, she would be disappointed. An unexpectedly normal week had flown by with no sign of them. I should have felt relieved at their absence, but instead, I'd felt slightly off all week. Despite trying my hardest to ignore the feeling, I'd caught myself about to text Lochlan several times. I shouldn't want anything to do with him after how he had treated me. I *didn't*. But I couldn't stop thinking about him.

I'd thought about him so much that I could have sworn I'd seen his Lexus following me to and from school a few times. And once or twice, I thought I'd spotted red eyes in the woods behind my house at night. It was probably just my imagination though.

Apparently my conversation with Kade last week had made an impact and they were finally giving me space. It's what I had wanted, so why wasn't I happy about it?

At least I had plenty of things to preoccupy me today. Besides the Halloween party, Reid had texted me a couple of hours ago, saying that he'd found "it." I'd immediately begged to meet up with him, but he'd burst my bubble by saying he wasn't available. Undeterred, I'd asked if he would be at the Halloween party. He said no, but would leave the paper under a rock beneath the football field's bleachers anyway.

When we arrived at the school in Isla's Mini around seven, I was beyond antsy to find the paper. Surprisingly, Aunt Tess hadn't made a fuss about me attending the party. As long as I was with Isla, she was fine with it.

Curbing the urge to zoom toward the football field right away, I shuffled through the entrance doors with Isla who beelined for the gymnasium. Music swelled around us, fast and upbeat. The overhead lights were dimmed, and colorful laser lights danced through the air. Spooky decor dangled from the ceiling and walls. The students buzzed with energy, and I wholeheartedly joined the fray, letting the excitement sweep me away.

Several girls gushed over our outfits and boys stared appreciatively. Isla basked in the attention, clearly a fan of the limelight. After a good half hour, I left her flirting with a couple of guys to check out the food. The attention was nice. Normal even. A feeling I so often craved. But every time one of those blue-eyed football players turned to speak to me, black eyes flecked with red came unbidden to my thoughts.

Freaking fates, what was wrong with me?

I shoved a Dorito into my mouth to distract myself. Maybe now would be a good time to sneak outside and grab the paper Reid left me. I was about to turn toward the rear exit when a voice nearly muted by the music said, "Hi, Kenna."

Surprised to find Hailey beside me, I squeaked a, "Hi," then bit my lip. Awkward silence descended.

She fiddled with a strawberry blonde curl, then blurted, "I like your costume."

"Oh, thank you. Isla picked it out." I glanced at hers. "I like yours too. Witch?"

"Yup." She flicked her black, pointy hat.

Without Isla here as an icebreaker, the strain of our relationship was definitely showing. I hated it, and I knew Hailey did too.

Deciding to rip off the band-aid, I said, "Is Peyton here?"

"Um, yeah. Well, she was supposed to be here but must be running late. Usually we all arrive together, but . . ." At the unspoken elephant in the room—*me*—guilt squirmed in my stomach. Before I could apologize for the umpteenth time, she stammered, "P-Peyton's been acting weird lately, especially the last few days. I'm just . . . I'm really starting to get worried."

I frowned, giving Hailey my full attention. "How is she acting?"

"Extremely moody and snippy. It's so unlike her. I think something is seriously wrong." Hailey's pale blue eyes welled with tears. She quickly blinked them away with a small laugh. "I don't even know why I'm telling you this. She hasn't exactly been nice to you this past month."

"I'm glad you did," I rushed to say, giving her arm a comforting squeeze. "I'll talk to Reid about it, okay? He's been opening up to me lately."

She sniffled and offered me a smile. "Thank you, Kenna. I miss hanging out with you and Isla."

"Me too," I said, truly meaning it.

She checked her purple sparkly phone, murmuring, "Oh, Peyton's finally here. I gotta go."

I watched her leave, feeling lighter but also heavier after our short conversation. I still felt responsible for the change in Peyton's behavior and wanted to help somehow. Maybe I'd try talking with her tonight. Glimpsing Isla on the dance floor with a football player, I decided now was a good time to slip out.

The evening was crisp and I shivered, crossing my arms and hurrying along the sidewalk. I nervously glanced over my shoulder, remembering the last time I'd taken this route. No one was there. August hadn't been in school all week, so I assumed Kade must have followed through with his threat.

I grimaced, hoping August had only been expelled and not killed.

The football field wasn't lit tonight, but the full moon cast off enough light to see by. I hurried over to the bleachers and peered underneath. Darkness greeted me. Argh, I shouldn't have left my phone in Isla's car, but this bodysuit didn't have pockets. Carefully ducking under the metal, criss-cross beams, I navigated by touch more than sight.

The tip of my boot finally glanced off a sizable rock and I bent to feel around. I found the rock and lifted it, breathing a sigh of relief when plastic crinkled beneath my fingertips. Thank the fates Reid had thought to protect the paper from water damage. I didn't want to discover this one half smudged too. Not knowing where else to put it,

I folded the plastic bag and tucked it inside my bra.

"What are you doing out here?"

The voice startled me so bad that I jumped and banged my head on a bleacher. *Ow.* I rubbed the bump and spun toward the voice, squinting to make out a face. My eyes widened. "Peyton?" She was the last person I expected to find.

She stepped closer and the moon bathed her dark complexion in pale light. I blinked. Was that . . . ?

"Are you bleeding?"

She swiped at her chin, barking a mirthless laugh. "It's not my blood."

"Oh." I cleared my throat, uncomfortable with the keen way she was looking at me. "Is it part of your costume? I can't really tell what you're supposed to be."

"I'm not *wearing* a costume, Kenna," she snapped, her eyes flashing a bright yellow. Shocked, I stumbled back a step, but she only pursued me. "This is all too real, thanks to you. I shouldn't even be here tonight, but I don't want to give up my life because of this. It's not fair. I wish it had been *you* that got attacked, not me."

"I—I . . ." I held my hands up when she came too close, but she batted them aside. "Peyton, you're freaking me out. Calm down."

"That's the thing. I *can't.* I'm always angry. Always one second away from exploding. This is all your fault!" Fear sucked the air from my lungs as she reached for me. Her nails were wicked long and sharpened to points. I pulled away but she was faster, latching onto my left wrist.

Peyton suddenly shrieked and yanked her arm back. One of her nails caught on my bracelet and, with a sharp tug, I felt the chain snap. I clutched my bare wrist to my chest, gaping at Peyton. Before I could say anything, she burst into tears.

"I . . . I ate Twitchy," she wailed and curled forward, sobs racking her body. "My sweet rabbit. I ate him, and . . . and I *liked* it. He was so warm and fresh. I'm a vegetarian, Kenna. *Vegetarian.*"

She fell onto her hands and knees, moaning loudly. Torn between running away and helping her, I remained frozen in place, wide-eyed.

"Please, no. I can't do this again," she whimpered. "I'm scared. I'm scared that my parents will find out what I am. They'll freak and disown me. I'll never see my family again."

"Peyton, where are you?" someone frantically yelled from across the football field.

She whipped her head up and fixed those eerie yellow eyes on me. "Don't tell him I'm here," she pleaded in a broken whisper. "Please."

"Peyton!"

I recognized the voice now. Reid's.

Worried and utterly confused, I crouched a few feet in front of her. "I don't understand," I whispered back, alarmed at how hard she was trembling. "Is he hurting you?"

"Y-yes," she stuttered, then shook her head. "I mean, no. He only wants to help, but it still hurts. I have to get out of here. *Help* me, Kenna."

I knew I couldn't deny her, despite her strange behavior. She wanted *my* help. This was my chance to finally make things right between us. As running footsteps drew near, I whispered, "Take my hand. I'll hide you."

She flashed me a wobbly smile and accepted my hand. When our skin touched though, her smile slipped. I tried pulling her up, only to be yanked down beside her.

"Peyton, what—" I felt it then. A rush of warmth where our hands touched. No, not warmth. *Heat.* I yanked my hand back but couldn't break free of Peyton's ironclad grip. "Peyton," I hissed when the heat became white hot. "Peyton, let go."

"I . . . I can't," she panted, a look of pure terror on her face. "I'm changing. It's happening. I can't stop it."

I winced as her deathgrip practically crushed my bones. I pried at her fingers, then gasped at the sight of our hands glowing a bright ruby red. Panic exploded through me. *"Peyton, let go!"*

She screamed, in fright and pain. Something dark rippled up her arms, something that looked a lot like *fur*. What the crap was happening? When an unearthly howl erupted from her, chills whipped up my spine.

"Peyton!" Reid skidded to a halt beside us and pulled at our linked hands. When he jerked away with a sharp hiss, I looked up at his frightened face. Freaking fates, his eyes were yellow too. I silently begged him to help us, unable to speak as the fiery heat consumed my every thought. "I-I can't. I can't touch your skin," he said weakly, and despair filled me.

He was suddenly gone, whisked away on the wind. A dark form swallowed up the space where he'd been. I was too delirious from the heat to react, and Peyton was still screaming, all but breaking the bones in my hand. The red glow had grown brighter, consuming our hands completely. And then, faster than I could blink, our touch was severed.

I fell back, gulping in much-needed air as the heat slowly dissipated. Peyton stopped screaming. I stared at the dark form hunched over her collapsed body.

"Is she . . . Is she—?" Reid said in a panicked whisper.

"She's alive, just unconscious. I'll watch over her. Now leave before you wolf out," a familiar voice said.

Kade.

Pain abruptly ripped through my body and I gasped, curling

forward to clutch my stomach. Before the agony could subside, hands encased in cold leather were cupping my cheeks, tipping my face up.

"Were you bitten or scratched?"

He spoke, the person I loathed. And missed. Crap, I had truly missed him. I could only stare at Lochlan's blazing red eyes, in too much pain to answer. He bent his head and breathed in deeply before saying, "You're not bleeding."

Then he plucked me off the ground as if I weighed nothing.

"She fully triggered the change, Kade," he said, pulling me tightly to his chest. "You know what'll happen. I'll handle this alone."

"Yes, drothen," Kade replied, before a new spasm tore through me.

I was too disorientated to resist as Lochlan carried me away. Or rather *flew*, shooting across the field at lightning speed. No problem. It wasn't like I needed to *breathe* anyway.

Seconds later, he stopped. A car door opened and I was placed inside. The seatbelt was buckled and door shut before I could twitch a muscle. I glanced over to see Lochlan in the driver's seat, revving the engine. He shot out of the parking lot, tires squealing as he raced down the road. The car rumbled with power, the scenery whipping by way too fast.

I stared at his shadowed profile, not at all bothered by the inhuman sight. When had it become normal to me? I started to ask where he was taking me, but groaned instead as fire ate at my insides.

"You'll get through this. I'll make sure of it," he said, but my spine pressed further into the seat as he sped up even more.

"S-slow down."

"No."

I gritted my teeth. "I need to check that Peyton is okay. Turn around."

"Kade will take care of her."

"Isla will wonder where I am."

"Kade will take care of her too."

"I lost my mother's bracelet. I *need* it."

A pause. Then, "Kade will find it."

Anger suddenly ripped through me and I snapped, "You're so stubborn and rude and infuriating!" The car careened around a corner and I clutched my seatbelt for dear life.

When he didn't reply, I inwardly called him more names and fumbled for the window switch. When I found it locked, I growled, "It's *hot* in here. I need air *now*." Fates, I was beyond cranky.

"Fresh air will only trigger the change faster."

"Change?" My shoulder rammed into the window as he barrelled around another corner. I bared my teeth at him, like a freaking *dog*. I gripped my suddenly pounding head and groaned, "What is happening to me?"

"Your skin made contact with a werewolf's," he calmly explained, as if mentioning werewolves was a commonplace thing. Seriously though. He just said *werewolf*. "I don't know how long you touched her though, so the side effects you'll endure is undetermined. But there's a full moon tonight. Expect some discomfort."

I snorted. Discomfort? I was way beyond that already. "I'm assuming by werewolf, you mean Peyton?"

His silence was answer enough.

"This is crazy, you know," I said, my ire returning. "First vampires, now werewolves? What's next, ogres?"

"Ogres aren't real."

"Good to know," I grumbled, tugging at the strings of my vampire cape. The material slipped off my shoulders and pooled at my waist.

"What are you doing?" Lochlan said warily.

"I'm freaking burning up. What does it look like I'm doing?" I snapped, not caring one bit how ornery I sounded. Fiery heat was pulsing down my spine and all I could think about was fresh air. I lifted my heavy mass of hair to cool off my neck.

Lochlan's gloved fingers tightened on the steering wheel. He jerked the car left and I fell against the window again. "Stop driving like a maniac!" I was seriously going to tear his throat out. Then eat it! Wait, that sounded weird.

"Only if you keep your clothes on," he replied sharply.

Seriously? My annoyance at him boiled over. "Well, you won't let me open a window, so what happens next is on you."

Grabbing the top of my bodysuit, I yanked. The zipper whined. The material ripped from my body, top to bottom. The car zigzagged and I shot Lochlan a look, catching his fiery gaze on me.

"Eyes on the road," I barked, too hot to bother with blushing at his perusal. In fact, I didn't care at all that I was practically sitting naked in front of him. Pulling my boots off, I sank back against the seat, bare except for my lacy red underwear.

Why had I worn lacy red underwear?

I waited for cool air to hit my skin, but relief never came. "It hurts," I finally choked out, desperation tightening my throat.

"I'm going to help you, McKenna," Lochlan said, switching to his soothing voice. "We'll be there soon."

"Where?" I gripped the door handle and squeezed.

"Somewhere safe."

Safe. Safe sounded good.

Because I didn't feel like myself anymore. It felt like my body didn't belong to me and I was just along for the ride.

CHAPTER 17

I must have passed out at some point.

One minute, I was drifting in a haze of searing pain, and the next, cradled in Lochlan's arms. I looked down at myself, surprised to see my cape tucked around me. I struggled to remove it and Lochlan pressed me closer to him, stilling my movements.

"You're killing me," he muttered, quietly enough that he probably thought I hadn't heard. But that was the thing. I could hear *everything*. The loud crunch of his boots. The wind whistling shrilly in my ears. His breathing.

His heart.

Thump thump, thump thump, thump thump.

Louder than a drum.

Overwhelmed by the intense noises, I pressed my ear tighter to his chest and closed my eyes, focusing on his heartbeat. Only his heartbeat.

The second I relaxed in his arms, the pain returned tenfold. My spine arched as every bone in my body spasmed. My eyes flew wide and I gasped. Or tried to. I couldn't breathe. Frantic for air, I thrashed in Lochlan's arms, so hard that he almost dropped me.

"McKenna, look at me."

Obeying the command in his voice, I focused on his glowing eyes, straining to see past the tears blurring my vision.

"Breathe," he ordered, his voice a firm yet soft caress.

I immediately dragged in air, choking as it went down too fast. My body screamed at me when the coughing jarred my inflamed bones. A strangled cry tore from my lungs. Hot tears rolled down my cheeks. Lochlan walked faster, which only made me hurt more. I whimpered, not caring how loud or pathetic it sounded.

"We're here," he said.

The sound of crashing water reached my sensitive ears, then I was being submerged. A blissful chill curled in and around me, dousing the heat. I heaved a sigh as the water chased the pain away. I let my head fall back, soaking my hair and immersing my ears. The blaring sounds dulled and I sighed again, closing my eyes.

For several minutes, Lochlan held me, allowing the water to cool my hot skin. Pain continued to seize me, but not as intensely. When my teeth started to chatter though, his arms shifted, lifting my head out of the water.

"Despite what you're experiencing, you're not actually a werewolf," he said. "You weren't scratched or bitten, which means there is no werewolf DNA running through your veins. These symptoms are only temporary, and your body can't handle the freezing water for long periods like theirs can."

I frowned. "How do you know it can't? I can barely feel the cold."

"Because I knew someone like you who died from hypothermia. She didn't feel the cold either."

I pried my eyes open to find his gaze far away, probably focused on a memory. "I'm sorry," I whispered, hoping he'd tell me more.

Instead, he blinked and wordlessly stirred into motion. I bit my lip, feeling the pain flare with every small movement. He walked slowly, but I still struggled for air by the time we reached land.

"Where . . . are we?" I panted, clutching at his drenched jacket.

"There's a small cabin up the hill. Hopefully somewhere no one will find us. Or hear you scream."

I stiffened. "What?"

"This isn't over. The change takes several hours and can last multiple nights. With how intense your symptoms have been so far, I don't expect them to go away anytime soon."

"But . . . I-I can't. I'm already exhausted and can't stand much more of this. And what do you mean by *multiple* nights?"

"For a werewolf, the pull of a full moon usually lasts two, sometimes three days. They normally lose control of their human forms and wolf out when the moon is at its fullest."

"What are you saying? That I'm going to—to turn into one?"

"I don't know. Maybe. Your situation is unique and unpredictable. You absorbed werewolf toxin through physical touch. Since your blood wasn't infected, you might not experience the full range of symptoms." He glanced down at me. "Whatever happens though, I'll help you through it, McKenna."

Freaking fates, if I turned into a wolf, I was going to seriously flip out. To distract myself, I said, "Why are you even here? I broke our deal. You've been gone for over a week. Why did you even show up tonight?"

He was silent for a moment, then, "You ending the deal didn't keep me away. There have been complications I've had to take care of. I almost didn't come tonight because of them."

"What kind of complications? Like a brother showing up you never told me about?"

He looked at me sharply. "Kade shouldn't have told you that."

"It's not his fault. I pestered him for an answer. At least he actually answers some of my questions," I said, laying the guilt on thick. "Why can't we talk about him? Everett, I mean." *Like how he's using*

August to threaten me, I knew I should add, but didn't.

Lochlan fixed his gaze on the dark path ahead. "He left Rosewood this morning. No need to discuss him."

Okay, then. Must be a sore point. I could relate, since I didn't have the best relationship with my aunt. I opened my mouth to change the subject, but the heat chose that moment to return with a vengeance. I hissed, pressing my forehead to Lochlan's chest. It lapped at my skin and I squirmed in his arms to be let down. His hold only tightened and my earlier crankiness returned. "Let me down."

"No. I don't want to be chasing you through the woods all night."

"*What?*" I struggled some more. "I'm not going to—"

"Yes, you will," he interrupted. "You've absorbed a wolf's instincts. The pull to hunt and run will be irresistible. And if your temporary wolf scents an animal in these woods, or even a human, you won't be able to control the urge to chase and kill."

"That's insane. Do you know how insane you sound?" I yelled. Okay, maybe I sounded a little bit insane too. Also, ouch. Yelling *really* hurt my ears.

Ignoring my outburst, he continued to stride up the path in silence. I almost asked what he'd do if I had the sudden urge to chase and kill *him*, but I doubted he'd tell me. If I went berserk on him, it would probably end with my head detached from my body faster than I could blink.

I couldn't deny his words though. A primal need to scent the air and explore the world around me was building. And something else was too, a sharp burn low in my belly. Not white hot, but undeniably intense and distracting.

Lochlan's stride faltered and I glanced up at him, a silent question in my gaze. He stared at me for the longest time, long enough that I panicked and snapped, "What? Is fur sprouting on my face or something?"

He looked away again. "Your eyes are glowing."

"What, like a werewolf's? Are they yellow like Peyton and Reid's were?" Holy crap, Reid must be a werewolf too.

"No. They're pale silver, like the full moon."

"Oh. Cool, I guess." I downplayed his words, because the comparison felt like a compliment, and that was doing weird things to my insides. Highly *inappropriate* things.

In the next breath, warmth rushed to the apex of my thighs. I sucked in a gasp, arching my back like a cat as pleasure zinged through me.

Lochlan completely froze, like he freaking *knew*.

Not possible, not possible, not possible.

When I peeked up at him though, his blazing eyes were on me.

No, freaking *no!*

"Let me down. Now," I demanded, my voice suddenly hoarse.

And, just like that, he did.

Standing on unsteady legs, I tightly pulled my sodden cape around me to cover my nakedness. I gestured for him to lead the way, refusing to meet his gaze. Even when he turned and resumed walking, I kept my eyes firmly trained on the ground.

What the crap had just happened?

I'd experienced sexual urges before, but nothing like *that*. Nothing so powerful and fiercely carnal that I lost all control. And the feeling was still there, a simmering boil deep in my core.

I only managed to walk a few feet when the feeling erupted like an angry volcano, forcing me to drop on all fours. Gulping in air, I dug my nails into the ground as a fiery need ripped through me. Surprised at how easily my nails slid into the packed dirt, I pulled them out again to inspect them. They were now long and wickedly sharp.

Like *claws*. Was I turning into a freaking werewolf?

"McKenna."

"Just . . . give me a moment," I panted, sliding my nails—er, claws—in and out of the earth again. Something about the motion soothed me. Eased the burning ache between my thighs.

Or so I thought.

Without realizing it, I'd been rubbing my legs together. A moan slipped past my lips as the friction intensified. At the airy sound, I froze, shocked at what I'd just done in front of Lochlan. I bit my lip and tried to stand, but the feeling had me ensnared. It continued to pulse through me in punishing waves, and all I could do was whimper.

My body *desperately* needed something. And I had a sinking feeling that I wasn't going anywhere until that need was fulfilled.

Lochlan crouched before me. "You're in heat," he said haltingly, as if the words had been forced from him. I didn't respond. I didn't know how to. Did *heat* seriously mean what I thought it meant? He cleared his throat, his voice almost guttural as he added, "It rarely happens, but when it does, the urges won't go away until the full moon has lost its pull, or . . ."

"Or what?" I said, still refusing to look at him.

"Or until it's taken care of."

I could actually *hear* Lochlan swallow, which only intensified the urges to the point of pain. I squeezed my trembling thighs together, gritting my teeth. Fates, it was *him*. My body was responding to him. "I think . . . I think you should go." I dug my nails into the earth again.

He didn't respond, and panic quickened my heartbeats.

"Lochlan. Leave."

More silence.

"*Lochlan*." My voice went shrill with desperation. Even saying his name sent a bolt of fiery pain through me.

"I can't," he eventually replied, and I internally screamed. "McKenna, look at me." My stupid head rose without my permission. My stupid eyes locked with his, and I bit back a whimper. "I can help you," he simply said.

Freaking fates, I knew *exactly* what he meant.

My body did too, eagerly responding by burning hotter and hotter with need and yearning. It wanted. It desperately wanted *him*. And it hurt to want. It hurt so bad. Biting my lip hard enough to draw blood, I forcefully shook my head.

He waited a beat, then, "I'll carry you to the cabin. You'll be more comfortable there."

I shook my head again. Any contact with him would be too much. I was afraid of what I'd do. He didn't push the subject further, which I was beyond grateful for. Still, my body was highly attuned to his. When he shifted to sit on the ground, I tracked the movement, wishing I could see his shape through the shadows. My imagination was doing a good job of conjuring it though.

At one point, I couldn't stop myself from wondering what he looked like naked. When my mind happily supplied the details, my mouth started watering. Was I seriously freaking *drooling* right now?

I remained on all fours, panting and trembling and burning with need for what felt like hours. The agony spread to my whole body, so sharp and brutal that I could hardly draw air. I fought against the urges. Reminded myself of how much I disliked Lochlan after the way he'd treated me. I silently cried, frustrated and scared. I should be stronger than this irrational need.

But, in the end, I lost. In the end, the urges consumed me entirely, and I could no longer deny them. In the end, I was powerless, absolutely powerless to resist.

I raised my trembling head, finding his eyes already on me. As if he'd been waiting for this very moment. I trembled harder. "H-how?" was the only thing I could manage to say.

But he must have known all along what would happen. Must have read my body language that was all but screaming for him. He shifted again, and a second later, he was behind me. My heart thundered when he gently grasped my shoulders and lowered me onto my side. Every nerve ending became painfully aware of him as he positioned himself directly behind me, his chest, stomach, and thighs brushing against me.

I couldn't breathe, couldn't breathe when he placed his gloved hand on the curve of my waist and said, "There are ways to touch without skin contact."

I almost combusted right then and there, my poor heart galloping in frenzied bursts. Every muscle in my body shook as I focused on his hand. He peeled the cape from my skin to expose my nakedness, but embarrassment couldn't reach me. Not when all I wanted was his touch, his hands exploring my body in places no man ever had before.

His hand returned to my waist and I fisted the cape beneath me, squeezing my eyes shut. With excruciating slowness, he inched his hand downward, sliding the cold leather over the contours of my stomach. My body bucked, slamming into him, and he released a sharp hiss. I gasped as he dragged me flush against his hardness and held me there.

My body responded eagerly, rubbing against the impressive length. His hand on my stomach pressed harder, stilling my movements. I released a whimper, *needing* . . . "Help me," I begged, not the least bit ashamed of the words. "Please."

His breaths on my neck grew ragged, and I unclenched my thighs, wordlessly asking for what I wanted. His hand slowly inched downward again, but to the place I desperately wanted it to go. I thought I would die waiting for him to finally touch me. Thought the flames would consume me completely and I'd never know what it felt like.

But then he did.

And I cried out breathlessly, arching my back.

When his fingers lazily moved against me, I almost blacked out from the sheer bliss of it. I writhed, desperate to make him go faster, but his other hand slid beneath me to cup my breast, anchoring me in place. I moaned, drowning in the sensations he slowly wrung out of me. Only thin leather and a scrap of lace separated our skin, and oh how I loathed the material. I wanted to feel all of him against all of me. I wanted him *inside* of me.

Then he did something unexpected, capturing my full attention. Through the leather, I felt him scrape a sharpened nail—no, *claw*—down my center. I screamed, my body trembling uncontrollably. He did it again and again, slowly, teasing me mercilessly. Unable to take much more, I panted his name, pleading with him. I *needed . . .*

And he gave, stroking my sensitive peak at the pace I needed, pushing me closer and closer to the edge.

Seconds later, I shattered under his touch, crying out as I came hard. His fingers continued to move, prolonging the utter bliss. It lasted so long, I almost didn't survive. When I eventually floated down, spent and satiated, he wrapped both arms around me and simply said, "Sleep, McKenna."

So I did.

My stomach cramped with hunger and growled loudly, dragging me awake.

What was that *smell?*

My stomach growled again even louder. I rolled onto my side and a million aches slammed into me at once, stealing my breath. Confused, I jerked my eyes open to a strange room. I struggled to sit up in the large unfamiliar bed that smelled primarily of lake water and dirt—or maybe the smell was me. That wasn't the scent my stomach was responding to though.

Where in the world was I? What happened last night?

The sun was shining through the room's sheer gray curtains, but I had no idea what time it was, or even what day. I racked my brain, trying to remember how I'd gotten here, but came up empty. Alarm flooded me, followed by panic when the gray and white comforter fell to my waist, displaying my half naked state. I yanked the bed's white sheet up to my neck, covering my red bra.

Wait.

A memory from last night finally surfaced. I dropped the sheet and reached inside my bra, but the plastic-protected paper Reid had left me wasn't there. "Shoot," I muttered, patting the bed sheets and looking under the pillows. Ignoring my body's aches as best I could, I crawled to the edge of the bed and plopped onto my stomach to peer underneath.

A throat cleared from behind me.

I quickly popped my head back up and looked over my shoulder. The blood drained from my face. Lochlan stood in the doorway—the human-looking version of him. He was casually dressed in charcoal jeans and a snug black t-shirt that showed off his well-defined biceps and vine tattoos. Awareness slammed into me like a freight train. My lacy-underwear-clad butt was sticking up in the air, giving Lochlan an eyeful.

I did the only thing I could think of, sliding off the bed to land in a heap on the carpeted floor. Ow. I rubbed the spot where I'd landed, then froze, holding my breath. Maybe if I remained perfectly still, he'd leave and we could pretend this never happened.

"McKenna."

I closed my eyes and silently cursed. It couldn't get much more embarrassing than this. "Yeah?" I said, grimacing as my voice squeaked. *Play it cool, Kenna!* Smoothing my expression into what I hoped was indifference—as if sliding off beds half naked was a morning ritual of mine—I sat up and reached for the bed sheet to cover myself.

"You need to eat."

I frowned as I wrapped the sheet around my body. "Um, okay."

Why was he here anyway? I was seriously missing some memories of last night.

"It will help with the cravings and the lingering urges," he added, and I paused to consider his words. When they still didn't make sense after a few moments, I casually stood, tripping a little on the long sheet.

"I could eat. But, um . . . I seem to have misplaced my clothes. And where are we?" And why was *he* here? I was still mad at him for being so rude to me last week. A thought came to me and the blood drained from my face again. "Please don't tell me I got drunk last night. I never do that."

Fates, we didn't . . . *do* anything, did we? It would explain my state of undress. But no. There was no way I would do anything that stupid. My eyes widened. Did he drug me?

My mouth dried and I pulled the sheet tighter. "Explain or I'm calling the police." Crap, where was my *phone?*

Lochlan took a slow step into the room and I tensed, preparing

185

to defend myself. But who was I kidding? He was a vampire! And I didn't . . . I didn't have the silver dagger. This was bad. Really really bad.

"It's okay," he said, using his dumb sexy voice to soothe me.

"No. It's not," I said forcefully, trying not to show my fear. "I can't remember what happened last night after the Halloween party. I'm practically naked in a strange bedroom, and *you* are here. It is definitely *not* okay."

His brows pulled together, the only emotion he revealed. "You'll regain your memories soon—sometimes it takes awhile for your body to adjust after a change. And you took off your clothes last night when you got too hot. Unfortunately, they can't be salvaged, but there's clothing in the dresser behind you." His expression smoothed, but his voice hardened when he added, "As for why I'm here, I have experience with handling this sort of thing. As soon as you're recovered, I'll take you home."

Apparently finished with our conversation, he turned on his heel and left me to speechlessly gape at an empty doorway. Was he mad at me?

Holy fates, what happened last night?

CHAPTER 18

I finished buttoning the white dress shirt, a color I hadn't thought Lochlan owned. Although it fell to mid thigh and was way too big for me, it sure beat parading around in a bed sheet. I froze when the heady mix of amber, sandalwood, and musk filled my nose. All on their own, my hands fisted the shirt and shoved the fabric in my face. As the scent—*his* scent—completely invaded my senses, my eyes drifted closed. Warmth kindled in my stomach and my heart fluttered erratically.

What the freaking crap?

I let go of the shirt and frowned at my bedraggled reflection in the dresser mirror. It was like staring at a stranger. The girl I saw had dark smudges under her eyes from yesterday's mascara. Her long, brunette hair looked wild, with twigs and leaves decorating it. And her nails . . . dirt was packed under the oval tips.

I had never seen this girl before. I didn't know her story, what she went through to get here. And how she *felt* was even more of a mystery. It was like she had climbed a mountain last night and was now feeling the bone-deep aches and tiredness from such an exertion. But she also felt rejuvenated, as if the exercise and fresh air had done her good.

It frustrated me to no end that I couldn't remember what happened. But even more frustrating was that I had to deal with Lochlan if I wanted answers. He was the *worst* at answering questions—if he felt like answering them at all. And if these clothes smelled like him, was this his room? It was tastefully decorated in neutral colors with the occasional red accent piece, but besides his clothes, there were no personal effects.

Suddenly, the walls came crashing down around me as reality reared its ugly head.

"Aunt Tess!"

Crap, crap, *crap!*

I flew across the room and yanked the door open before remembering I didn't have pants on. No time! I charged forward, seeking the exit. Pants didn't matter anyway. I was already doomed, no matter what I was wearing. I halted halfway down the hall.

Maybe it was better if I didn't go home. There was no way I could explain my absence to Aunt Tess without her freaking out. And if she *did* know about vampires and discovered I'd spent the night with one, she'd probably ship me off to Timbuktu.

Besides, I would be eighteen in a little over a month. I could manage on my own until then. Or maybe I could crash at Isla's. Even if my aunt discovered where I was staying, she wouldn't force me to move away when I was nearly a legal adult, would she?

Yes, she would, my pragmatic mind said.

Argh! This was really bad. I was so close to being free of her and I'd ruined everything!

I lurched into motion again, muttering, "I can handle this. Just get out of here first."

The hallway ended at a second floor landing, and I noticed right away that the setup was all wrong. Lochlan's house by the lake had banisters overlooking the gabled front windows. There were no windows on this floor. Just a carpeted stairway leading down to the first floor.

When I caught sight of the front door below, I decided to worry about where I was later. I clambered down the stairs, surprised to see my ankle boots on a shoe rack at the bottom. Hurriedly slipping them on, I grabbed the door handle, then made the mistake of breathing.

The intensity of the mouthwatering smell almost bowled me over, my stomach immediately cramping with hunger. And not a little cramp either, but a raging PMS one. No, more like a I'm-in-labor-and-about-to-pop one. I leaned against the door as my knees threatened to buckle. Every breath I took made the stomach pains worse, so I inhaled shallowly, exhaling through my mouth.

When the pangs became tolerable, I carefully opened the door and sought my escape. I had no idea where Lochlan was or where on earth I planned on going next, but leaving this place was my first priority. The chill morning air sent goosebumps racing up my legs the moment I stepped onto the wraparound porch. Crap, I should have grabbed pants. I would pay for that poor decision.

All thought of pants fled my mind when I caught sight of the view though.

"Hoooly fates," I breathed, completely awed by what lay before me. The house—or maybe cabin was the right word—sat atop a small mountain range, overlooking a glittering lake below. The whole area as far as the eye could see was covered in dark green pine and fall-colored oak trees. The swell of neighboring mountains could be seen in the distance, and a fathomless blue sky soared overhead.

No sign of civilization. Or a car.

Oh.

Oh no.

"Well, that's just peachy," I muttered, clutching my still-aching stomach. I descended the porch steps and turned in a circle, taking in the two-story log cabin and overgrown trail leading up to it. "You've got to be kidding me."

How did I *get* here? By helicopter?

"Looking for something?"

I whirled at the sound of Lochlan's voice and found him leaning against the front door, arms casually crossed. My stomach did a funny lurch at the sight of him, at the way his eyes slowly roved up my bare legs. I passed off the feeling as more hunger pains. "Yes," I answered, deciding that honesty was the best approach. "I'm looking for a way off this mountain. I can't be here right now."

He tilted his head and black hair fell into his eyes. "And when the sun goes down, how will you explain your behavior to your aunt?"

I wrinkled my nose. "Huh?"

He uncrossed his arms, slowly stepping onto the porch. "The panting, the moaning, the screams," he said, taking another step. "The sweating, the elongated fingernails, the stripping of clothes."

He descended the stairs, and my heart sped up. Something about his words or approach was causing my skin to flush. "This isn't over yet. The moon's pull is still too strong. Even if you don't fully change into a werewolf tonight, how will you explain your violent mood swings? Your incessant need to hunt and consume raw meat? Or your need for . . . *other* things."

My breaths were now coming in quick bursts, my heart thundering inside my chest, because his words were starting to make sense. Memories of last night were coming back, memories of me touching Peyton and everything that happened after. I slapped a hand over my mouth as more and more memories poured in.

Nope. No way.

That didn't happen. That didn't happen either. And that *definitely* didn't happen.

I didn't freaking allow that. I didn't. I couldn't have.

"Freaking fates," I groaned, shaking my head in disbelief. I had allowed Lochlan D'angelo to touch me intimately. And I had *liked* it. More than liked it. In fact, my body was warming in the worst of ways just remembering the details, how he had used a claw to—

Straightening my spine, I started to walk. I walked so that I couldn't think. I walked so that Lochlan couldn't see my flushed skin, so he couldn't figure out that my body was still reacting to him.

The overgrown trail leading down the mountain wasn't too steep, but I kept tripping anyway in my haste to create distance. I forced myself to speed walk and not sprint so I wouldn't break my neck. Not that the distance would make any difference. He would pursue me as he always did, and it would only take him seconds with his vampire speed. I was stuck here until the werewolf inside me, or whatever it was, disappeared. And according to Lochlan, I had at least one more day of this, whatever this was.

And, fates help me, I was scared to death.

Scared of what tonight would bring. More of last night? More . . . urges? For *him*? For his touch, for the pleasure he wrung out of me, for the incredible way he made me feel? Yes. I knew I would want that. I could feel it underneath my skin, a need I couldn't deny.

And so I continued to walk. To desperately clear my head and rid my thoughts of him. Of his face, his voice, his touch, his scent. *Gah.* I almost whipped his shirt over my head and chucked it into the woods. I couldn't escape him!

Several minutes later, I reached the lake. Still no sign of a car. Sighing, I walked to the tip of the dock and sank onto its wooden planks. I would have stayed there all day—listening to the birds chirp, scenting the rich air and feeling the wind caress my skin with my newly heightened senses. I would have stayed despite the late autumn chill numbing my fingers and toes. But the hunger became too much. I knew what my body craved. I knew what that smell had been up at the cabin.

It was all I could think about now.

So, despite the *other* thing I would find in the cabin, I trekked back an hour later. I was officially a slave to my stomach. It didn't care that we would have to face Lochlan again. My stomach only cared about the meal I had been depriving it of for far too long. The hike up left me dizzy and nauseous. My heart pounded too rapidly, my breaths too shallow. But I made it.

I found Lochlan inside, sitting at the kitchen's breakfast nook I'd tracked with my nose. He hadn't followed me to the lake, which surprised me. But I supposed he knew, just like he'd known last night, that I would eventually succumb to my carnal cravings.

I hated that he knew. Hated that I was giving in, yet again.

But the last of my resistance fled when I caught sight of *it*. A plate of rare, bloody steak sitting opposite Lochlan on the table—the scent that had woken me from sleep earlier. My stomach growled like an angry bear, and I could have sworn I heard Lochlan chuckle under his breath. My gaze refused to meet his though, and not because of last night. My eyes were fixed on the food and only the food. Nothing else mattered right now.

My stomach and throat were tight as I slid onto a kitchen chair in front of the loaded plate. There was a fork and knife on either side, and I picked them up with trembling fingers. Saliva pooled in my mouth when I cut into the steak, and I quickly sealed my lips shut so I wouldn't drool. Raising the forkful of meat, I slowly placed it into my mouth. But when the taste exploded on my tongue, I lost control.

The cutlery clanged against the table as I grabbed the steak and viciously ripped into it. I lost track of time and place, my entire focus on devouring the fresh, tender meat. When I finished far too soon, I licked the juices from my fingers, savoring every last drop.

The sound of movement raised the hair on my arms. I froze, a growl sticking in my throat. My eyes flashed upward and latched onto Lochlan, whose direct, unflinching gaze forced my senses into high alert. My lips peeled back in a silent snarl, but he didn't heed the warning. In fact, he seemed to be challenging me.

Refusing to look away, I held his gaze. And the longer I did, the brighter his eyes became. From black to wine red, they seared my retinas with their intensity. The breath stuttered from my lungs and I reached down to pinch my thigh. He was suddenly up out of his seat, his tall form looming over the table. I shot up too, unwilling to give an inch.

He slowly came around the side toward me, holding eye contact the entire time. The closer he came, the harder it was for me to bear the weight of his gaze. I finally relinquished a step, then another, stopping when the cold metal of a fridge pressed into my back. But I didn't look away, because I knew that's what he wanted. For me to back down.

Not gonna happen, I told him with my eyes, even as I trembled under the intensity of his stare.

He ever so slowly followed the path I took, his face set in determined lines. Closer, closer, closer. Reaching my position, he raised a hand, then the other, placing them on the fridge either side of me.

He wasn't wearing gloves. I stopped breathing.

This game had suddenly become dangerous. I knew it, and I was betting that he did too. Oh, he most *definitely* did. The glint in his deep red eyes turned wicked as one hand left the fridge. My eyes started to water from the strain of holding his gaze when all they wanted to do was check on his hand's whereabouts.

A strangled gasp left me a moment later as I felt his fingers slide down my clothed arm.

Stop that, I silently commanded, narrowing my eyes.

He tilted his head, face relaxing as he sent his reply. *No.*

I clenched my hands into fists when his fingers stopped just shy of touching them. Then they reversed their course, traveling back up. The whole time, my heart threatened to leap out of my chest, equally terrified and thrilled at the precarious predicament. Stupid heart. I needed to end this. Now. Before something worse than werewolf symptoms flooded my body.

"Do you want more?" he suddenly murmured, and curled a finger around a lock of my hair.

I felt the contact to the very tips of my toes, but nothing negative happened. I guessed only skin contact could do that supernatural trigger thing. I licked my lips, not failing to notice how his eyes flickered, like he'd almost broken the staredown to watch my mouth. Victory swelled in my chest. "More what?"

"Steak. But if you do, you'll have to move."

At the mere mention of food, my concentration broke, and I looked behind me at the fridge. Immediately realizing my mistake, I whipped my gaze back to his and growled, "You cheated!"

Pure male satisfaction was etched on his face as he straightened, tugging gently on the strand of hair before releasing it. "Don't feel bad," he said and gestured for me to move aside so he could open the fridge. "You lasted longer than most. I'd even consider your inner wolf an alpha female."

I opened my mouth to retort, then paused, wrinkling my nose. "Is that what just happened? Some territorial thing?" My mouth snapped shut. Did I seriously just act like an animal over *food*?

Lochlan seemed to be enjoying this way too much. I'd never seen his face so animated before—besides the bouts of rage, of course. "Every living creature has an instinct to protect what they deem is theirs—even humans. Vampires and werewolves are natural predators though. We can't help but fight for dominance." He closed the fridge and I eyed the container he held. But when he added, "I just happen to be more alpha than you," I glared up at him.

"You cheated, plain and simple. I didn't know the rules."

"We could try again, if you like," he practically purred, and my heart gave a pathetic jolt. Who *was* this man, and where had dour Lochlan D'angelo run off to? Whoever this new version was, my body let me know quite clearly how it felt about him by heating up in all the wrong places.

I cleared my tight throat and dropped my gaze to the food container once more. "Um, I think I'll just take that." He didn't immediately hand it over, and I squirmed on the spot, keeping my eyes averted. When he finally did, I wanted nothing more than to hide in a corner and eat where he couldn't assert his *alpha*-ness again. But I behaved like a civilized person and reclaimed my seat at the table.

Now that my stomach wasn't trying to gnaw a hole through me, I savored the meat, and even used my utensils. The steak wasn't cooked at all, as if it had come straight from the butcher's. I should be thoroughly repulsed that I was eating it, but wasn't. Its presence, however, sparked my curiosity—and raised suspicion.

Swallowing a bite, I looked to the side where Lochlan was leaning against the kitchen counter. "Where did you get this meat anyway? Did you go shopping while I slept?"

Or did he already have the fridge stocked for this very purpose?

I shoved that thought aside. He couldn't have known ahead of time. Could he?

"Hunting, actually," he said, and lazily crossed one booted foot over the other. "That's deer meat, fresh off the bone."

At the news, I expected my stomach to rebel. Nope. It seemed to like knowing that *Bambi* was filling it up. But knowing that Lochlan had bagged me a deer was a different matter entirely. A strange feeling swelled inside of me, a fullness beneath my sternum. I quickly busied myself with cutting more meat, refusing to dwell on what it could mean. "Um . . . so you shoot then?"

"Not really. I wasn't prepared to have a gun with me anyway."

My eyebrows inched upward. "Did you *catch* it?"

He inclined his head.

"With your bare hands?"

Another nod. His left cheek indented, briefly flashing his sole dimple. "The deer didn't suffer," he said after a moment when I continued to stare.

A crazy thought came to me and I gulped, focusing on my plate again.

"You can ask," he said quietly, and my heart thumped extra hard. Was he always this intuitive or were my expressions that transparent?

I fiddled with my fork, wishing he would just tell me and not make me ask. But I had the distinct impression that Lochlan D'angelo never gave away information for free. If I wanted answers, I'd have to work for them.

Gripping my fork tightly, I forced my gaze to his, then expelled the words in a rush. "Did you drink its blood?"

"Yes," he said without pause. Before I could digest this admission, he muttered, "Revolting stuff."

I almost choked on my spit. "Then why drink it?"

He flicked the barest of glances at my neck, so quickly that I almost missed it. That's all it took for my senses to go on high alert though. *Danger*, my mind screamed. *Predator*. But the usual instinct to run wasn't there. It was replaced with a powerful need to defend myself. I raised my steak knife an inch, angling the tip toward him.

His eyes flashed when he noticed my reaction, but he didn't move. "I won't drink your blood, McKenna. You don't need to fear me."

I warred with myself, wanting to believe him but still overcome with doubt. "How can I trust you when one minute you tell me not to fear you and the next that I should?"

A muscle jumped in his jaw as he unflinchingly held my gaze. "You can't trust me. You should never fully let your guard down around a predator. But I'm telling you right now that I won't harm you. I'll make do with animal blood while we're here, even though my body demands more. I know what the consequences of touching you are, and I'm not willing to take that risk."

At his words, my heart skipped nervously, but there was no stopping me from asking, "What are the consequences of touching me?"

He stilled, deathly so, and I struggled to remain seated. I had undoubtedly struck a nerve with that question, but I wouldn't back down. I needed to know. I needed to know what I was capable of. "If I tell you," he slowly began, watching me closely, "and you use the knowledge against me, then I won't be able to protect you from myself."

A chill swept down my spine at the barely concealed threat, but I nodded anyway, urging him to continue.

"If our skin touches the way yours did with that werewolf last night," he said, straightening to his full height, "then you would manifest vampire symptoms temporarily." I swallowed, having already guessed as much, but I was wholly unprepared when he added, "I, on the other hand, would be dead."

CHAPTER 19

I scrambled out of my chair so fast that it tipped over backward. Lochlan did his speedy vampire thing and caught the chair before it could hit the floor. I quickly backed away, hands raised in front of me. Cursing, I tucked them behind me instead.

"You knew all this time?" I couldn't keep the accusation and panic out of my voice. "You knew and still almost touched my hand a few minutes ago? I could have killed you! Fates, I-I grabbed Kade's finger. I could have killed him too. Wait, is Peyton really okay? She was in pain and I touched her for so long. I—"

"I checked in with Kade. She's fine. More than fine, actually. Now come here."

I gawked at him. "W-what? No."

Determination glinted in his eyes, and he stalked toward me. My earlier courage vanished and I fled into the living room, catapulting over a sofa. When I straightened, he was inches away, reaching for me. I yelped as he grasped my upper arms and pulled me close. Only a handful of inches separated our faces.

"I'm not that easy to kill," he said, near enough for his breath to warm my cheeks. "Do you think I'm afraid of you?"

"Let me go, Lochlan," I gasped out, desperate for space but unable to move. I was painfully aware of his gloveless fingers on my arms. Only a thin shield of clothing protected him from my lethal skin. "You should have told me."

"And this is exactly why I didn't. Nothing has to change."

"This changes *everything*," I cried, balling my hands into fists. "You should fear me more than I should fear you. I don't want to hurt anyone."

His expression noticeably softened, and seeing that aloof mask slip for the first time—seeing the way it transformed his face into something achingly beautiful—was too much.

I bit my trembling lip, then forced myself to say, "You shouldn't be near me, especially if I get angry again like I did last night. Just leave me here. I'll be fine on my own tonight."

"I can't do that," he replied, absentmindedly stroking my arms to comfort me.

"Why?" I said, raising my voice. "It doesn't make any sense for you to help or protect me. So *why* are you doing it?"

His lips thinned. "Because it's my duty. It's my responsibility to protect and watch over you."

Hurt stabbed my chest, which was dumb. I'd known for quite some time that I was merely a "job" to him. Still, I had hoped for a different answer, especially after the intimate moment we'd shared last night. "And why do I need protecting?" I asked quietly, partly resigned that he wouldn't tell me.

He clenched his jaw. "If I tell you, you'll either run or try to kill me."

I arched an eyebrow. "I've stuck around this long, haven't I? And I'm not the killing type, so try me."

He looked at me skeptically. "At the very least, you'll hate me."

"Argh, just tell me!"

"Nearly half of the supernatural world wants to use you or see you dead."

A heavy silence settled between us as I stared in shock.

He released a tired sigh and stepped back, letting go of my arms to shove both hands through his hair. "I shouldn't have told you."

I blinked. "No, I . . ." My voice died as the full meaning of his words sank in.

I just don't want you dead yet.

Yet, yet, yet.

Lochlan was one of them. He wanted me dead too.

I pressed a hand to my roiling stomach. "I . . . excuse me." Turning, I walked as calmly as I could toward the hall bathroom and carefully shut the door. I barely reached the toilet in time. The meat I'd just eaten violently gushed from me. The force of it squeezed tears from my eyes, leaving me trembling and shell shocked.

Lochlan wanted me dead. I didn't care about the nameless, faceless others who did. Only that he did.

Lochlan. Wanted. Me. Dead.

Why didn't that sink in before? And why did the realization suddenly *hurt* so much?

When I was empty and spent, I flushed the toilet and cleaned myself up. The shock had been replaced with a resolute calm as my survival instincts kicked in—far too late, but better late than never. If killing me was Lochlan's end goal, I needed to be prepared. Even if I'd had a silver dagger with me, stabbing him and escaping this cabin wasn't a smart idea. If I missed his heart, he would only pursue me and no doubt finish me off.

No, I needed information. Knowledge. An ace up my sleeve to buy myself more time.

I can handle this, I told my reflection, ignoring my trembling hands. I had to. No one could protect me now but myself. I could pretend that all was well. I'd been doing it for years.

I inhaled a steadying breath. In, out. In, out. Then quietly opened the door.

Not surprisingly, Lochlan was waiting for me when I emerged. He searched my face impassively for a moment, then paused. Something like concern flickered in his eyes, but it had to be an act. Maybe he'd been pretending this whole time, which made me feel sick all over again.

"Um, I think I'm going to lie down for a bit," I started, relieved when my voice didn't shake. "You're right. Maybe you shouldn't have told me."

Nothing like a guilt trip to make someone back off.

He nodded wordlessly and let me go, but I felt his eyes on me the entire way up the stairs. Closing myself in the room I'd vacated this morning, I sat on the bed and waited. My only hope was that he would leave the cabin at some point out of hunger or boredom. With his vampire hearing, he'd immediately know that I was up to something.

Time wasn't on my side though and I struggled not to tap my foot impatiently. Once the sun went down, the werewolf symptoms would probably flare up again.

Oh *crap!*

I gripped the bed tightly as a terrible thought came to me. What if my body didn't care that Lochlan wanted to kill me and responded to him again tonight? Freaking fates. I shoved the problem aside for later, renewing my focus on the movement downstairs.

The afternoon slowly dragged by as I strained to hear. Maybe an hour passed, then finally—*finally*—he moved. It wasn't his footsteps that I heard, but a snick as the front door closed.

Carefully removing my boots, I tiptoed to the bedroom door and cracked it open, listening for sound. I even snuck out and peered down the stairs. When I was convinced he'd left, I began my search. First the dresser, meticulously checking through the clothes without disturbing them too much. Then under the mattress and inside the closet. I scoured every inch of the room, but came up empty.

No problem. That would have been too easy anyway.

A second bedroom across the hall proved to be an unfruitful search as well. There wasn't even a trace of Lochlan's scent in that room, which made me wonder where he had slept last night. No luck in the upstairs bathroom either. I even checked the toilet tank.

Heading downstairs, I briefly paused at the front door and listened for footsteps. I soon turned and searched the hall bath, my movements becoming desperate. Nothing there. I ransacked the living room, lifting cushions and rugs. I checked the fireplace mantel and even bent to feel around inside, getting sloppy by disturbing the ash as my time ran out. It *had* to be here. I dove into the kitchen and pulled open cupboards and drawers, pausing when I found an exceptionally long and sharp knife.

I shook my head and slammed the drawer shut. It wasn't silver and therefore probably useless. My stomach rumbled when I peered into the fridge, but I ignored the hunger pains. Eventually, I stopped to lean against the kitchen table and rack my brain. The paper could have fallen out when Lochlan drove me here, or while I was submerged in the lake. But I could have sworn I felt it shift against my skin when he had . . . when he had . . .

Blowing out a breath, I squeezed my eyes shut. But the memory persistently floated to the surface, just behind my lids—of his hand cupping my breast and kneading the flesh. I gripped the table as warmth flooded my body, weakening my knees. I struggled to dispel the phantom feeling of his hands on me and focus on what I suspected.

That he had discovered the plastic-protected paper inside my bra and removed the information I so desperately needed while I slept.

I should be furious at the invasion. I was. But also completely turned on at the thought of him slipping a hand inside—

"*Gah!* Where is it?" I hissed to distract my aroused body.

"Where's what?"

I whirled with a muffled shriek, clutching my chest. Lochlan stood in the kitchen doorway, cell phone in hand. He slipped it inside his jeans pocket and my eyes shot to the spot. Of course. His *pocket.* I inwardly cursed. The knowledge I sought was probably in the one place I could never reach.

I had to play my hand carefully. I had no idea what Lochlan thought of the three dark princes story, only that he didn't want Reid telling me about it. That had to mean something. It was the only possible weapon I had against a supernatural being so much faster and stronger than me.

"Oh," I said, tucking hair behind my ears to hide my nervousness. "I lost something a friend gave to me. I thought maybe I'd dropped it in here somewhere."

I held my breath, waiting to see if he'd reveal anything.

He didn't. His face had returned to its usual impassiveness. I tried not to show my disappointment when he avoided the topic entirely by saying, "I take it you're feeling better now?"

"Um, yeah. You just caught me by surprise earlier. It's not every day you hear that people want you dead." I laughed lightly, but watched his expression like a hawk. Argh! Still nothing. When he chose to stare at me instead of respond, I reached down and pinched my thigh.

"What's wrong?"

I blinked in confusion. "Huh?"

"Your leg. You're pinching it. You do that when something's bothering you."

"I . . . what? How do you even—" I spluttered, completely caught off guard. Huffing, I crossed my arms. "It's been a stressful twenty-four hours. A lot is bothering me."

He shook his head and stepped into the kitchen. The room immediately felt smaller and I resisted the urge to pinch my thigh again. "No, this is different. Your stress has something to do with me."

My heart jumped into my throat.

"There, see?" he said before I could deny it. "You're nervous."

I released a breathless laugh, further cementing his point. "I—it's because you're doing that eye thing." Why the crap did I say that?

"What eye thing?" He took another step.

"You know, where you try to read my thoughts with your eyes," I blurted, unable to shut up. My backside hit the table, reminding me that I had no room for escape.

"I can't read thoughts," he said, his voice sliding into dangerous sexy territory, "but I can sense your mood changes and emotions. Hear your thundering heartbeats." Every cell in my body sprang awake as he stepped into my personal space, saying quietly, "Smell the blood racing through your veins."

"Lochlan," I warned, albeit breathlessly. He was *way* too close, and my body was going haywire. I uncrossed my arms and gripped the table's edge, hoping he couldn't detect my reaction to his nearness.

But I knew the jig was up when he slowly bent to breathe me in. My heart pounded fiercely and his eyes shot up to mine. "You feel desire, but also genuine fear. Why? What has caused you to fear me?"

Horrified, I tried to look away, but he grasped the nape of my neck, angling my face toward his. I jumped at the contact, eyes widening as I waited for something awful to happen. When nothing did, I focused on his hand, realizing he'd touched the collar of my shirt, not my skin. Still, I felt no relief. Not when Lochlan's gaze demanded an answer.

"S-stop," I stammered, as the need to answer him grew with each passing second. He was using thrall on me, and it was working this time. "Don't . . . don't m-make me."

"Then just tell me," he said, his voice rumbling through my insides. "Tell me why you're afraid."

"Because . . ." My nails dug into the table as I tried to withhold the words. But they were slipping, slipping from my control. I had no choice. I had to *speak*. The words were yanked from me against my will, and I burst out, "Because you want to kill me."

I bit my tongue, but it was too late. The damage had already been done. Anger that he'd forced me to speak and fear for how he'd react charged through me. I bit down harder until the coppery taste of blood filled my mouth.

Lochlan's gaze shot to my lips, sending another jolt of fear through me. I swallowed and he tracked the movement. As panic set in, he flicked his eyes up to mine again. "You believe I want to kill you?"

I pursed my lips, expecting him to pry the answer out of me again. Surprised when the pull never came, I decided to answer honestly anyway. "You said you didn't want me dead yet. That means you want me dead at some point. So just do it already. Rip my head off or something. But if you take your time, I won't go quietly. I'll—"

I gasped when he suddenly pushed himself against me. The table scraped across the floor and struck the wall from the impact. Still grasping the nape of my neck, he leaned forward and rested a hand on the tabletop. The position bent me backward, leaving my lower half pinned against his.

Every drop of air fled my lungs at the contact. He aligned his pelvis with mine, slowly forcing my thighs apart. I was too overcome with shock to make a sound.

His hardness pulsed against me through our clothing. My body immediately throbbed in response, excited at the foreign new feeling. My shirt rode up, allowing his jeans to rub against my lacy underwear.

He brought his head low, low enough to whisper scant inches from my ear, "Does this feel like a man who wants to kill you?"

Struck speechless, unable to do anything but tremble as heat surged through me, I whimpered breathlessly.

He slowly ground his pelvis against mine and my eyes rolled back. I moaned as the length of zipper on his jeans created the most delicious friction. I immediately wanted more, craving the intimate connection yet needing it to stop at the same time. I couldn't think properly, couldn't remember why this was a bad idea. Why I didn't *want* this.

"Why," I panted, sucking in a gasp when he relentlessly rocked against me. "Why are you doing this?"

"Because I can," he replied huskily, continuing to rock. "Because you want me to. Because I can't stop thinking about touching you. I want to touch you in every way possible. Especially your skin. I want to know what it feels like. What *you* feel like."

His words only inflamed the friction between us. A visceral need swelled inside me. I released the table and dug my fingers into his back. A pleased growl rumbled in his chest and he increased the pace, until I was lost, utterly lost to the sensations lifting me higher and higher. Nothing else mattered but finding that highest peak, and I was close. I could feel it, a destination I had to reach at all costs.

When I finally reached the top, my entire body stiffened as pleasure blasted through me. I fisted Lochlan's shirt and screamed, shooting so high that I saw stars. Soon after, the sound of splintering wood reached my ears, followed by a rough groan from Lochlan as he shuddered against me.

Our breathing was labored, our limbs trembling as we slowly came down together. All without our skin touching. But, as I struggled to regain rational thought, I knew that I wanted more.

More of him. More of this.

No. *More* than this.

I wanted to touch his skin. *Desperately* so.

The ache increased the longer we stayed pressed together, and I couldn't help myself. I just wanted one touch. One little press of my skin to his. So my hand slid over his ribcage. Up his spine and shoulder blade. Until my fingers were inches away. Inches from pulling down his shirt and touching his—

In a frenzy of movement, he caught my wrist and spun me around, locking both arms to my chest. "*Witch*," he hissed, tightening his hold. "Always preying on my weaknesses. Always waiting until my guard is down. Always *using* me—"

"Lochlan," I frantically squeaked when his grip became painful. "I-I didn't mean to. I'm sorry. I don't know why I did it. *Please*. Please don't hurt me."

He froze. Then released me in a rush.

When I turned, he was gone.

CHAPTER 20

The sun drifted below the treeline and I shivered, rubbing my arms. Abandoning the view for the toasty indoors, I headed back inside the cabin and closed the door. Even with the lingering werewolf symptoms and addition of sweatpants, my skin still felt chilled after what had happened.

Three hours had passed since the "kitchen table mistake" as I was now calling our latest encounter. After his outburst, Lochlan had made himself scarce, leaving me shaken over his words—and the highly intimate moment we'd shared.

We had both obviously lost our minds. At least I could blame my horniness on being in heat, but what was *his* excuse? He had attacked me with his groin and then called me a *witch*, for fate's sake. I should be livid. I *was* livid—but confused too. And hurt that he treated me so harshly after we'd experienced something so . . .

Perfect.

I snorted at my own idiocy, shaking my head. That experience had been *far* from perfect. First, he'd used thrall on me, then lulled me into complacency with a mind-blowing orgasm. Lochlan D'angelo was controlling and manipulative, a bad boy through-and-through. I had never thought myself capable of helplessly falling for the dark and mysterious brooder type. I thought I was smarter than that. But, despite the clear danger, I could no longer deny my intense attraction for the vampire.

When another hour slowly ticked by and he still hadn't returned, I started to pace. Restless energy itched beneath my skin. Needs built that weren't my own. I stopped in the kitchen to guzzle some water and froze at the sight of the table. Jagged lines marred the light oak surface, marks that hadn't been there before. As I inched closer to inspect them, though, I remembered a sound I'd heard, right before Lochlan had fallen over the edge with me.

My throat constricted and I stumbled back.

Those were claw marks. From *his* claws.

My body responded by pulsing heat through me in waves. The force was so sudden that I dropped my cup and doubled over in pain. Glass shattered against the slate-colored tiles. I bent too far and sprawled onto the floor, landing on the shards.

"Fates," I hissed as glass split open my right palm. Blood immediately seeped over the tiles, and I fisted my hand to stem the flow.

The cabin's front door crashed open, startling me. I almost cut myself again as I scrambled to face the oncoming threat, my hackles raising—if I *had* hackles. *You aren't a werewolf, Kenna. Get a grip!* A growl slipped from my throat anyway when a towering dark form appeared in the kitchen doorway a second later.

I knew by the shadows surrounding him that it was Lochlan. Still, I hid my injury, my *weakness*, as his sharp red gaze took in the mess. Something felt different about him, something that put me on edge. His shadows swirled as if agitated, and with my heightened senses, I could smell him.

Underneath the amber, sandalwood, and musk was another scent, one more potent and undeniably *him*. The moment I breathed it in, my body responded. Heat doused me, my underwear dampening with arousal. I squeezed my thighs together and gritted my teeth against the pleasure-pain.

"McKenna," Lochlan said roughly, still framing the doorway. He didn't even have to say it. I knew what he meant, what he was offering.

Panicking, I shook my head. "No. I don't want you to touch me like that again." As if in complaint, my core throbbed in agony. A whine slipped past my throat that sounded way too much like a wolf's. I tightly fisted my injured hand, adding, "Not even if I beg."

And I would. Because I *did* want his touch. So badly that it hurt.

"Please," I said desperately, when all he did was stare. "Please promise me."

Instead of answering, he entered the kitchen. My entire body tensed, but he bypassed me, pulling open a drawer. He lifted out a towel and ripped it clean in half. Dampening one strip from the kitchen sink, he returned to crouch in front of me. His scent immediately invaded my senses, nearly choking me. I cringed back, seeking escape as unmet need splintered through me.

Before I could, his gloved hand shot out and captured my right wrist. I curled my upper lip back in a silent warning. He only tugged me closer. Brushing a thumb over my clenched fist, he asked me to open for him. I resisted, knowing he just wanted to help, but having him near made me want him even more.

Maybe I didn't *really* want him though. Maybe I only temporarily did, a byproduct of this screwed-up werewolf situation. Either way, my body shook as I continued to deny it.

But I wasn't the only one shaking. Lochlan's fingers trembled almost violently when he slowly peeled back my fingers to reveal the cut.

"Are you okay?" I asked, worried at how off he was acting.

He stilled, flicking his gaze up to mine. At the raw pain I saw in his eyes, my chest tightened. "This wasn't supposed to happen," he said and wrapped the dry towel strip around my injury. "Not to me. Not to us." Even his voice sounded pained. When the makeshift bandage was secure, he grabbed the damp towel half to clean my blood off the floor.

The moment he started though, he paused, inhaling sharply. The shadows around him billowed outward, further obscuring his features. But I still saw. Still saw him drop the towel and slowly touch the puddle of blood. When he hissed, a chill snaked down my spine. The shadows shifted to reveal his gloved hand. He lifted it. Higher and higher. Until it was inches from his face.

I didn't understand what was happening at first. I'd become used to his nightly appearance as Shadow Man, forgetting for a moment what he truly was.

But when he said, "Can't . . . stop," I remembered.

"Lochlan," I said, reaching for him, but it was too late.

He brought the gloved finger that was smeared with my blood to his lips. Inhaling a ragged breath, he tasted the blood. His red eyes closed and he released a groan. The gutteral sound vibrated through me, curling my toes.

Instead of feeling repulsed at the primal display, I had the strangest urge to growl approvingly like a feral dog. I wanted him to do it again. To bask in his carnal nature the way I wanted to bask in mine. We were the same, he and I. Predators of the night.

I licked my lips and scooted closer to him, mindful of the glass. My entire body was on fire, kindled awake by the match he had struck. I ached to press my lips to his and taste my blood on his tongue. To finally take what I wanted most. *Him.*

But before my fingers could touch him, he caught my hand. The bandaged one. "Don't," he said curtly, and I froze. When he didn't release me though, nervous excitement filled me. As if responding to the signals pouring from my body, he gasped for air, tightening his grip.

The bite of pain cleared my feverish mind, enough for me to stammer, "Lochlan, I-I think we should . . . I need some fresh air." I gulped, still struggling with the need to jump him. When his grip only tightened further, I yelped, all thoughts of humping his leg gone. Tugging to get free, I snapped, "Let me go!"

The same unpredictable anger I'd experienced last night rushed through me, and I watched with morbid fascination as my nails lengthened to claws. Our eyes locked at the same time. Without warning, I lunged at Lochlan. Caught off guard by the move, he didn't stop me from taking him to the floor.

Before I could sink my claws into him though, he reversed our positions. I landed flat on my back, my flailing arms and legs pinned within seconds. Rage built, hot and sharp. I snarled at him, baring my teeth. The longer he held me, the angrier I became.

And with that anger came crippling pain.

I howled in agony, sounding more animal than human. The pain only fueled my anger, and I doubled my efforts at attacking Lochlan for imprisoning me this way. I wanted his blood under my claws. To violently rip into his flesh. My muscles seemed to densify, lending me inhuman strength, but he was still stronger than me. No matter how hard I fought to free myself, his hold remained ironclad.

Several minutes into the struggle, he wrangled both my wrists above my head, pressing them to the floor. Still unable to pull free, I bucked and writhed against him, seeking vulnerable skin to bite.

"Kade, come now," he suddenly said, his tone sharp and commanding. "I'm losing control."

I was lucid enough to know what that meant. He was calling for backup. "Fight me," I spat, jerking a leg loose only for him to corral it back. "Just you and me. Don't let him interfere."

"Too late," he said, his voice so gruff that I barely recognized it. "I need him. I can't do this."

"Coward!" I snarled, my only thought on challenging him. I strained so hard to get loose that mind-numbing pain exploded through me. My skin, my *bones* burst into flames, and I screamed. It felt like my muscles were stretching. My bones shifting and bending into unnatural shapes.

The scream ended in a keening howl. My fury switched to panic, and I fixed frightened eyes on Lochlan. "It—it wants out. It's trying to come out. I can feel it. Please help me. I-I don't want to be a were-wolf."

"You need to calm yourself, McKenna," he said forcefully. "Focus on slowing your heart rate. Focus on breathing. You can stop the change if you get control of yourself."

As something pricked at my arms, chafing against my shirt, I struggled to see above me. "What's happening? Am I growing fur? No, no, no—"

"McKenna, look at me." At the command in his voice, my eyes were yanked back to his. "Take a breath. Good. Now another. Keep breathing."

I did as instructed, not even caring that he was using thrall on me. I was *that* freaked. After a minute of breathing, I whimpered, "What color is it?"

"Silver."

"Freaking fates."

"Just keep breathing. Don't focus on that right now. You're not a werewolf. You don't need to change. Say it."

I clenched my teeth as more pain shot through me, hissing, "I'm not a werewolf. I don't need to change."

"Good. Again."

So I did, repeating the words over and over until the fur receded and my bones settled. Exhausted, I sagged in his grip, beads of sweat peppering my skin. "Never let me touch a werewolf ever again," I rasped, my throat raw from screaming.

Lochlan shifted his hold on my wrists to a more comfortable position. "Werewolves only experience the pain of transformation a couple days out of the month. The first few times are the worst, but the more they transition, the easier it becomes. After a few years, they can change within minutes instead of hours. Once they learn control, they can live their lives with minimal disruption from their beast form, only changing for a short time."

"So how come I haven't changed yet? How come I was able to fight it off on my first try?"

He hesitated for a moment, studying my face. "Because you're different. You don't have to follow the rules like the rest of the supernatural world. It's why so many of them want to use or kill you."

I swallowed. "Including you?"

His eyes shuttered. "I thought I made myself clear earlier. I don't want to kill you."

Only half an answer. Did he want to *use* me? I bit my lip, uncertain if I wanted to know. Not right now anyway. Instead, I asked, "How do you know so much? Are there supernatural schools, or a supernatural encyclopedia maybe? The internet hasn't helped me at all."

"There are a few schools for the supernatural, yes, but most of my knowledge comes from personal experience. I write down everything I learn in a journal."

"Can I see it?" I wasn't sure why I bothered asking. Journal was probably code for a diary where he kept his deepest, darkest secrets.

But the more questions I asked, the more distracted I was from my pain. And the more he answered, the thirstier I became to hear him speak. He'd never opened up to me this way before, and I didn't want this moment between us to end.

When he didn't answer right away, I became acutely aware of our positions. His gloved hands still held my wrists, his legs curled around mine. The rest of him hovered directly above me, dangerously close.

"I'm surprised you want anything to do with the supernatural world after what I've told you," he finally replied, distracting my mind from inappropriate thoughts.

"Well, I'm a part of it, aren't I? I'd rather face the monstrous truth than hide in the shadows."

Another hesitation. Then, "It's safer in the shadows."

I tilted my head to the side. "Is that why you cloak yourself? You never let me see what you look like in this form."

He stiffened against me, averting his gaze. "You wouldn't like it."

I blinked at him in surprise. Did he think I would be afraid of him? Or did his reservations go deeper than that? I opened my mouth to assure him, but he suddenly hissed, tightening his legs around mine.

"What are you doing?"

I frowned. "Doing what?" Then I felt it—my breasts were pushing up against him. I peered between us, startled to find my spine arched. "Uh, I don't—" A gasp left me as I managed to rub our bodies together from chest to pelvis.

Freaking fates, my body had gone rogue.

Lochlan hadn't moved an inch. This was *all* me.

"Stop," he grunted, yet didn't shift away when I did it again.

Heat sparked low in my belly, dulling my ability to think

rationally. "Maybe we should," I said breathlessly as need trembled through me. "Just one more time."

He swore sharply and turned his head away. "I'm trying to honor your request."

"Well, don't. I don't care about that." I whimpered when he lifted his body an inch anyway. "Please, Lochlan. I want you to touch me. *Please*."

A growl rumbled deep in his chest. My core throbbed in response. I struggled against his grip, desperate for contact. "Stop, McKenna," he gritted out. "I can't lose control."

"But I want you to," I cried, wanting him so badly that tears sprung to my eyes.

Shouting a curse this time, he jerked away from me. In a flash, he was up and halfway across the kitchen. The move was so sudden and unexpected, I wasn't prepared. I didn't see the wicked blade arcing through the air until it was too late.

"No!" My voice rang through the silence that followed, clanging through my skull.

I stared, horrified, as the shadows thinned, revealing the knife hilt deep in Lochlan's abdomen. I gasped out his name and scrambled to my feet.

Before I could move toward him, he held up a hand. "*Don't*, McKenna."

"What? Lochlan, you need *help*. Fates, this is really bad. Let me—"

"I'm *fine*," he barked, even as he slumped against the kitchen counter. "But you won't be, not if you keep talking like that. You can't say those things to a vampire, especially not to me."

"I'm sorry. So sorry. I couldn't help myself. I'm just so—"

"It's not your fault." The shadows receded even more, as if he didn't have the strength to maintain them. "You're my responsibility and I'm failing you. That's why I called Kade, because he can protect you from me. But I need you to stay away until he arrives."

My stomach cramped, responding to the pain in his voice. I instinctively stepped toward him, but he released a warning growl, freezing me in place. I growled back, frustrated and scared that he would bleed out right in front of me. "I don't understand! No one needs to protect me from you. Now please let me—"

"*Kenna.*" At his sharp use of my nickname, the words died on my tongue. He straightened from his slumped position and pinned me with a severe look. "I am seconds away from losing it. All I can think about is plunging my fangs and cock inside you. Doing so would kill me, but I can't seem to care right now. So if you value my life and your virtue, then run. *Run* before I destroy us both."

Shock barrelled through me at his blunt words. Did he just say—?

"*Run!*" he thundered, and yanked the knife from his stomach.

At the sight of his red, glistening blood on the blade, I stumbled back. The knife clanged against the tiles as he dropped it and doubled over. The need to help him was overwhelming, but I continued to back away, mindful of his words. When I was inches from the kitchen door, his head lifted and he zeroed in on me with a keen predator's stare.

Holy. Freaking. Fates.

He hadn't been kidding. He was losing it.

I bolted from the kitchen.

Seconds later, he tore after me.

Fear pumped through me as I raced past the living room toward the entrance hall. Not just fear for myself, but for him. Even if he did catch me, touching my skin could kill him. Forces beyond our control were driving our actions, and I was terrified that one or both of us was about to die.

I was feet away from the front door when he snatched me out of the air. I screamed as he hauled me against him, growling like a beast who'd captured his prey. Reacting instinctively, I jabbed an elbow into his stomach, right where the knife had been.

I expected a roar of pain. A pause in his movements. *Anything.* But he ignored me completely, solely focused on dragging me to the side and pinning me against the wall.

"Lochlan. Lochlan, look at me," I said frantically, latching onto his shirt. He easily pried my fingers loose and locked both arms above my head. I kicked at him, but he firmly pressed his thigh between mine. "You could *die*. Snap out of it, Lochlan. You don't want to do this."

"But I do want to," he panted, trembling violently. "Your scent is everything. It's a siren's song I can't ignore. I am powerless to resist, nothing but a slave. My control is gone. I have to . . . *claim*."

Ice froze my insides as the shadows completely fell away, revealing the monster within. It was Lochlan, yet wasn't. His skin was as dark as his hair, his eyes as red as rubies. And his teeth . . . two sharp fangs glinted in the hallway's light. He opened his mouth wider and lowered his head, aiming for my neck.

"Lochlan, don't!" I screamed.

CHAPTER 21

The front door banged open with a powerful whoosh. Lochlan suddenly reared back and roared in agony. A force violently wrenched him away. He hit the opposite wall with a meaty thud, and a lamp crashed to the floor. Before he could fall, a towering dark form pinned him face first to the wall. Silver flashed high in the air, then slammed into Lochlan's back.

He grunted this time and slumped unconscious. The dark form stepped back, letting him thump to the floor. I wordlessly clutched my throat, frozen in place. My eyes remained glued to Lochlan's crumpled body, to the twin silver *daggers* embedded in his back.

I blinked.

Silver. Silver could *kill* vampires.

"Lochlan," I gasped and flung myself forward, desperate to pull them out. I landed beside him and searched for signs of life. Was I too late? Was he . . . was he—

"Whoa, little Kenna. I wouldn't touch those if I were you," a familiar voice said, sounding *way* too flippant after what he'd just done.

I threw Kade a death glare. "He'll die! I can't believe you stabbed him."

"Oh, he's in excruciating pain, but he won't die. I didn't hit his heart. Those are just to weaken him while I—" He froze and sniffed the air. "Holy mother of Moses, it reeks of pheromones in here! Are you in *heat*? No wonder Loch called me. He was probably going out of his mind with—"

He paused to sniff again. "Wow, you *both* reek. I'm gonna open some windows and clear the air. This horniness is highly contagious, and Loch is definitely not the threesome type."

My jaw dropped. Heat infused my already heated face. Did he seriously just say that?

Kade strode down the hall and, yup, started opening windows. Shoot me now. "Loch didn't do anything, did he?" he called, too busy sliding the living room windows open to see my deer in headlights expression. "He's a saint if he kept his hands to himself while this was happening though. Mating calls are *potent*."

Wait. *Mating* call?

He sniffed again, whipping his head toward the kitchen, then to me. "Why do I smell your spilled blood? Did he hurt you?"

Remembering what happened between us on that kitchen floor, my mouth opened and closed like a gasping fish. When Kade's expression switched to alarm, I quickly shook my head. "I—I cut myself. H-he tasted my blood though. Just a drop."

His red eyes narrowed. "Before or after he called me?"

"Before. Why?"

"Just a theory. Is that when he lost control?"

My cheeks flamed hotter, and I flicked a glance at Lochlan's unconscious form beside me. *No*, I almost confessed. *That's when I lost control.* "Around that time, yes. But he's felt off ever since . . . Well, earlier today, I tried to touch him. His skin, I mean." When Kade's brows hiked upward, I hurried to add, "I-I didn't mean to. It just happened. But it set him off. He . . . he called me a witch."

"Well, you are."

Caught off guard, I sputtered, "E-excuse me?"

Kade cringed, shooting a quick look at Lochlan as well. "Whoops. Don't tell him I let that slip."

Okay, now I was thoroughly confused.

Before I could question him though, Lochlan muttered what sounded like, "You'll pay for that."

My body immediately responded to his voice. Relief poured through me, followed by an ache to be closer. My body didn't care that he'd almost bitten me. It didn't care that he'd wanted to steal my virginity. In fact, my body *wanted* him to take it.

A now familiar need spread through me like wildfire, heightening with each passing second. I reached for a dagger, determined to ease his suffering so he could ease *me*.

I had to have him. All of him. It was the only way to extinguish the flames trying to eat me alive.

The moment I touched the dagger's silver hilt though, I was yanked away. A pair of arms banded around my midsection and hoisted me up.

"Scratch that," Kade grunted, and stalked down the hall with me in tow. "Loch needs protection from *you*."

I spluttered, twisting for one last glimpse of Lochlan before Kade marched me up the stairs. "But I-I need him. I won't try to touch his skin again, I promise. He makes the aches go away." *Freaking fates,* did I seriously just say that out loud? What was wrong with me?

Kade guffawed, clearly amused at my expense. "I bet he does. But that's what a cold shower is for. You'll thank me later."

Since escaping his firm grip wasn't an option, I tried distracting him with questions. "Why did you say that I was a witch? Do you mean a *witch* witch? Or just a—"

"Oh, I'm not falling into that trap again," he said with a chuckle. "Loch's going to have my head as it is."

We reached the second floor landing without pause, continuing down the hallway. Desperate, I blurted, "Can my touch kill all supernaturals? Or just vampires?"

He stiffened, but didn't falter as he corralled me inside the upstairs bathroom and flicked on the light. "I'm surprised Loch gave up that bit of information so soon. As far as we know, just vampires. Basically, skin contact with a supernatural allows you to temporarily steal their essence. Werewolves retain their humanity, so even if you fully sucked out their toxin, they'd simply resort to being human again."

The showerhead spit water as he cranked the handle, his gloved fingers still latched onto my arm. "Vampires are different though," he continued, peering down at me with a grim expression. "Whether you're a Venturi or Feltore, ties to your human genes are severed at creation. If you absorbed the entirety of our vampire essence, there would be nothing left to keep us alive."

I gaped, thoughts of breaking free dwindling. "Fates, if I'm so dangerous to vampires, then why are you helping me? I know that supernaturals want me dead because of what I am. So why risk getting in their way? I even thought Lochlan wanted to kill me, but"—Heat curled up my neck when I recalled what he'd done to prove otherwise—"now I'm not so sure."

Kade snorted. "Loch struggles to articulate his feelings with actual words. Don't worry. After this weekend, killing you will be the last thing on his mind."

That didn't exactly comfort me. "But why are you and Lochlan help—"

"Okay, this interrogation is over. In you go," Kade singsonged, clearly avoiding the elephant in the room. With one fluid motion, he deposited me in the bathtub directly under the freezing cold spray, clothes and all.

I sucked in a startled gasp, coughing when water caught in my windpipe.

Kade groaned. "Choking again? You're so fragile."

I pried at his gloved fingers, sputtering, "Because you're d-drowning me!"

He shifted his hold so I could breathe again. "Sorry," he said, sounding flustered. "I'm not aware of this stuff like Loch is. I've forgotten what it feels like to be human. With the last girl, he—" Kade suddenly coughed to cover up his words, but I'd already heard.

And my reaction was instantaneous.

A bitter tang coated my tongue, followed swiftly by a sharp stab of anger. "What do you mean the *last* girl?" I said through clenched teeth, curling my hands into fists. When he glanced away, fury washed over me. "Kade Carmichael, tell me at once! What game are you playing at?"

"It's not a game," he rushed to say, tightening his grip when I struggled to pull free.

"Tell me what you were going to say, or I'll . . . I'll scar your pretty face with my claws!"

"Whoa!" He caught my wrist as I swiped for his cheek, then the other. "You think my face is pretty?" At my growl, he quickly added, "Look, you being in heat is fogging my brain, so I'm gonna shut up now. I've said way too much already."

I narrowed my eyes to slits and spat, "Say more or I'm going to shout at the top of my lungs that you're hurting me."

Shock contorted his face. "You wouldn't," he whispered, sounding like a kicked puppy.

But I was too incensed to care. Too freaked. Too *jealous* at the mention of another girl. Just the thought of Lochlan caring for her the way he'd cared for me—*touching* her intimately—boiled my blood. I opened my mouth and screamed, "*Help!*"

Kade immediately released me with a curse, backing away. Seconds later, shadows darkened the doorway and Lochlan was there, his presence sucking all the air from the room. It was impossible to tell if he'd removed the daggers with the shadows churning around him. His gaze thoroughly roamed my drenched body before fixing on Kade.

Slowly raising his hands, Kade faced him, his broad back an effective barrier between me and Lochlan. "We're drothen, Lochie. You know I wouldn't touch her."

"That's the only reason you're still alive, *drothen*."

I flinched at his harsh reply, briefly regretting my rash outburst. But greater than the regret was my need for him, a need the cold water hadn't doused.

As if scenting my need, Lochlan audibly inhaled, flicking his eyes to me over Kade's shoulder. "Let me through, drothen, and I'll forgive your actions."

Kade chuckled darkly. "If I did, you wouldn't forgive me in the morning. Come back when you're thinking with your brain and not your dick."

Lochlan released a low, warning growl.

"So sexy," I whispered. Two pairs of red eyes shot my way. Crap, my mouth needed to be stapled shut.

"Not helping, little Kenna," Kade said, his jaw rigid. I shrugged sheepishly, but couldn't find it in me to apologize. This exchange was seriously turning me on. Narrowing his eyes at me, he faced Lochlan again. "How about we settle our differences outside? We could both do with some fresh air. It reeks in here."

I stuck my tongue out at his back.

"After you," Lochlan said with an exaggerated sweep of his arm. Thick tension filled the air. I held my breath in anticipation. This confrontation was about to reach a tipping point, and my raging hormones were all for it.

But I wasn't prepared—not even a little bit—for the lengths Lochlan would go to get to me.

As Kade stepped forward, Lochlan blurred into motion. I could barely track the flash of silver, but Kade did. He blocked the dagger's trajectory and punched Lochlan square in the face. Gasping, I lurched forward. Kade whipped around and shoved me back. I slipped on the tub's slick surface and fell hard, striking my head against the tiles.

Lochlan bellowed. Glass broke with a splintering crash. I blinked to clear my vision, spotting Kade climbing off the vanity where Lochlan had thrown him. Groaning softly, I touched the tender bump on my head. Distracted by the sound, Lochlan didn't see Kade barreling toward him. The impact sent them both careening into the hallway, where they resumed fighting.

Woozy from the blow to my head, I slumped against the tub and simply listened to the violent brutality mere feet away. I cringed with every pained grunt. Squeezed my eyes shut when plaster cracked and crumbled from the force of their hits. Clutched my aching head when a door flew off its hinges and banged against the wall.

The blow had knocked some sense into me, and I no longer wanted them to fight—especially over me. I just wanted the throbbing to stop. In my head, between my legs, and throughout the rest of my body. Moaning, I curled into a ball and lay flat in the tub. I shivered from the shower's cold spray yet continued to burn up inside.

"I'm not a werewolf. I don't need to change," I whispered. It wasn't the same without Lochlan.

The fighting lasted long into the night, until eventually, the crashing sounds faded. I strayed in and out of consciousness, crying out when waves of fiery pain and need shot through me. Lochlan hadn't entered the bathroom once—not from lack of trying though. I could hear the way he responded to my pain, cursing Kade and threatening him bodily harm. But Kade never let him reach me.

I suffered alone, trembling so hard that I remained in the tub, too exhausted to move. I knew that I should warm myself, but that would mean getting up. I even left my clothes on. The sodden material helped cool my boiling skin. Tears burned my eyes and I let a few of them fall.

Hours later, when only running water broke the silence, I succumbed to my exhaustion. Darkness dragged me into a restless slumber.

No mouth-watering scents woke me from sleep this time. Rather, it was the feel of fingers working at the buttons of my shirt that had my eyes flying open. The fingers stilled. I rubbed my gritty eyelids, struggling to see clearly.

The room I'd slept in last night gradually came into focus, bathed in soft early-dawn light. I glanced at the dresser and sluggishly blinked in surprise. The solid oak was tipped over, its attached mirror smashed. I peered down to where I'd felt the fingers and found them still there, gently grasping a shirt button. I noted the gloves, realizing my upper body was cradled in a pair of arms. I followed a clothed arm upward, expecting to find Kade at the end.

When I found Lochlan instead, his features cast in shadow yet unmistakably human, I merely stared. Emotions warred for my attention, but I was too tired to process them. When I didn't pull away from him, he continued to unbutton the shirt, watching my face closely the entire time.

I fleetingly wondered where Kade was, even worried for a split second that Lochlan had killed him. I wondered about his own injuries too and wanted to check that he was okay.

Before I could inquire though, he quietly said, "All is well."

The tightness in my chest loosened. I still had so many questions, but was quickly distracted by the careful way he undid my shirt. There was no aggression in his movements, nor seduction. Only gentleness. When the last button came undone, he slid the damp shirt off my shoulders. Cool air hit my bare skin, and a shiver racked my sore body. I bit back a groan and he paused, then proceeded to remove the shirt, his movements painstakingly slow.

The way he tended to me now almost felt like an apology. I didn't know what to think, only that my body sank into his careful ministrations, completely at ease with his presence. The heat I'd grown to expect when near him didn't flare up. In fact, the heat had vanished entirely, leaving me chilled to the bone. The shirt fell away, exposing my red bra and bare abdomen, but the urge to cover myself didn't come.

Not when he was looking at me with nothing but attentive care.

He reached for the waistband of my pants, and I didn't stop him from lifting me to tug them off. When I was naked before him with only a few scraps of lace covering me, he leaned forward to pull the bed covers back. Neither of us broke the silence, continuing to wordlessly watch each other while he tucked me in.

When he was finished, exhaustion pulled at my eyelids again. They drifted closed. He remained on the bed for a few moments. Then slowly stood and stepped toward the door.

My body tensed in protest and I murmured, "Don't leave. Please."

He paused. No doubt debating the wisdom of staying. I didn't press further, letting him decide. When I heard him toe off his boots though, my heart fluttered with relief.

The bed dipped as he laid down beside me, but he kept his distance. Minutes ticked by. I tossed and turned, unable to get comfortable. Finally, Lochlan sighed and rolled toward me. Reaching out, he turned me to face away from him and settled an arm over my waist. I snuggled back against him, releasing my own sigh as the restlessness eased.

Eventually, his stiff body relaxed against mine and he whispered, "Sleep, McKenna."

I felt the tug of his thrall, and gratefully followed its pull. Within seconds, I drifted into dreamless nothing.

CHAPTER 22

By the time I woke up again, Lochlan was gone. Not out-catching-a-deer gone, but *gone* gone.

I unfolded the note he'd left me on his pillow and read it for the sixth time.

McKenna. You're free to leave upon waking. Kade will take you home. On your list, you asked if there was a way to defend against vampire thrall. In the vial I've left for you is my blood. One drop consumed daily will protect you from all compulsions, including mine. I have also returned to you your bracelet. Unfortunately, it's broken. I believe it was spelled to protect the wearer against vampire thrall, perhaps even more. If you have access to another, I encourage you to wear it. —L

The glass vial and broken bracelet were now tucked away in my borrowed pants pocket. The red rose I'd also found on his pillow was currently being twirled between my fingers while I recalled yesterday's events. Surprisingly, I had woken with my memories intact. Every. Single. One. But when I'd found myself alone in the bed, I'd only felt confusion.

After everything Lochlan and I had experienced together this weekend, his abrupt departure left me shaken. My chest had ached the minute I'd discovered him gone. It still did, two hours later.

Did he regret sleeping beside me? Touching me? Admitting how his body had reacted to mine? Was he too ashamed to face me now that the werewolf symptoms had lessened? At least I was no longer oozing mating call pheromones, as Kade had so eloquently informed me.

The rumble of Kade's electric blue Mustang died as he turned off the engine to face me. "Got everything? Need me to carry you?"

I shook my head with a small smile. "No, I'm fine." He'd been acting like a mother hen all morning, doting on me hand and foot. I had already told him several times that my head injury wasn't his fault, but he still looked guilty.

He appeared to be unscathed from last night's fight though. Not a single bruise or scratch on him. The cabin hadn't fared so well. Nearly every room had been destroyed, like a tornado had ripped through them. When I'd expressed my utter shock, Kade had merely waved a hand, saying, "A maid will take care of it."

I rubbed at the seam of my right palm for the umpeenth time, still amazed that the cut had disappeared so fast. "Werewolf healing," Kade had explained, which made me want to ask a dozen more questions. I hadn't though. Asking them would require energy that I didn't have. As soon as I drove my car home from Isla's, I was taking an extra long nap.

When Isla came bursting through her front door though, I knew the nap would have to wait a little while longer. As she hurried down the driveway, reality hit me. My throat tightened. "Does she know about what happened?"

"Yes."

Sweat dampened my palms. "You won't make her forget everything, will you? She's . . . I need her."

"We know." Kade cast me a sympathetic look, and I fought off a sudden urge to cry. "With her father being the county sheriff though, it's a huge risk letting her know the truth. Most humans who know about vampires want us dead, so we keep a pretty low profile. But we know what she means to you and that you need someone to talk to. Well, someone *human* anyway. You can always talk to me," he added with a wink.

A tear slipped free and I quickly brushed it away. "Thank you. You're a good friend, Kade." Vampire or not, he really was.

His face split into a huge grin. "I know. But don't thank me. Loch gave the green light—which he never does, by the way."

The master of secrets had allowed Isla to keep her memories? Warmth filled my chest when I thought about what that could mean. Flustered at my reaction, I ducked my head. A couple days ago, I'd been mad at Lochlan, even disliked him. But after this weekend, that anger and dislike seemed petty after all he had done for me. I felt so many other things now, so many that I was having trouble sorting through them.

Isla tapped on the passenger side window, and I set aside my conflicted emotions for later. When I stood from the car, she took one look at my disheveled appearance and wrapped me in a tight hug. "Girl, I've been so worried about you. Kade told me what happened. I can't imagine going through all that."

My face flushed and I had to clear my suddenly dry throat. "Uh, what exactly did he tell you?"

She pulled away to look me in the eye. "It's okay. I know that your touch affects supernaturals and that you absorbed Peyton's werewolf. I can't believe she kept that a secret from us all this time! We could have helped her. Thankfully, that won't be a problem anymore."

I frowned. "What do you mean? Lochlan told me she was fine."

"Oh, she is. More than fine. You fixed her!" Isla said, squeezing my arms as if to thank me. When I stared at her quizzically, she bent to scowl at Kade still in the car. "You didn't tell her?"

"Whoops. Slipped my mind," he muttered sheepishly.

She straightened with an eye roll. "When you and Peyton touched, you ended up sucking all the werewolf toxin out of her. She's just a regular old human again."

My mouth fell open. "W-wait. She didn't turn into a werewolf this weekend?"

"Nope. All her symptoms went away. The heightened smell, hearing, animal urges—everything. She's completely back to normal. And she's been begging to see you all weekend, by the way, wanting to thank you for curing her."

Holy. Freaking. Fates.

I poked my head into the car and gave Kade the stink eye. "You didn't think I'd want to know about this right away?"

He coughed uncomfortably, avoiding eye contact. "I've kinda been distracted."

"You suck." I ignored his spluttering and straightened, my next question aimed at Isla. "How did Peyton become a werewolf anyway?"

Her dusky blue eyes brightened. "Girl, Peyton gave me the *full* scoop. So get this. On your first day of school, Reid thought he'd accidentally scratched you. He saw your claws the night of the bonfire, so assumed you lost control and wolfed out on August. That's why he started following you around, because he felt responsible for turning you and wanted to help you learn control.

"Anyway, he was going to invite you into his pack the day of the lakehouse, but he couldn't suppress the change and had to leave in a hurry. Unfortunately, he didn't get far enough away and found you and Peyton in the woods. That's when he accidentally bit and turned Peyton. She endured the transformation into wolf form last month and hated it so much that she blamed you for not saving her. Ironic, since Reid had initially tried to save her from *you*.

"Then, right before the Halloween party, she couldn't control her urges and ended up eating her rabbit. Poor little guy. It freaked her out so bad that she went to the party, desperately wanting to feel normal again. That's when she saw you, and"—Isla shrugged—"you know the rest."

I absorbed the news in silence, letting the pieces click into place. When the entire picture was clear, I blinked, muttering, "Well, crap."

That whole messed-up situation had been my fault.

Isla's expression flipped to concern. "Ah, Kenna, I'm so sorry. This was too much."

The car door opened and Kade was suddenly in front of me, tilting my chin up with a gloved hand. "You okay? What do you need? Should I take you to the hospital?"

I would have laughed at his excessive concern if I wasn't so tired. "I'm fine, really. Just need some more rest." In my peripheral, I caught Isla gawking at Kade, probably from witnessing his vampire speed. Her stare slipped to his backside as I added, "I might not be able to go home though. I'm sure my aunt is all set to move after I disappeared for the weekend."

Isla's gaze flew to mine, her cheeks pinker than her dyed hair ends. "Oh, you don't have to worry about that. I told her you were spending the weekend with me."

My brows rose. "And she believed you?"

"I think so. She didn't seem upset or anything. I used your phone to call since you left it in my car."

Relieved, I slumped against the Mustang and Kade's hand fell away. "Could I borrow some clothing before I go?" I tugged at the long hem of Lochlan's shirt, this one a dark blue. "She might get suspicious if I walk in like this."

Isla's lips curved into a mischievous smirk. "Of course. But when you're feeling better, I need details as to why you're dressed like that."

"Me too," Kade said, sliding me a wink.

Heat engulfed my entire face and neck.

Fates. I was so screwed.

"So how was your weekend at Isla's?" Aunt Tess asked.

Although it was a normal question for a dinner conversation, the words rang through the dining room like a death knell. My loaded fork paused halfway to my mouth, and the meatball tumbled off, plopping into the red spaghetti sauce. I quickly stabbed it again.

"Oh, um, it was good. Just didn't get enough sleep," I replied with a weak smile and raised my fork.

She casually sipped her iced tea, but her eyes were sharp over the cup's rim. I popped the meatball into my mouth, chewing slowly in the uncomfortable silence.

"Where's your bracelet? I've never seen you without it."

Caught off guard by the subject change, I swallowed too fast and a chunk of meatball lodged in my throat. I grabbed my drink, guzzling half the glass before meeting her keen stare. "In my room. It broke. I must have worn out the clasp."

Her knife scraped across the plate as she cut into a meatball. "Hmm, that's a shame. I know how much your mother's bracelet means to you. If you give it to me, I'll fix the clasp."

Outwardly, I remained calm and murmured a soft, "Sure, thanks. I'll give it to you after dinner." But inwardly, panic revved my heart rate into overdrive. If what Lochlan had written in the note was true and my bracelet was spelled to ward off vampire thrall, then maybe my parents or Aunt Tess knew that vampires were after me. Combined with the jewelry box's contents, I was almost certain.

Yet I looked my aunt in the eye and didn't say a word. If she knew that I knew, she'd force me to tell her everything. Which was why I needed to sneak the jewelry box back down to the basement as soon as possible. If she chose to swap my bracelet for the unused one instead of fixing it, then the box needed to look undisturbed.

I excused myself and went up to my bedroom half an hour later. Earlier today, I had added the vial of Lochlan's blood, along with the silver dagger he'd given me, to the jewelry box. I removed the box from the armoire now, careful not to make a sound. Not knowing where else to hide the items, I shoved the vial and dagger in the bottom of my underwear drawer alongside my extra cash.

I had so many questions about the blood in that vial. Did Lochlan expect me to *drink* it? Wouldn't that turn me into a vampire or something? Argh. There was so much for me to learn.

One thing I knew for certain: I needed to start wearing gloves.

I didn't want to experience being a werewolf *ever* again. And who knew how many supernatural beings were out there. During the daytime, they all looked human. I may have eluded supernaturals for nearly eighteen years, but I'd already run into several this past month. It was time for me to protect my skin from theirs.

After Aunt Tess went to bed with my bracelet in hand and I'd returned the jewelry box to the basement, I could barely keep my eyes open. A few werewolf side-effects still lingered, but Kade assured me they would disappear in the next few days. Those weren't keeping me awake long past my bedtime though.

I couldn't shake the feeling that something was missing. It wasn't the bracelet, or the numerous unanswered questions. No, it felt like a piece of *me* was missing.

At around three in the morning, I finally gave up on sleep, whipping the bed covers back with a huff. My bare feet hit the cold floor and I shivered in my red tank top and cropped yoga pants. I needed to unpack my warmer sleepwear before the snow arrived, something I hadn't seen in a few years while living down south.

Grabbing my sketchpad, I padded to the window seat and pulled back the curtains, letting the moonlight spill inside. Drawing always quieted my mind, similar to how a good book did. Like getting lost in a fictional world, creating something out of nothing distracted me from the stresses of reality. Sometimes, I painted with oil on canvas, but the soothing strokes of pencil on paper really spoke to me.

They allowed me infinite control over my subject. I was the master of their fate, in charge of each and every little dash and line.

Unconsciously, I flipped to the half-finished drawing of Lochlan. I squinted in the dim light, critiquing my linework. His nose was all wrong. It should be narrower and straighter. After fixing that, I studied his intense eyes for a while. The longer I stared at them, the more settled my body felt. Still happy with how they looked, I focused on his stern eyebrows, then brought out my eraser again. They should dip down over his eyes a bit more.

Sometime later, I jerked awake. This time, I managed to grab my sketchpad before it slid off my lap. A cold awareness skated across my exposed skin, alerting me to his presence before I caught the flash of red in my peripheral. I whipped my gaze to the window but was too late. The rooftop below was empty.

Oh, no you don't. Not this time.

I snagged a hoodie from the end of my bed and sneaked out of the room. I paused at the bottom of the stairs to grab my boots before hurrying toward the back slider. Soundlessly slipping outside, I hopped on one foot to yank on my boots, then shot across the yard.

In no time, the woods loomed before me. A short while ago, I never would have run headlong into the darkness toward an unknown predator. I would have stayed safely behind locked doors where the possible serial killer couldn't reach me. But I no longer feared the shadows. Not when I knew what awaited me inside.

I plunged past the treeline without hesitation, my breaths fogging the crisp air before me. Even with the bright moon lighting my way, the pine trees were thick, and it grew darker the farther in I went. The lingering werewolf senses I'd absorbed helped a little, but they were definitely fading.

Red glowing eyes failed to greet me. I knew he was here though. I could feel him, a dark caress against my neck and cheeks.

I slowed, straining to hear over the crunching of leaves and pine needles beneath my boots. Finally, I stopped, turning in a circle only to come up empty. I shivered from the cold, pulling the hoodie tightly over my thin tank top. Except for my breathing, the air was perfectly still. Not a single sound disturbed the night, not even the wind.

Doubt trickled in. Had I imagined I saw him? Was I seeing and feeling things out of exhaustion? The hair on my neck suddenly stood on end at the sensation of being watched. I swallowed, nervously searching the darkness. "Where are you?" I whispered.

"Here," a voice whispered back in my ear.

I gasped and spun, but no one was there.

The hair on my neck raised again. I turned and choked back a scream as red eyes filled my vision. At the familiar shadows curling around his faint silhouette, I sighed in relief. "Were you trying to scare me or something? Because—"

"You shouldn't be out here," Lochlan cut in. "I could have been anyone."

At the chill rolling off him, I shivered and crossed my arms for warmth. "I knew it was you."

"How?"

Frustrated at the coldness in his voice, I threw my hands in the air. "I don't know how to describe it. I can feel your shadows or something. I didn't feel anything around Kade or that other vampire, so I just knew it was you. And for whatever reason, you're feeling extra ornery tonight."

He gave me nothing, not even a condescending snort. He simply stared in that unnerving way of his, stripping me bare with his eyes. Finally, he said, "You were drawing me."

Wait, what? He *saw*? Freaking fates, shoot me now.

Heat scorched my face and I looked everywhere but at him. "I-it was nothing. I just draw whatever's on my mind." Whoa, I did *not* mean to say that. "In fact, I was going to draw Kade next."

Silence.

"Anyway," I continued, beyond flustered and embarrassed, "maybe you should stop spying through my window if you don't like what you see."

His response was to step toward me. Nervous butterflies erupted in my stomach, and I shuffled backward, only for a tree to halt my progress. Before I could inch sideways, Lochlan's arms shot out, trapping me against the trunk. My eyes flew to his, and what I saw there stalled the breath in my lungs.

"I don't dislike what I see," he said, his voice a silky purr. "And I didn't intend to spy on you. I only wanted to make sure you were feeling better."

At his words, a thrill raced up my spine. I desperately dug my blunt nails into the tree, afraid my body would go rogue on me again. "You could have just texted," I whispered.

"I don't like texting," he whispered back.

"A phone call then."

"Not good enough."

"Why?"

"Because I can't sense your emotions that way."

I dug my nails in harder. "And now? What do you sense?"

Danger, danger, my mind screamed.

His face had inched closer to mine, as if pulled to me by magnetic force. I heard a scraping sound either side of my head, as if the claws within his gloves were gouging the tree. And his eyes . . .

They had dipped to my mouth more than once, lingering.

We were playing a dangerous game. And neither of us could seem to stop.

239

CHAPTER 23

"I shouldn't have come."

The abrupt statement slapped my face like a cup of ice water. "W-why?" I sputtered as he pushed away and stepped back several feet. I shivered, keenly feeling his absence.

"Because this can't happen. It's impossible." He turned around, the shadows rising as he shoved both hands through his hair.

The rejection stung. I knew that it shouldn't. That the connection between us was twisted and nonsensical. But I couldn't let him go. At least not without closure. "Is it my touch?" I pressed, stepping forward. "Because of what I can do to you?"

He stilled, but didn't face me. "Yes," he said, and my chest tightened at the admission. "But that's not all," he continued, looking over his shoulder at me. "I made a vow a long time ago. I can't break it."

I frowned. "What kind of vow?"

He stared at me for a moment, then shook his head. "I have to go."

"Wait!" I lurched forward when his shadowy form quickly receded, afraid that this was it. This was goodbye. I wasn't ready. I would never be ready.

Expecting him to vanish like he'd done so many times before, I was shocked when he actually stopped and turned my way. So shocked that I struggled to find my voice. Swallowing, I blurted, "At least tell me what I am. After all we've been through together, I deserve to know that much."

And he did. Finally, after weeks of prodding him for an answer, he said without pause, "You're a Syphon."

I blinked, then slowly rolled the strange word on my tongue. "A Syphon."

He nodded. "A rare subsect of witch, so rare that you're currently the only one living of your kind. You don't possess your own magic, but have the ability to absorb and use the essence of any supernatural being or object. A long time ago, Syphon witches were nearly hunted to extinction. Ambrose, the vampire king, put a bounty on their heads. They were all marked for death."

Whoa. Information overload. Not that I was complaining. He was *finally* giving me answers, and I was grateful. But a witch? A *witch* witch? And I was the only one of my kind? "How did you know? That I was a Syphon, I mean," was the first question that popped out.

"The scent of your blood. All Syphons have a signature wintery mint smell."

Goosebumps erupted over my skin. My blood smelled like a breath mint? Well, that wasn't weird or anything.

I sobered then, focusing on the most troubling thing he shared. "Why did the vampire king want to kill off my kind?"

"Jealousy over their unique power. Fear of what they could do. Revenge for what one of them did to his son. The usual things that cause lifelong feuds and wars."

"That was a long time ago though, right? The king is dead and things can change. I mean, we're in the day and age of diversity and tolerance. Supernaturals don't seriously want to kill me because of an old feud . . . do they?"

I pinched my thigh, not caring that he noticed. Something told me that I was getting to the meat of this story and I wasn't going to enjoy the aftertaste.

Lochlan stepped toward me, saying, "The king is still very much alive, McKenna, and so is the feud. One thing you need to know is that vampires are very set in their ways, especially the king. The passage of time won't change that."

I gulped, forcing myself to remain still while he approached. "And how long have your kind been hunting mine?"

He reached for me and I stiffened, nervous of his intentions now that I knew the truth. Cold leather skated across the back of my hand, making me jump. He freed my thigh from further bruising, dislodging my fingers and entangling them with his. "A hundred and thirty years."

I didn't know what shocked me more: his answer or that he was holding my hand.

Struggling to concentrate on the conversation and not the press of his fingers, I said, "But that would make the king—"

"Immortal. He's around five hundred, give or take a few years."

Uh . . .

A few more moments ticked by, then . . .

Oh. *Oh.*

"So . . . does that mean you're immortal too?"

"I'm one hundred and forty-nine."

My mouth dried. Freaking fate balls, I was attracted to a one hundred and forty-nine year old *man!* He didn't look a day over twenty though, so did that make it okay? Wow, I couldn't believe my brain went there.

Lochlan waited patiently while I gawked at him as if he were a museum exhibit. Crap, he was old enough to *be* an exhibit.

What really shook me though was my calm reaction to the news.

I mean, I was internally freaking out a tiny bit, but I wasn't exactly running for the hills. To be honest, I didn't really care about his age or immortality. It even excited me, knowing he had two lifetimes worth of information in his head. He must know a *lot* of cool stuff.

"McKenna."

"You're in highschool," I said, as if the revelation was more shocking than him being immortal.

He lapsed into silence again, carefully studying my face.

"I mean . . . that's kinda funny." I bit my lip, struggling not to laugh.

"About that." Lochlan let go of my hand. "I can't attend the school anymore."

The urge to laugh died. "What, why?"

"It's too dangerous for you to be around me. My movements are being watched. That night the vampire attacked you—he had friends. I've already disposed of two that were lurking on my property, but if there are more, they'll keep coming. And if word gets back to the king where you are, he'll send a small army here to retrieve you. No one in this town will be safe."

The blood drained from my face and I sank back against the tree.

How could this be happening? A month ago, I was just a girl who wanted to lay low until her eighteenth birthday so she could live life on her own terms. And now? A bunch of supernaturals wanted me dead. Laying low might not be good enough, not if my friend's lives were in danger. I'd already allowed selfishness to hurt one person I cared about. I wouldn't do that again.

"I have to leave," I said numbly, forcing my body upright. All the moving made perfect sense now. Aunt Tess must have known. She must have been protecting me all along, just like she said. Fates, I was such an idiot, stuck in my pathetic little world. I had to leave *now*.

How many more lives would I ruin if I stayed?

No, I wouldn't cower with my head in the sand, but I wouldn't stay and jeopardize the lives of others either.

I started to walk.

"McKenna."

The sound of Lochlan's voice was like a dagger through my heart. I would have to leave him behind. Kade and Isla too. Even Aunt Tess. Tears threatened to blur my vision, but I kept walking.

"Kenna."

No, stop *talking*. It was too much. It made me want to cry. *Truly* cry. And I couldn't do that. Once I did, I'd never stop.

Wind stirred my hair, then he was in front of me. I tried to skirt around him, but he wouldn't let me. A million emotions I couldn't process rose up and I lashed out, "Let me go, Lochlan. I have to pack." I'd take one suitcase with me, maybe two. Any more than that would slow me down. He blocked my path again and I growled in frustration.

"You're going to run after all we've been through?" Anger lined his voice, but something else did too. Hurt maybe.

"I have no choice," I said, exasperated. "People could get hurt because of me. They already *have*. It's better for everyone if I just keep moving."

"Running for the rest of your life is no way to live."

I stopped to look him in the eye, not bothering to mask my pain. "You're right, it isn't. I've spent fifteen years on the run. And never staying in one spot long enough to form lasting relationships sucks. Not knowing what stability feels like sucks. Always wondering when the dreaded moving boxes will come out again sucks. Running *sucks*. But better that than . . . than people *dying*."

I shoved past him, and he let me this time.

"None of this is your fault, McKenna," he called after a few moments. "I brought this into your life. I put you in danger by getting too close."

I froze in my tracks. Then marched back to him. "And why did you? Why did you get so close?"

When he let the silence stretch between us, the pain of his nearness became too much. I moved to step away but he caught my chin between his gloved fingers. "I had to," he said roughly. "I couldn't stop myself." His fingers slid up my jaw. "But then I wanted to. I needed to."

"That's not an answer," I whispered, wishing he would stop touching me, then wishing he wouldn't. "Tell me why."

His hand slowly snaked behind my neck to draw me closer. "You will hate me."

I swallowed, letting him pull me to him. "I can't hate you. I've tried."

"You will. It's inevitable," he insisted, and slid his other hand to the small of my back. "And when you do, this will all be over. You and me. Us. You won't want this. You won't want anything to do with me. And I'm . . . I'm not ready for that yet."

My heart fluttered at his bold confession. The last of the space between us vanished as he fitted my body against his. My head emptied for a moment, too focused on the way we fit together—and how it felt. His hard length rested on my lower stomach, thoroughly capturing my attention. As if he knew where my thoughts had strayed, he pressed on my back, letting me feel him more fully.

I chomped on my lip to suppress a gasp, stammering, "I-I won't hate you."

"You will," he said, then whispered so quietly that I almost missed it, "What I wouldn't give to kiss you right now."

I forgot how to breathe. I clutched his jacket as my legs threatened to buckle.

When his head dipped toward mine, I forgot everything. Everything except the anticipation of our lips touching. My eyes drifted shut. His warm breath caressed my mouth. I trembled, but held perfectly still.

Waiting.

Waiting for our skin to *finally* touch.

He softly hissed and pulled back. "We can't. I shouldn't have done that."

All the air fled my lungs in a disappointed rush. He was right, but that didn't make me want to any less.

"I won't let you run away," he said after a moment, sliding his gloved fingers into my hair. A pleasurable shiver racked me as his claws gently scraped my scalp. "Not without me. I think you should stay though. I'll continue to protect you. I'll keep you safe. But I'll keep my distance from now on, for both our sakes."

He put space between us as if to prove his words, letting his hands fall to his sides. With effort, I released his jacket, knowing he was thinking more rationally than me at the moment. He was right again. We needed distance from each other. Only pain and suffering would result from our closeness. A simple kiss could kill him. I couldn't risk that, no matter how badly I craved to know what his lips felt like pressed to mine.

I rubbed my arms to ward off the chill sinking into my bones. "I can't promise not to run," I said when the silence stretched. "It would be safest for everyone that way. But I'll lay low for now and try to at least graduate from highschool. You need to let me know right away if more vampires come looking for me though."

The shadows around his head dipped as he nodded. "Deal. Do

you still have the vial of blood I gave you?"

"Yes, but"—I wrinkled my nose—"do you actually want me to drink it?"

"A drop every day will suffice. You'll experience no adverse effects. It's only meant to protect you from vampire thrall."

Not quite ready to drink blood, despite his reassurance, I said, "I think you're right about my bracelet protecting me from vampire thrall. I was able to resist you up until this weekend when I didn't have it on. My aunt immediately noticed that I wasn't wearing it and offered to repair the clasp. I'm pretty sure she knows about vampires."

"She does."

I blinked, caught off guard by his certainty.

Before I could question him, a yellow glow through the trees caught my eye, coming from my aunt's bedroom. Even though I knew she couldn't see me, I crouched, whispering, "I need to get back. She can't find me out here."

"Hold on."

In a flash, Lochlan picked me up and zoomed through the trees. I barely had time to squeeze my eyes shut against the cold wind before we stopped. He carefully released me beside the slider door while I caught my breath. "Uh . . . thanks."

Without a word, he stepped back. Wings of panic beat at my chest as I waited for him to vanish. Acting on impulse, I grabbed his hand. We both tensed, but I didn't let go and he didn't pull away. "When will I see you again?" I whispered.

He lowered his gaze to study our linked hands, answering quietly, "I don't know. But I'll be watching. Always." He freed his hand, raising it to skate a thumb across my cheek. "Stay safe, McKenna."

I knew what would happen next, but I wasn't ready. He disappeared in a rush of wind, leaving me cold and hollow inside.

When I snuck back inside the house, I held my breath, expecting Aunt Tess's door to fly open at any moment. It didn't. And at breakfast the following morning, my bracelet was on the dining room table, looking brand new and completely fixed.

CHAPTER 24

Many things changed during the month of November.

Aunt Tess left the house a lot—without explanation, of course. Peyton and Hailey started hanging out with me and Isla again. Reid invited us to every one of his football games, letting us hang out with a few of his "pack mates." I kept a silver dagger hidden in my boot at all times, even at school. The first early winter snow had fallen, making it easier for me to wear gloves without looking weird.

And, like he promised, Lochlan kept his distance. No texts, phone calls, or school appearances. No notes or roses on my windowsill. Several days had passed since I'd felt the cold presence of his shadow self. Or seen the glow of red eyes in the woods at night.

The only thing that didn't change was Kade. He continued to attend the school, assuring me that no new vampires had been spotted in Rosewood. He still refused to answer most of my questions about supernatural stuff and wouldn't allow me to visit their house again. He cheered me up the best he could, though, while I struggled to cope with each passing day.

Ever since the weekend spent with Lochlan, something inside me had changed. There was a hole in my chest. I could actually feel it, like a hollow rock was embedded beneath my sternum. No matter how hard I tried to fill it with school and friends, it remained empty, leaving me morose and listless.

Then there were the sleepless nights. No matter how tired I was, my body's restlessness woke me every few minutes. I could no longer hide the dark circles under my eyes, nor properly focus on school-work. My friends had noticed, especially Kade and Isla. Nearly a month had passed since the weekend at the cabin when they cornered me after school.

"What are your plans tonight?" Kade asked as I shut my locker and tucked a limp strand of hair behind my ear.

"Um, I've got an English Lit paper due on Monday that I haven't even started yet, so—"

"Good," Isla said and grabbed my bag, slinging it over her shoulder. "Call your aunt and tell her you're having a Friday night slumber party at my place."

"But—"

She marched for the exit before I could protest.

Kade draped an arm over my shoulders and steered me after her. "No buts, little Kenna. You desperately need this. Holy Moses, when's the last time you ate? You're boney."

I scowled at him, but swallowed my retort when I saw his genuine worry. I looked away with a shrug. "I haven't been very hungry lately."

To be honest, I was getting worried myself. Maybe my time as a temporary werewolf had messed with my body. But it wasn't like I could research what side effects Syphons experienced after absorbing supernatural powers. I hadn't touched a supernatural since—that I knew of anyway—and faithfully wore my new bracelet and gloves. I hadn't touched the vial of Lochlan's blood either, still uneasy at the thought of drinking blood.

After a quick call to Aunt Tess, I waited for Isla to hand me my bag. She tossed it to Kade instead. Flashing my car keys, she pocketed them. "Kade's driving you. We'll pick your car up later." She gave me a hug, then hurried to her white Mini.

Uuuh.

Unprepared for their scheming, I allowed Kade to usher me inside his Mustang without comment. We were halfway to Isla's house before I found my voice. "Why can't I drive?"

"Because you'd try to escape." He engaged my door's child lock.

I rolled my eyes. "Escape what? I like going to Isla's house."

He rubbed his lips together and refused to comment. Whatever. I settled into the seat and closed my eyes.

Several minutes later, they popped back open. "You passed Isla's house."

"So I did," was his only reply. "Hand me your phone for a sec."

Frowning, I placed it in his waiting palm. "What—"

"Thanks." He stuffed it in the front pocket of his jeans.

"Seriously, Kade, what are you up to?" I didn't for one second think to be scared. He had been nothing but a solid friend to me this past month, like how I imagined a big brother would treat me. But I didn't enjoy surprises. I'd had enough of those over the years with the dozens of unexpected moves.

He flicked a glance at me. "I'm staging an intervention. I know you'll be against it, and I understand why, but you need to get better. Once you are, you can chew me out all you want."

My stomach swooped with nerves. I didn't like the sound of that. Before I could question him further, he raised his phone and said, "I've got Kenna. I'm taking her on a little retreat, but I'll be dropping her off and leaving her unprotected."

Shouting burst from the phone. Kade held it away from his ear with a grimace. When the shouting ceased, he added, "You can't ignore this, drothen. No matter the risks, she needs you." He ended the call with a sigh and white-knuckled the steering wheel. "That went well."

I gaped at him, utterly shocked at his betrayal. "You called Lochlan? You *know* why we can't be near each other. I can't believe you're doing this."

"I know, I know," he said, clenching his jaw. "But this separation is killing you both."

I threw my hands in the air. "What are you talking about?" Kade had officially lost his marbles—or *would* be, when I was done with him.

"I'm Loch's drothen," he said, his expression grim. "We're bonded by blood and a century's worth of unshakable loyalty. I can feel what he feels. Know when something's wrong. He's been suffering ever since that weekend you two spent together."

Startled by his impassioned speech, my anger fizzled out. "Okay, so maybe we picked up the same virus. But we're not *dying*, Kade."

"He hasn't fed in over a week," Kade said in a strained voice. "Vampires need fresh blood every few days or we become weak, physically and mentally. We're immortal and won't die from blood starvation, but the pain of it is like razor blades scraping across your veins. Death is preferable to that agony."

A terrible, helpless feeling pressed down on me. Lochlan was experiencing that? "Why isn't he feeding then?"

"I'm guessing for the same reasons you aren't," he answered matter-of-factly. "If I'm right, the desire for sustenance will return once you're together again."

I pinched my thigh, trying to wake up from this crazy nightmare. How the fates had we gotten ourselves into this mess? Being together could kill us, but being apart could kill us now too? This situation was seriously screwed up.

I flopped back against the headrest. "This is too much."

"I know, little Kenna," Kade said regretfully. "I'm truly sorry."

But his regret didn't stop him from driving me to the middle of nowhere. It took me way too long to figure out where he was taking me. By the time I did, he was already parked and rounding the hood to pull open my door. Cursing, I grabbed the handle and fruitlessly tried to keep it shut. He had the door open and my seatbelt undone before I could curse again.

"Don't make me do this the hard way, Kenna," he warned with a stern look. I set my jaw, letting him know that I wasn't doing this without a fight. He sighed and reached for my arm, his hand safely encased in a glove. I lashed out and kicked him in the kneecap, flinching when he grunted in pain. Still, I scrambled to escape my awaiting fate, throwing myself into the driver's seat. I had the door halfway open when Kade pulled it wide, unbalancing me.

With a gasp, I tumbled out of the car head first. Kade swooped me into the air before I could hit the ground, draping me over his shoulder like a towel. "Kade, put me down right this—"

He shot forward at vampire speed, sucking my enraged words away. Seconds later, he set me on my feet and stepped out of kicking range. "The door is unlocked, your overnight bag is packed, and the fridge is stocked," he said in a rush, retreating as I swiped at him. "Just don't kill each other for the next twenty-four hours and you'll be feeling better in no time."

"Twenty-four *hours?*" I snarled, advancing on him. "Don't you dare leave me here that—" He vanished in a blur of motion. "Kade Carmichael, get your butt back here right now so I can kick it!"

Silence settled over the snow-dusted mountaintop. My frustrated scream startled a flock of birds in a nearby pine tree. They frantically flapped into the endless blue sky, escaping the way *I* wanted to escape. Grabbing my school bag Kade left for me, I stormed inside the cabin, too cold and angry to enjoy the breathtaking view. I slammed the door shut and dropped my bag so I could pace the hallway and living room, barely noticing how pristine everything looked since the last time I'd seen it.

"Oh yeah, it's totally acceptable to *kidnap* your friend. As if they didn't already feel like crap. It's for your own good, you say. This will solve all your problems, you say. Well, I have news for you, buster," I yelled, snatching up a white couch pillow. "This"—I threw it across the room and picked up another—"won't"—I threw that one too, narrowly missing a turquoise vase on a side table—"help!"

I grabbed the two remaining pillows and chucked them both toward the hallway. But they never hit the ground. My heart leapt into my throat when I saw who had caught them.

Tall and imposing as ever, Lochlan's presence sucked all the air from the room. Dressed in charcoal gray slacks and a black button-down shirt, he appeared older than I remembered. Or maybe the dark bruising under his eyes made him seem so. His normally shiny obsidian hair hung limp and dull over his forehead, partially shadowing his dark eyes. His face was paler too, cheeks gaunt and sallow-looking.

He looked as awful as I did, and the thought of him suffering the way I had this past month tore at my heartstrings. Still, I couldn't go to him, couldn't comfort him. We weren't supposed to be near each other, and I knew he didn't actually want to be here.

I bit my trembling lip and forced myself to turn away, to pick up the pillows I'd thrown. My body ached as I bent over to retrieve them, as if punishing me for turning my back on him. I straightened with a grimace, moving slowly toward the couch.

"McKenna."

Every muscle in my body painfully seized at the sound of his voice. The silken quality was now raw and gravelly, but I violently responded all the same. Breathing became impossible, and I dropped the pillows to clutch at my heart before it exploded from my chest. I doubled over, gripping the couch for dear life as I struggled to remain standing.

"Why?" I whispered, digging my nails into the leather. "Why is this happening?"

He didn't respond, didn't move toward me. I was relieved. And frustrated. And so freaking *confused*. We held our positions for what felt like an eternity, me trembling uncontrollably against the couch and him stiff as a board in the hallway. Until I couldn't stand it any longer. I was weak, my body screaming with a need I didn't understand but knew I couldn't fight.

There was only one thing I could do. One thing that would ease both our suffering. I knew the consequences, knew that he could very well refuse me, but I was so tired. So freaking tired of fighting, of staying away, of ignoring what I felt.

A tear slipped down my cheek as I raised my eyes to his and uttered one word. "Please."

For an awful second, I thought he'd ignore my plea. Thought he'd turn his back on me and walk back out that door. Then he was moving, not away but *toward* me, erasing the space between us in three long strides. Then stopped. Inches separated us. Terrible, terrible inches.

"P-please," I said again, not caring how desperate I sounded. "Hold me."

His chest rose and fell sharply as I reached out with trembling fingers to tug at the pillows he was strangling. His grip eased and they tumbled to the floor. He continued to hold himself back, the tendons in his neck bulging from the strain. A deep groove bisected his brows, his eyes twin pools of pain.

And I couldn't . . . I couldn't stand it a moment longer.

I stepped into him, initiating contact. When he still didn't move, I twined both arms around him and pressed my face to his chest, breathing in deeply. Amber, sandalwood, and musk enveloped me, trickling inside to partly fill the hole beneath my sternum.

At the warmth, at the soothing relief, I heaved a sob.

The sound stirred him awake and he was suddenly everywhere, his arms tightly locked around me, one gloved hand cradling the back of my head. The hole filled up to overflowing and I fought to be nearer, fitting myself to every part of him I could reach. He wedged a leg between mine, pressing his thigh to my core. I moaned into his shirt, digging my blunt nails into his back. He growled in response, sliding a hand down to cup my backside.

He ground his thigh between my legs and pure energy charged through me, splintering my vision to white. I cried out and arched into him, asking for more. His leg continued to move against me and I rode it without restraint, needing the release more than anything.

As we clutched each other, there was no confusion. Only a surety that this was *right*. Us. Together. Everything made sense.

He squeezed my backside, using the grip to press me more firmly against him. My movements grew frantic. I chased after the pleasure, panting as it intensified to the point of pain. But it was the best kind of pain, so wild and reckless that I begged for *more*. Until my body burst from its moorings in sheer ecstasy.

My head fell back and Lochlan grasped the nape of my neck, holding me while I shuddered from the pleasurable aftershocks. When I sagged in his grip, utterly spent, he tucked me against his chest again. For several minutes, he made no move to pull away, and neither did I, content to hear the steady rhythm of his heart.

An angry growl suddenly erupted between us, startling me. A soft chuckle surprised me even more. I tipped my head back in time to see the most devastatingly beautiful thing I'd ever laid eyes on.

Lochlan was smiling.

CHAPTER 25

"I think that was you."

His mouth was moving, but I couldn't seem to concentrate on the words. Not when his lips were still tilted in the most alluring way. Lochlan was unquestionably handsome, but with the addition of a smile, there wasn't a word adequate enough to describe him.

"Holy fate babies," I breathed, realizing too late that I'd spoken out loud. When the smile deepened, revealing his left dimple, I almost keeled over from a heart attack. "S-stop that."

"Stop what?" the mouth said.

"Stop"—I swallowed loudly—"smiling."

The lips cruelly teased me, forming the most charming lopsided grin. "Why?"

"Because I—I can't handle it." Fates, I was so lost. So lost that I wanted to name his mouth. And dimple. They deserved names. My fingers curled into his shirt. Oh, how I ached to touch his lips, to feel how soft they were.

A vicious rumbling cleaved the air again.

"That was definitely you."

I blinked. "Huh?"

"Your stomach growled. You're hungry."

Oh, I was definitely hungry. I wet my lips, still focused on that delectable mouth. But it pulled away. The arms around me retreated too. My eyes shot up to Lochlan's. His gaze was hooded as he walked backward toward the kitchen, his movements completely at ease now.

"Let's get you something to eat, solemae." A startled look suddenly passed over his face and he stumbled back a step. I raised an eyebrow at his blunder, the first I'd ever seen him make. I'd never seen him look startled either. Before I could question him though, he slipped into the kitchen.

Weird. And what had he said? *Sow-luh-may?* Was that vampire lingo for Syphon?

Shrugging, I took a moment to smooth my hair and straighten my clothes, suddenly self-conscious of my appearance. I'd definitely lost weight—my stonewashed jeans hung low on my hip bones—but the miraculous return of my appetite soon overroad my bout of nerves.

I entered the kitchen and stopped short at the sight of the clean floor. I stared at the spot where Lochlan had tasted a drop of my blood, where he helped stop me from turning into a werewolf. Heat immediately rushed to my face. The scarred tabletop caught my eye next, where Lochlan and I had . . . where we had . . .

My face flushed scarlet.

Fates, there were too many memories of us in this room. They practically saturated the air.

Lochlan closed the fridge and turned toward me with a container in each hand, reminding me of our heated standoff over food. He paused to assess my face and stiff posture, his own expression clear once again. "What are you thinking right now?"

My eyes widened. "Uh, nothing." I cleared my throat and motioned at the containers. "What's in there?"

His knowing look further warmed my overheated body. Flustered, I searched for a safe place to rest my gaze. The kitchen counter.

That was relatively safe. We hadn't made any memories on it. I hurried over and hopped on top instead of sitting at the table where I'd have to stare at his claw marks.

He didn't say anything, but I could have sworn he huffed a laugh. I expected him to carry the food to the table, so when he headed my way and placed the containers beside me, I struggled not to fidget. His nearness made me highly aware of everything he did.

First, he removed his gloves. Slowly. Fates alive, I didn't realize that watching someone peel leather off their fingers could turn me on, but now I did. After that torture, he removed the container lids. Slowly. Gripping the counter's edge, I peered inside and pretended interest in the contents when I couldn't even focus on what it was.

Lochlan grunted in disgust, muttering something about blasted cheesecake. "This is all yours," he said, and reached across my legs to pull open the cutlery drawer—slowly. *Fates!* He grabbed a fork and slid the drawer shut, taking his time, of course. But he wasn't done yet. No, he was just getting started with this new level of pain I'd never experienced before.

"Excuse me," he murmured, stepping into me before I could hop down. I sucked in a breath as he leaned over to open a cupboard, then positioned himself between my legs. Clinking sounds came from the cabinet while he no doubt searched for a plate, but all I could concentrate on was the way his hips gradually pressed against my inner thighs, spreading them apart.

My eyes drifted shut and I fought back an embarrassing groan as my core lit on fire. It was as if the orgasm from minutes before had never happened. My body was primed and ready to receive another one.

"The universe has a cruel sense of humor," he said, his warm breath teasing my hair.

"Hmm?" I muttered as my poor brain fogged. When I felt him wrap a strand of my hair around his finger, I tensed and popped my eyes back open.

His face was inches from mine, his gaze fixed on my mouth. He looked . . . starved. My nervous energy returned tenfold and I made the mistake of wetting my lips. He greedily tracked the movement, following the darting motion of my tongue. The flecks of red in his black eyes brightened, a feral gleam entering their depths.

When his head lowered an inch, my heart banged against my chest, both desire and uncertainty filling me. I wasn't stupid. I knew what he wanted. Fates, I desperately wanted it too. But even one little kiss could end in disaster. Not only that, but the feral look suggested another need, one far more deadly.

He was hungry for blood.

My heart continued to thunder, a fact he didn't miss. His gaze slid over my jaw and neck, fixing on my pulsing artery. I struggled to breathe, to think rationally. One half of me wanted to push him away, but the other half wanted to know what it felt like to have his fangs plunge into me. To have him ravenously drink from my vein.

A thrill surged through my body, powerful and dangerous. I swallowed hard, biting back a whimper when his gaze ate up the movement. "You . . . you should feed," I whispered, then gasped at his growled reply. Oh fates. "I-I mean, from wherever you usually do it. Not me."

The sound of ceramic breaking startled me and I jerked, bumping my head on a cabinet. Lochlan responded to my unintentional retreat by gripping my hair, forcing my neck to arch back. I stopped breathing when he growled again as if demanding I hold still—as if I were his prey.

"Lochlan, don't," I said softly, trying not to make any sudden moves. "You'll get hurt."

His grip tightened and I squeezed my eyes shut, dreading and anticipating what would happen next.

"Push me away," he demanded through gritted teeth. "Now, before I lose control."

Was he serious? Did he really think I was strong enough to—

"*Please*, McKenna."

Shocked by his plea, I reached up and shoved his chest. He might as well be a brick wall, yet he surrendered a few inches, his hold on my hair loosening. I pushed again and earned a few more inches. I started to shimmy off the counter when he released me entirely, violently throwing himself backward.

The kitchen table exploded in a shard of wooden splinters as he crashed into it, severing the top in two. I pressed both hands over my mouth. Before I could do anything stupid like rush to help him up, he grunted, "Fridge."

Avoiding the broken plate shards on the floor, I dashed to open the fridge. Inside were several plastic containers and a tall, metal thermos. Going with my gut, I grabbed the thermos and turned. Then shrieked and dropped it when I found Lochlan standing inches away.

He easily caught the thermos, his gaze locked on mine. His fingers shook as they unscrewed the lid. It fell and clanged across the floor, but I didn't dare pick it up. I didn't dare move a muscle while he raised the thermos to his lips and tipped it back, drinking the contents deeply.

My mouth dried as I watched his throat work, then realized with a start that his eyes were still on me. Something about watching him drain the thermos felt extremely intimate. Like I was watching him perform an erotic act. I couldn't help but be jealous of that thermos.

When he lowered it and licked his lips, I caught the barest hint of red on his tongue. Blood. Of course it was. Fates, I'd just been aroused at the sight of a vampire consuming blood.

His shoulders released their rigid hold and he sighed as if a great weight had been lifted from him. "I apologize if I scared you," he said, searching my face. "I wanted to wait until after you'd eaten, but . . ." He looked away with a frown, then bent to retrieve the thermos cap.

"I wasn't scared," I quickly assured him, as something like guilt twisted his mouth. In fact, being afraid hadn't even crossed my mind. "But I didn't expect this strong of a reaction from either of us. I thought it would go away, now that I'm not in heat."

Well, that wasn't embarrassing to admit or anything.

Raising his eyes to mine, he shocked me by saying, "I've always hungered for your blood. The additional pheromones only enhanced that hunger. As for today, I went too long without feeding. My control was weakened."

I gulped, unsure how I felt about that admission. "And . . . the other thing?"

"What other thing?"

Crap, he was making me *say* it. "The earlier thing in the living room," I blurted, already regretting my candor. "And the . . . the—"

"The thing on the counter?" he finished for me, the color of his eyes warming to a burgundy red. At my affirming nod, he stepped toward me. "It's called sexual attraction. Lust. I'm sure you've experienced that before."

I quickly stepped back, stammering, "N-not like this, no. This is . . ."

"Intense? Consuming?" he offered, pursuing me across the kitchen. "Confusing? Distracting? *Infuriating?*"

I nodded mutely, relieved that I wasn't the only one feeling these things.

He backed me against the counter and leaned forward, but only to set the thermos down. Straightening, he stepped away again and jerked both hands through his hair. "It's why we're here right now," he said, clearly agitated. "Time and distance have only exasperated the problem. But being near you again is almost more painful. This shouldn't have happened. I can't—"

He glanced away with a muttered curse. "Eat, McKenna," he said after a moment. "I need some fresh air but will stay nearby. You'll be safe."

Then he did what he did best and vanished.

Releasing a frustrated sigh, I ignored the mess Lochlan made of the kitchen and hopped onto the counter again to eat my strawberries and cheesecake. While I demolished the food like a starved animal, I stewed over his words.

Attraction? Lust? Yes, I definitely felt those things for him. Hearing *him* admit that thrilled me. And also unsettled me. Because attraction and lust sounded so shallow. What I felt for him went deeper than that.

An hour ago, I'd practically felt dead inside. But the moment I'd seen him again, *touched* him, I'd come alive. Every part of me had sprung awake, bursting with fullness, with *rightness*. I didn't crave his touch simply for the carnal pleasure of it.

His touch brought me to life.

Somewhere along the way, the attraction had grown into attachment. I longed to be near him, to hear his voice, to banter with him, even when he annoyingly disappeared mid-conversation. I longed to know his thoughts, to learn his life story. I especially longed to see him smile again.

Those were the feelings he'd failed to articulate.

Attraction? Lust? Our connection was so much more than that.

But what if he didn't feel the same way? What if this thing between us was merely a case of lust for him?

To think that he only desired my body and not the rest of me soured my stomach. I set aside the remains of my cheesecake and slid off the counter, suddenly needing some fresh air of my own. I peeked inside my school bag, hoping to find some gloves before remembering they were in my coat pocket. My sketchpad was in there though, so I pulled it out.

Escaping into a new drawing was just what I needed to distract my mind. Lochlan probably wasn't coming back for a while anyway. That boy could brood. Although, calling a century-and-a-half-year-old immortal vampire a *boy* sounded ridiculous.

Before my brain could dwell too long on that impossibility, I picked up the white parka I'd discarded in the foyer and left the cabin. The cold air immediately helped clear my head, yet I found myself following Lochlan's shoeprints in the snow. His car was nowhere to be seen, and I wondered why he and Kade chose to park so far down the hill. Probably to keep me from hijacking their vehicles.

After several minutes of walking—more like skidding—down the slope, I paused as the prints forked in opposite directions. One pair must have been Kade's. The other veered right toward the lake, so I took that route, deciding to sit on the dock again. My butt would undoubtedly freeze, but I had a sudden itch to draw the lake with pines encircling it and majestic mountains poking their heads overtop.

I rounded the bend leading down to the water and stopped dead in my tracks. Because there, standing at the edge of the dock, was a half-naked Lochlan. Despite the near-freezing temperature, he'd removed his shirt and shoes. I didn't know if he'd heard my approach with his heightened vampire senses, but he continued to stare out at the lake, so I let myself stare at him.

Even from several yards away, I could see the powerful line of his broad shoulders, the deep groove of his spine, and the dimples just above the waistband of his pants. My mouth dried at the sight of such symmetrical perfection. The dark twisty vines tattooed on his arms were now on full display, curling up both muscular biceps to disappear over his shoulders.

I wanted to draw him like this. I'd never wanted to draw anything so badly in my life.

When time slowly ticked by and he hadn't moved, I couldn't resist the itch any longer. I spotted a boulder beside me and tiptoed to it, careful not to make a sound as I dusted the snow off and perched on top. Not long after, my butt and fingers went numb from the cold, but I didn't move or pull out my gloves. Capturing this breathtaking sight, so unguarded, so *beautiful*, was all I could think about.

As the sun slowly dipped toward the mountain peaks, my pencil glided across the paper, transforming a blank canvas into the regal strength and sensual power that was Lochlan. I didn't know how much time had passed, but as I finished shading in the shadows on his back, he moved.

I tensed, ready to retreat the second he turned. But he didn't.

His arms flexed while he fiddled with something at his waist. Then the unthinkable happened. He removed his pants. I almost swallowed my tongue, too shocked to look away or even blink. I'd never seen a naked man before, and certainly had never *spied* on one while they undressed. Fates, I was a peeping tom!

But I couldn't stop staring, utterly transfixed by how perfect he was. And I was only glimpsing his firm, perfectly-rounded backside. I couldn't imagine how the front must—

266

He suddenly dove into the lake.

I gasped and scrambled to my feet, not caring if he saw me. What was he *thinking?* Panic shot through me and I charged toward the water, slipping and sliding the whole way. The panic only grew the closer I got. I hadn't seen him surface yet. The lake was nearly cold enough to freeze over. If he didn't emerge soon, he could die of hypothermia.

I reached the dock and ran to the very end, almost skidding off the side and into the water in my haste. I dropped to my knees and peered into the blackened depths. When I couldn't find him, my heart twisted painfully. "Lochlan!" I frantically screamed, dropping my sketchpad so I could claw at the buttons of my coat. I was a terrible swimmer, but I'd never forgive myself if I just sat here and let him drown.

Before I could finish yanking off the coat, though, he breached the surface near the dock in a spray of freezing droplets. I cried out in relief and reached for him, then quickly withdrew. My touch would only cause him further harm. I scrambled to pull on my gloves with trembling fingers, then reached for him again. "Take my hand."

When he didn't comply, when he continued to tread water just out of reach, I snapped, "*Now*, Lochlan. You'll freeze to death!"

His lips parted in surprise. "McKenna," he said after a beat, his tone almost gentle.

I growled, fear riding my words. "Why are you doing this? Is death really preferable to being near me?" I knew I sounded unhinged, my voice cracking with emotion, but I didn't understand. I didn't understand how he could do this to me.

A strangled sob heaved from my lungs before I could stop it. I bit down on my lower lip, but more followed. Angry and confused, I struggled to keep tears from falling.

"Turn around, McKenna. I'm coming up," Lochlan said over my hysteria, then, "You're getting an eyeful if you don't."

I managed to scoot back and avert my gaze as he rose from the water. The dock shifted under his added weight. I listened as he zipped up his pants and knelt behind me, but refused to turn around. I was too mortified at my outburst. After a moment, he pulled me back against him.

At first, I resisted, a ball of tension in his arms. But when he continued to hold me, when I felt his warm breath stir my hair, I melted into his embrace.

"Vampires can't drown or freeze to death," he said in soothing tones meant to calm me.

I swiped a gloved finger at an errant tear. "I know. I forgot." I looked up at the sky to halt the waterworks. "Sorry."

"For what? For caring? You have nothing to be sorry for. I should be the one apologizing for scaring you."

"No. For crying. I don't know what's wrong with me. I haven't cried in years."

He pulled me more firmly against him. "Nothing's wrong with you, McKenna. Tears just mean you're tired of fighting. Of staying strong. There's no shame in taking time to heal."

I sniffled, surprised at his insight. "Do you cry?"

A pause. Then, "I have."

"What, like once a hundred years ago?" I quipped, brushing away another tear.

His chest expanded against my back and he sighed quietly. "Every time I lose someone."

I stilled in his arms. Oh. "I'm sorry. That was insensitive of me."

"No need to apologize," he said, pulling his leather wristwatch from his pants pocket. "I have to go."

Alarm trickled through me. Crap, was he upset? "Is everything okay?"

"Everything's fine. I just need a moment to transform."

Transform?

Oh. *Oh.*

I worried at my bottom lip, recalling my own semi-transformation. "Does it hurt?"

"Not anymore. Not in a long time."

Before I could lose my courage, I said, "I want to see," then held my breath. Yeah, we'd just shared a vulnerable moment, but something told me I was pushing my luck with this request.

Sure enough, I felt him stiffen. "I've never let anyone watch me transition into my true form before."

Wow. Okay, this was serious, like stripping him of his virginity or something. Although, I doubted he was a virgin. I mean, come on. He was almost a hundred and fifty.

Still, I wasn't giving up that easily. I turned in his arms to face him, letting him see my utter sincerity. "Please share this part of you with me. I won't be afraid."

His lips thinned. "I saw how you reacted to my face when I had you against the wall the night I lost control."

"What? That's because you were about to *bite* me. Lochlan, please." Although my fingers trembled, I reached up and placed my gloved hand on his cheek. His own hand shot up to grasp mine, but he didn't remove it.

A spark of vulnerability flickered in his eyes, so raw and open that my heart turned over for him. Overwhelmed, I dropped my gaze to his sculpted chest. But it was what I found there that wholly captured my attention.

An intricate tattoo of a rose stretched across his heart.

Not freshly-bloomed, but one that wept. Its head was drooped, its wilted petals curling at the ends. Several had broken off and were scattered across his right pectoral as if blown away by the wind.

The thorny vines twining up his arms met in the middle of his chest, viciously twisting around the rose as if to choke the very life out of it.

"Beautiful," I breathed. "Everything about you is beautiful."

Caught up in the moment, I lifted my other gloved hand and touched the rose. Lochlan's whole body jerked, as if I'd plunged a dagger into his heart. Startled, I yanked both my hands away. "I'm so sorry. Did I hurt you?"

Crap. Was there a hole in my glove? They were brand new!

"No," he said quickly, but I wasn't convinced, not when he was struggling to *breathe.* "You didn't hurt me," he continued when I wrung my hands. "Your touch was simply . . . unexpected."

Still not convinced, I stood and stepped away. "I-I should leave." Besides, his transformation was obviously a personal matter for him. I had no right to—

"You can stay," he said, standing as well.

My heart knocked against my ribs at those three words. His willingness to let me watch rendered me speechless. Something between us had shifted once again. The newness scared and excited me, quickening my pulse. I merely nodded, shuffling back a few steps to give him space. Moments later, it happened.

The change began at his fingertips, lengthening his nails to sharp black claws. A chill shivered up my spine at the sight, but I didn't move. His skin darkened next, the color bleeding from olive to inky black. The darkness raced up his arms and torso, swallowing the tattoo. His face was the last to fall into shadow, to change into something otherworldly. Beastly, even. His skin and hair became the same hue, and his eyes . . .

A blazing red erupted from their depths, completing the transformation.

When it was finished, I waited for the swirling shadows to envelop him. To hide the wicked fangs I knew were lurking behind his lips. But they never came.

He stepped toward me, and I immediately felt the cold presence of his shadow self. When I stayed where I was, tipping my head back as he drew closer, he said, "This doesn't strike fear into your heart?"

As I caught the barest peek of fang, a tremor shook me. Not from fear, but something else entirely. With his dark, imposing form towering over me, I should be running. I should be terrified and screaming. But all I did was stare at him and say, "I don't know. Should it?"

Silence fell, the only sound an occasional bird call.

Then he blinked and slowly shook his head. "In all my years, I've never met anyone like you, McKenna Belmont. I didn't think it possible for someone like you to exist."

Any reply I would have had faded as his expression transformed to one of bewildered awe. Witnessing a being so fierce and powerful look at me that way snatched the air from my lungs.

He turned then, allowing me a moment to catch my breath. He bent to pick up his discarded clothing, but that wasn't all, I realized with a start. That wasn't freaking all.

He had my *sketchpad* in his clawed grip.

I lurched forward and swiped for it, but he easily dodged the attempt. "Lochlan, don't," I warned as he flipped it open. He froze, and I knew without a doubt which drawing he'd found. My face flamed, but I made another attempt and he let me snatch the sketchpad away this time. I tucked the newest drawing of him close to my chest and dropped my gaze.

"It's a good likeness," he said after a painful moment of silence. When I didn't respond, he added, "You have a lot of talent, McKenna. You should be proud of your work."

I peeked at his face, barely able to pick out his features in the growing darkness. At the soft expression there, butterflies erupted in my stomach. "Thanks."

Without warning, he blurred forward and swept me off my feet. His arms tightened around me as I gaped up at him, wholly unprepared when he said, "I'll pose for you whenever you'd like. But next time, just ask. It took me a while to figure out what you were doing back there."

My gasp of utter mortification was lost to the wind as he sped us up the mountain.

CHAPTER 26

The sexual tension between us slowly returned with the sun's departure. Our earlier vulnerability and light banter gave way to thick silence and hooded looks.

Now that I knew Lochlan lusted after me, even *without* the werewolf pheromones, distracting myself with English homework was fruitless. It didn't help that he was *torturing* me by leaning against the fireplace, jotting notes in a black journal. The kitchen was still a wreck, so I'd opted for the living room couch. I should have gone upstairs to my room, but neither of us seemed capable of leaving each other's presence.

Hours later, he finally made the first move, wordlessly heading upstairs to take a shower—probably a cold one.

While I waited for the bathroom to free up, I debated over a most vexing dilemma. Wear a t-shirt to bed that smelled of Lochlan, or subject myself to the scrap of satin I'd found in my overnight bag. I didn't know whether to blame Isla or Kade for packing my sleep attire, but I had a bone to pick with them when I got my phone back.

Seriously though. A short red *nightie?*

Grumbling, I slipped it over my head and peeked at my reflection in the new dresser mirror. It was worse than I thought, barely covering my black underwear and showing cleavage for miles. "Curse you, Isla and Kade."

I eyed the dresser, once again tempted to wear one of Lochlan's t-shirts. I firmly shook my head and turned away. My hormones were already raging. No need to make things worse by enveloping myself in his scent.

Hearing the bathroom door open, I gathered my toiletries and paused to listen. When a second door down the hall clicked shut, I scampered across the hallway to brush my teeth and wash my face. Minutes later, I poked my head into the hall. All clear. I dashed across and slipped inside my bedroom, breathing a sigh of relief that he hadn't seen me.

I tucked the toiletries back in my bag and promptly rammed my hip against the bed's footboard. I hissed quietly, but that's all it took. The door banged open, and Lochlan's tall form filled the frame. I froze with one hand pressed to the insta-bruise on my hip, mouth opening to chew him out for barging in.

The words caught in my throat when, for the second time today, I saw shock stamped across his face. His eyes slid down my body, taking in every inch of exposed skin.

I felt his gaze like a caress, slowly trailing up my legs to my inner thighs where it stopped. My body flushed in response, growing embarrassingly wet. His nostrils flared as he no doubt scented my arousal. *Freaking fates.* I squeezed my thighs together against the growing ache.

I wanted him, and I knew he wanted me too. With a single word, I knew he'd have me on that bed, finding ways to pleasure me that didn't involve skin contact. My knees weakened just thinking about it, but I wouldn't go there again. Not if this was only lust for him.

So when he swallowed and roughly said, "You okay?" I straightened my shoulders and hardened my resolve.

"No, I'm not," I replied tightly. "This isn't okay."

His brow furrowed. "You haven't been sleeping," he said, and slowly stepped into the room. "You're exhausted. I can help you."

I can help you.

My eyes rounded when I recalled the last time he'd said that. I scrambled over the bed in record time, clumsily landing on the other side. "Oh, no you don't!" I said forcefully, swiping hair out of my face. "Just . . . just stay where you are."

He frowned, clearly confused.

A guy like him probably isn't used to being rejected, I reminded myself. *And who in their right mind would? He's panty-melting hot!*

Muttering a curse, I dug my nails into my palms.

"What's wrong?" he said, taking another step.

"No!" I yelled, pointing at him. "Stop right there."

His brows dipped low, partially shadowing his red eyes. "What happened?"

I barked a laugh and threw my hands in the air. "Where do I start? Vampires and werewolves exist and I'm a freaking witch. I'm afraid to touch people now and a bunch of supernaturals want me dead. But that isn't what's bothering me, Lochlan. It's *you*. For so long, I've craved connection. Like the deep, meaningful kind that is all-consuming. The kind you can feel in your very soul.

"Then you admit you're attracted to me. Even *lust* after me. But you know what? I'm. Not. Okay. With. That. Why? Because I don't just want a physical connection with you. No matter how much my body wants it, I need more. But I'm worried that you don't. I'm worried that all you want from me is sex, and I'm *not* okay with that."

Shocked that I'd revealed so much, I crossed my arms and hugged myself tightly, feeling vulnerable. I almost ordered Lochlan to leave so I could dive under the bed covers and never emerge. But I held my ground, knowing that I'd done the right thing by standing up for myself.

He hadn't moved a muscle while I spoke, his face utterly impassive. I fought to hold still, to lock my jaw and accept however he reacted. If he walked out that door, I wouldn't go after him. If he laughed at my words, I'd know he wasn't good enough for me. I prepared myself for the worst, but wasn't prepared in the least for his response.

"It's not merely lust for me," he said, conviction strong in his voice. "You're not just a job, and death will never be preferable to being near you. What I feel for you is so much more than physical attraction. We have an undeniable connection. But . . ."

He raked a hand through his hair, his movements suddenly jerky and agitated. "An unexpected bond has formed between us. Such a thing rarely happens in the supernatural world, especially between a vampire and witch. On top of that, you're a Syphon. This bond is impossible, yet our bodies want nothing more than to complete it."

Joy at his confession soared through me, then trepidation as his last words sank in. "By *complete it*," I began, watching his face closely, "do you mean . . . have sex?"

He dipped his head in an affirming nod.

My legs failed to hold me up and I sat down on the bed. Holy fates. So it wasn't *us* that wanted to have sex, but our bodies? What did that even mean? I chewed on my lip, trying to fully grasp this new revelation. "What happens if we don't complete the bond?"

"Probably go through more of what we've been experiencing, only worsening with time. I had hoped time apart would sever the bond naturally, but apparently a formal rejection is required from one or both of us."

Hoped.

He had *hoped* the bond would be severed?

At the realization, an ugly ball of hurt and anger burrowed into my chest. "So that's why you stayed away this month? To *sever* this bond between us without even telling me? Why don't you just *reject* me while you're at it."

I jumped up, every inch of me shaking with rage. I didn't even understand what this bond was. I didn't even know why I was reacting so strongly. But the mere thought of it being stripped away made me want to tear apart this room. And it hurt. It hurt so much knowing Lochlan didn't want it.

At my words, anger sparked in his eyes as well. "It's not that simple. But yes, I stayed away in hopes that our bond would lessen. I told you that night in the woods behind your house, McKenna. I care for you, I won't deny it, but I made a vow over a century ago that I never intend to break."

"*What* vow?" I said even louder. When he refused to answer, I lost all control, shouting, "So help me, Lochlan, tell me or I'll—"

"That I would never tie myself to a witch ever again," he roared, his shadows lashing out to whip around him. Startled, I flinched back. "That I would never let my guard down or get close enough for one to hurt me. That I would never trust one. Or care about one."

His face fell. The anger crumbled and the shadows withdrew. "Then I found you. And I can't get you out of my head. You're *everywhere*, and I can't let you be. It's killing me."

When his voice broke, a piece of my heart broke too. Sorrow filled me, and I whispered, "You should have just killed me when we first met. If you hate witches so much, why torture yourself by being around me? Just reject me and free yourself from this pain our connection brings."

His face twisted in agony. He swiped a hand over his mouth and the pain vanished, safely locked behind a mask of indifference. "I took something from you," he said, and slid a hand into his pants pocket. When he pulled out a folded paper tucked inside a plastic bag, I went numb inside. He held it out to me, and I barely had the strength to accept it.

"I don't regret taking it," he continued as I retreated a step, not knowing whether to open it now or wait. "I wanted to do things differently this time. I was hoping you'd never have to be burdened by the full story, but my plan failed. It'll be safer if you know so you can better prepare for what lies ahead."

Dread ate at my stomach. The way he spoke gave me anything but comfort. And he wouldn't look me in the eye. Guilt poured off him in waves. "And what lies ahead?" I asked quietly, clutching the paper to my chest like a lifeline.

"Open it," he replied, jerking his chin toward the paper.

Fear tied my insides into knots. I knew that fear wouldn't stop me though. I had been searching for answers my entire life. Now that I had them grasped in my hand, nothing would stop me from discovering the truth.

I flicked a glance at Lochlan—at the sadness weighing down his proud shoulders—and hesitated.

You will hate me, he had said. *You won't want anything to do with me.*

Even though my heart was currently bruised, I didn't hate him. But what if knowing the full truth destroyed the last of what remained between us?

I inhaled a fortifying breath and focused on what I needed to do. Carefully removing the paper with trembling fingers, I opened it. But before I could start reading, Lochlan spoke again, reciting the whole thing from memory:

"Three dark princes, monsters were they.

Cursed in their true forms, they must pay.
Bound to the night, along with their kingdom.
'Til the hundredth year, or a cure can free them.
Beyond that time, the curse remains.
But night becomes day, a monster to stay.
Only one can free all, before it's too late.
An elusive maiden, with a touch that slays.
Drawn to her blood, the three must choose.
As one follows another, but never two.
Together or divided, they must agree.
A threat, she is, but also the key.
A sacrifice must be made, to end this curse.
A choice given, the hardest to learn.
Without this choice, doomed their kingdom be.
And in shadow it falls, for an eternity."

When he finished, all I could do was stare, thoroughly confused. "What does this have to do with me?"

His expression was grim, his gaze resolute as he said, "Everything. Without you, the entire vampire species will be exposed for what they truly are. Without you, the world will fall into chaos."

CHAPTER 27

I was in shock.

Yup, shock explained why I wasn't freaking out right now.

"Is that why you transform every night?" I asked Lochlan, who remained rooted in place at the room's center. "Is it part of this curse or whatever?"

"McKenna," he called softly when I made another lap around him. I was still in a barely-there nightie, but whatever. He'd seen me in less.

"And how many years have passed since this curse began? Sounds like an important detail," I mumbled mostly to myself, consulting the paper. I hadn't given the words much thought the first time I'd read them, but hearing Lochlan recite the story and seeing the whole thing together made it seem so *real*.

"Wait, who are these three princes, and what did they do to deserve this curse?" I was guessing they must have done something *really* bad.

"You need to properly deal with this," Lochlan said, tracking my progress with his eyes.

"Huh?"

"Run. Shout. Scream. Hate me for telling you. You need to process your emotions."

I paused to glance up at him. "Despite my recent actions, I'm not much of a runner or screamer. And why should I hate you? I mean, I'm shocked—and upset about our bond thing—but this is bigger than us."

Frustration flashed in his eyes. "You should hate me because I dragged you into this. Because you're part of a century-long curse. Because out of the vampires who need your help, half of them want you dead. And if the curse isn't broken in time, we'll be stuck in our true forms forever, even during the day. How do you think humans will handle that?"

My mouth rounded in a silent O.

"Yes, oh."

I launched into motion again, gesturing with my hands. "But we can figure this out. With your protection, I'm sure I can—"

"It's my duty to track down the next Syphon," he interrupted sharply. "I recite the prophecy to her if she's unaware of it, then deliver her to King Ambrose and his council. I have to bring you in, McKenna. I've already broken several rules by delaying the inevitable."

I slammed to a halt, nearly tipping over. If he was trying to shock me, he'd succeeded.

Lochlan huffed a bitter laugh at my stunned expression. "Exactly. And now you know. Now you know what my purpose here is and why I got close to you. Go ahead and hate me. They always do."

I swayed as my world came crashing down. I couldn't breathe. I couldn't think. This didn't . . . this didn't make *sense*. My throat and chest tightened painfully. "They?" I whispered.

A muscle jumped in his jaw and he looked away. "The previous Syphons. '*As one follows another, but never two.*' For nearly a century, there has always been one living Syphon, but never two at once. When she dies, a new one is born. Thus the cycle repeats itself—until the curse is broken or the one hundred years are up."

I clutched at my stomach. "W-was my mother a—"

"No," he quickly interjected, a tortured look on his face. "She wasn't a Syphon. The gene is rare and often skips several generations. It's why I've been on the move for nearly a century. Finding a Syphon is harder than locating a needle in a haystack. I've only found six in the last hundred years, including you."

A tear slipped down my cheek and I didn't bother wiping it away. The truth stung more than I expected. I'd known it was Lochlan's job to find me, but knowing there had been others made me feel like a cheap game piece. Something that could be used and discarded if it didn't measure up.

I'd foolishly thought Lochlan had searched for me alone. I'd foolishly thought he'd only protected and comforted *me*. And the things he made me feel? He had no doubt made others feel as well.

I wasn't special. I wasn't one of a kind.

Not to him.

Our time together was expiring. I was a package to be delivered to a vampire king who hated witches. Who *killed* them. I was a means to an end, nothing more.

I had only ever wanted the truth. My whole life, I had wished for nothing else. And now I knew one thing without a shadow of a doubt.

The truth *sucked.*

"Do you want to reject me and our bond?" Lochlan said when the silence thickened. "You should. I wouldn't blame you." His jaw hardened, eyes like molten ice as he waited for my reply.

I shivered. It wasn't his frigid expression that chilled me to the bone, but knowing that he wanted me to sever our bond—the one and only special connection we had.

Too much. It was too freaking much.

"I, um." My voice cracked. I tried again, the words barely intelligible. "I'm really tired. I just . . . I need a little time to think. Please."

Unable to face him, I lowered my gaze. The only sign that he'd heard my words was to ball his hands into fists. He squeezed them so hard that his claws punctured his skin. I winced as blood trickled over his knuckles and fell to the floor.

I kept my eyes averted, unable to bear seeing the coldness in his. Or worse—nothing at all. I couldn't bear seeing the truth anymore, that everything between us had been a lie.

So I turned and crawled into bed, curling up into a tight ball beneath the covers. I didn't hear him leave, but when the light flicked off, I knew I was alone.

Despite how exhausted I was, despite how numb with shock and sadness, I tossed and turned like I had for the past four weeks. Just when I was about to scream in utter frustration, I felt something warm and soft drop onto the mattress near my fingers. I jerked my eyes open to find him by the door, cloaked in shadow once more.

"That should help you sleep," he said quietly, then slowly backed away.

I ached to call him back, to beg him to lay beside me. To *pretend* that nothing between us had changed. But I didn't. I couldn't. Everything had changed, and there was no avoiding it. I let him go, ignoring my body as it whimpered miserably.

My fingers tangled in the fabric he'd left behind. I brought it to my face, breathing deeply. His shirt. Still warm from his body heat and strong with his scent. Tears pricked my eyes and I let them fall, cradling the shirt against the hole slowly expanding inside my chest.

By morning, I felt nothing but a soul-deep numbness.

Any desire to hate Lochlan for his part in this mess or run from what awaited me was missing. Hating and running wouldn't solve anything anyway. Lochlan still had a job to do, and despite the unbearable tension between us, I knew he wouldn't let me go. His duty was to hunt. He'd had a century to hone his skills. There was no way I could outrun him.

We silently rode toward Isla's house where my Honda was parked. I hadn't failed to notice the dark circles under his eyes or the rigidness of his shoulders. A wall had erected between us, one that kept us from comforting each other. Still, I itched to dispel the silence, if only to hear his voice.

But what could I say?

So, when are you taking me to the vampire king? How long should I pack for? How am I going to break this curse exactly? If I fail, will they kill me? Was this bond between us ever real, or was it merely an attempt to trap me so I wouldn't run away?

Yeah. I couldn't say any of those things, especially the last one. I wasn't ready for the truth. Maybe I'd never be ready for the truth ever again.

When we arrived at Isla's, the sky was a sea of turbulent gray, a perfect match to my mood. Snow wasn't far off, and I wanted nothing more than to hurry home so I could shut myself in my room for the entire rest of the weekend.

I opened the car door the minute Lochlan pulled into Isla's driveway. Before I could escape the silence though, I heard him say, "McKenna." I squeezed the handle and waited, still unable to face him. He sighed wearily, and my chest throbbed at the sound. "We'll talk more about this soon," he said, his voice dull and hollow. "I won't stay away long. Your suffering will be minimal this time."

I wanted to cry. And scream. He hadn't pressured me to reject the bond, but I knew he wanted me to be the one to do it. Was this his way of being chivalrous? Well, it *sucked*. And until I had the guts to do it, we were stuck with more days like the last four tortuous weeks we'd spent apart.

With a small nod, I slipped from his Lexus and walked to my car. Isla's white Mini wasn't in the driveway, so I assumed she was out. Probably grabbing coffee at Mama Jo's, something I desperately needed right now. My keys and cell phone were on the driver's seat, so I didn't bother checking to see if she was at home. I wasn't ready to talk about everything that had happened anyway.

The moment Lochlan pulled out of the driveaway and drove from sight, the hole beneath my sternum yawned wide. I shoved down a sob, but tears blurred my vision as I navigated the roads.

Aunt Tess was vacuuming the living room when I got home. I slipped past while her back was turned and wearily climbed the stairs to my room. The thought of taking a long nap sounded appealing, but I probably wouldn't sleep much. I sat on my bed and pulled out Lochlan's shirt, not the least bit sorry that I'd stolen it.

After everything he had done, I deserved this one small comfort.

Burying my nose in the fabric, I breathed him in and immediately felt less hollow. I curled up on the bed and closed my eyes, pretending that the scent surrounding me meant he was in the room, watching me drift to sleep . . .

Ring, ring, ring.

Jerking awake, I flailed around on the bed, trying to silence my pesky phone. I found it in my jeans pocket and pulled it out. Isla's name flashed across the screen and I hesitated, wondering if I was ready to answer her questions. Before the call could go to voicemail, I picked up with a groggy hello.

"Kenna? Kenna, is that you?"

The panic in her voice jump-started my brain and I quickly sat up. "Isla, what's wrong?"

"Kenna, a vampire is stalking me. I'm in the girl's restroom at Mama Jo's. Can you please come get me? I'm sure if there's two of us, he'll go away."

"*What?*" I hissed. Even as I inwardly wrestled with the news, I scrambled out of bed and dashed for the door. "Hold on, Isla, I'm coming. How do you know he's a vampire?"

"H-he has fangs. I saw them. *Hurry*, Kenna. I don't know what he wants."

Icy tendrils of fear wrapped around my heart. There were only two things he could want: to drink her blood or use her to get to *me*. Both options would have terrible outcomes if I didn't get help. Sure, I could try to touch him, but vampires had fast reflexes. What if I missed? Isla could very well pay the price if I screwed up.

I was pounding down the stairs when my phone dinged, announcing an incoming call. The most shocking sight greeted me when I checked to see who it was.

Lochlan.

He *never* called.

For a spite-filled moment, I considered ignoring him and handling the vampire problem alone. Grimacing, I pushed aside my wounded pride and did the smart thing. Isla's life was at stake here.

"Isla, I'm on my way. Call if anything changes." I almost told her to call her dad, but the situation might not be that serious. No need to oust supernaturals unless there was no other choice. Then again, maybe the police could protect me from them. Who was I kidding? They'd lock me up in a mental institution if I told them everything I knew.

I hit the first floor at a run, breezing past a startled Aunt Tess in the kitchen. Crap! I'd have to explain away my hasty arrival and departure to her later. I accepted the incoming call. Before I could utter a word though, Lochlan's voice thundered from the other end.

"McKenna, where are you?"

Fates! I held the phone away from my ear and slowed to a fast walk. "I'm about to leave my house. Something is—"

"*Don't*," he barked. "You'll be safe inside. It's warded against vampires."

Annoyed at his tactless order, especially after the night I'd just had, I snapped, "Isla needs me. She said a vampire is—"

"It's a *trap*."

Growling, I unlocked the front door and whipped it open. "Would you stop shouting? You're hurting my ears." I slammed the door shut behind me and turned. "Also—" At the sight of the tall figure standing on the porch, I flinched back, nearly dropping my phone.

"Hello, Miss Belmont," the man said, his use of my name immediately putting me on edge. I didn't recognize him, yet a strange sense of déjà vu shivered through me all the same. He appeared to be in his early twenties, handsome in a military sort of way, with sun-kissed skin, cropped black hair, and a powerful build that suggested he worked out a lot. But there was a cruel tilt to his full lips. A malicious glint in his pale green eyes.

"McKenna, don't—"

"I'm Everett," the guy said, cutting Lochlan off. "We crossed paths on your first day of school here. You might not remember though. It was, shall we say, a *quick* introduction. But I think it's time we officially meet."

"*Everett*," Lochlan roared in my ear. "If you touch her—"

"August, fetch Miss Belmont for me," Everett spoke over Loch-

Ian's shouting, and stepped aside to allow a familiar, blond-haired brute to saunter up the stairs.

"Miss me, vixen?" August sneered, the scars running down his face puckering grotesquely.

He suddenly lunged across the porch at me. I fell back against the door and wrenched it open, stumbling through the entrance. When I tried to close the door though, he shoved it back against the wall with a bang. He grabbed my arm and I shrieked, lashing out to kick his kneecap. Cursing, he dragged me over the threshold anyway.

The moment my feet touched the porch again, Everett's arms were around me. He plucked the phone from my fingers and brought it to his ear. "I suggest you come quickly, brother. I'm quite displeased with your recent actions and might take out my anger on the girl. You know how creative my punishments can get." His hold around my waist tightened painfully, wringing a whimper from me.

Lochlan's roar abruptly cut off as Everett crushed my phone like a piece of paper.

"You really have my brother in a frenzy," Everett said, loosening his hold, but not enough for me to wiggle free. "If I didn't know any better, I'd say he has *feelings* for you, which is impossible. Still, I'm curious to find out why he's kept you to himself all this time."

He didn't give me a chance to speak, already turning toward August.

"Come here, boy."

August's eyes glazed over and he shuffled forward obediently. Securing me with one arm, Everett grabbed August by the nape of his neck.

"You've served me well but are no longer needed. Don't resist." Faster than I could blink, he jerked August toward him and violently sank his teeth into August's neck.

No, not teeth.

Fangs.

A scream lodged in my throat and I fought like a wildcat to break free, prying at the arm banded around my waist like a steel cable. With a jolt of surprise, I noticed he wore gloves. Of course he did. He was Lochlan's brother and a *vampire*. Which meant that if I touched his skin . . .

I yanked up his sleeve and bared his wrist. Grabbing it, I squeezed, willing the red, fiery glow to appear. He stiffened and loosed a warning growl. When nothing happened though, he continued feeding.

Why? Why wasn't my touch killing him? Had Lochlan lied to me about that? Had it just been another tale to control me?

Awful sucking noises filled the air, punctuated by high-pitched gurgling sounds from August. But he didn't move. He didn't freaking *move.*

I didn't know how long it took to suck someone dry of their blood, but I could hear Everett's long pulls and see August's shoulders slump. I had to do something. *Now!*

In my panic, I hadn't considered my one other advantage. A surprise Everett would never see coming. I slowly lifted my leg and reached for my boot, sliding out the silver dagger Lochlan had given me.

Without hesitation, I stabbed it into Everett's thigh as hard as I could.

The blade sunk past skin and tissue, embedding deep into his muscle. Everett bellowed and stumbled back, releasing me. But he didn't let go of August. Eyes blazing with fury, he grabbed both sides of August's head and wrenched it sideways.

A sickening *crack* rent the air, a sound I would never forget. Just like that, Everett snapped August's neck like he had my phone. The light in August's green eyes dulled and his body tipped over to thud against the porch.

Every inch of me froze in terror. Everett pinned me with an angry glare, bright red blood smeared across his lips and chin. The horrific sight sent adrenaline rushing through me, unlocking my limbs. I almost dove back inside the house. I needed to call the police, even if it would expose supernaturals. Maybe with all the noise, Aunt Tess already had.

I was just about to make my move when a vaguely familiar car chose that moment to pull up the driveaway. A guy with a baseball cap emerged from the expensive vehicle, and a wave of relief swept through me. Changing tactics, I bolted down the porch steps. "Help! Call the police!"

Catching sight of Everett, the pizza delivery guy sprinted toward me, so fast that I thought we'd collide. My boots skidded in the gravel as I tried to avoid him, but he grabbed my shoulders and whirled me toward his car. "Stay," he said with a piercing look, then shot toward the porch.

He reached Everett a second later. Instead of restraining him though, he laid a hand on his arm as if making sure he was okay. What the—? "No!" I screamed. "He's a killer! Get away!" But my warning fell on deaf ears. He peered down at the dagger in Everett's thigh, then ripped it out.

Everett grunted in pain. Shockingly, so did Pizza Guy, dropping the dagger to clutch his hand. Was the skin smoking? It was. His freaking hand was *smoking*. Every internal alarm I possessed screamed at me to run as fast as humanly possible.

But Aunt Tess was still in the house. I couldn't leave her here. While I struggled with what to do, a small whimper came from inside Pizza Guy's car. I squinted to see past the tinted windshield and spotted a pale face framed by blonde hair. I blinked until the features sharpened and I recognized who it was.

Disbelief crashed into me, then horror when I realized the danger she was in. I lurched forward, poking my head inside to gape at the person in the passenger's seat.

"Isla?"

CHAPTER 28

"Kenna, I'm so sorry." Isla's chin wobbled as she choked out the words. Tears and mascara streaked down her blanched cheeks, her hair in wild disarray.

I was missing something important here, but I didn't have time to ask questions. "Isla, get out of the car and run. I think Pizza Guy might be a vampire too."

"I-I can't," she stammered. "He told me to stay, so I have to."

"*What?*" I hissed. "Isla, we don't have time for this. We have to go *now.*" I dashed around the car and yanked open her door. "Get out!"

"I can't," she wailed, twisting her phone in her hands. "It's the thrall, Kenna. I have to do what he tells me. He made me call you to lure you outside. I'm so sorry."

"Oh, Isla," I whispered as sobs shook her shoulders. I bent and pried the phone from her grip. "I'm going to fix this. I'll—"

"Hand it over."

I whirled, yelping when I found Pizza Guy behind me. Before he could stop me, I dialed the police. When I heard someone pick up, I blurted, "There's two men at my house trying to kill me. My address is—"

He yanked the phone away and crushed it the same way Everett had. "Tut tut, my pet. No need for that," he crooned, dropping the destroyed electronic. "We'll get this sorted out in a minute when my brother arrives."

At my bewildered look, he sighed in mock exasperation. "He didn't tell you about me? I'm offended."

Stalling for time while I tried to come up with an escape plan, I said, "What did you do to Isla?"

His amber eyes lit with delight, and he licked his bottom lip seductively. "Oh, you've got fire. I like playing with fire. And don't you worry about your little friend. I take much better care of my servants than Everett does."

I shifted, blocking his view of Isla. "Servant? She's *not* your servant."

He threw me a devilish smirk and crossed his arms. "On the contrary, fiery one. A human's sole purpose is to service a vampire's needs. We're at the top of the food chain, and humans are simply . . . food." When he chuckled at the sickening joke, anger shot through me.

"Well, I happen to know your weaknesses. And when my friends get here, they'll help me remove your head and burn it to ash. Or maybe I won't wait and just do *this*." I lunged forward, taking him by surprise. His eyes rounded as my outstretched fingers reached for his bare hand. Arms plucked me up midair before I could make contact, banding around my middle.

"Stab me again and I'll snap your little neck," Everett's deep baritone rumbled through my back. He drove home the threat by squeezing me tightly, nearly crushing my ribs. Tears sprung to my eyes as all oxygen was forced from me in a painful rush.

The deafening sound of squealing tires and exploding gravel suddenly blasted through my ear canals.

"Let the fun begin," Pizza Guy hummed.

One second, I was being pulverized by a bear hug, and the next, thrown clear of the action. I hit a thin patch of snow and tumbled a few feet, the wind completely knocked out of me. I rolled over just in time to see Everett's body soar through the air and smash into my Honda's rear windshield.

I struggled to sit up, then froze when I saw who had thrown Everett like a ragdoll. Lochlan was storming down the driveway, a vengeful god with fury slashed across his face. Even in midday, shadows twisted angrily around him. His eyes blazed red, fixed on the man climbing off my ruined car. I must have moved or made a sound, because his attention suddenly snapped to me.

My breath hitched as I bore the weight of his wrath. Although not meant for me, I wrestled with the need to cower before him.

"Kade, get the girls out of here," he said, his voice barely containing the inferno raging within.

"Don't go anywhere near my car, *Feltore*," Pizza Guy drawled, sliding in front of the passenger door as Kade approached.

"Loch, you've disregarded the rules long enough," Everett called, lightly dropping to his feet as if he hadn't just plowed through glass. "Troy and I are done waiting. We've come for what is rightfully ours as well."

Something flickered in Lochlan's eyes, something so foreign that it took me a moment to place. But when I did, my heart thundered frantically.

Fear.

Lochlan D'angelo was afraid.

His anger quickly drained away, his eyes bleeding to black. The fear vanished next, replaced with a stone wall of indifference. He turned to Everett. "Listen to me. I—"

"No, I'm done playing games with you," Everett interrupted, slashing a hand through the air. "I gave you a chance to fess up *weeks* ago. Did you really think I'd buy that lame story about setting up a trap for the Syphon in her hometown? I know you too well. It's why I followed you here and used a human to force your hand. Now let's go before any more damage is done."

Lochlan's hands slowly curled into fists, and he shook his head. "You're not taking her anywhere."

Everett's head jerked back in surprise, but it was Pizza Guy—Troy—who said, "What's with the possessiveness, Loch? She's a *Syphon.* Just tie her hands together and stuff her in the trunk so we can call it a day. Time's running out, a fact you seem to have forgotten." He headed toward me then, as if planning to stuff me in the trunk himself.

"Troy," Lochlan said, the word so deathly soft that goosebumps erupted over my flesh. "Stand. Down."

"No, Loch," Everett replied, a muscle feathering in his clenched jaw. "*You* stand down."

There was a single moment of frozen time, as if the world held its breath to watch what happened next. Then . . .

Chaos.

Everett and Lochlan rushed each other, like two trains barrelling down the same track. Kade zipped toward Troy and tackled him to the ground. I allowed myself a second to gape at the utter brutality playing out before me, then scrambled toward Troy's car.

Isla was still glued to her seat, so I didn't bother with words this time. Crawling over her, I unbuckled her seat belt and grabbed her hand. Then pulled with every last ounce of fear, confusion, and desperation coursing through my veins. With a yelp, she tumbled out of the vehicle and hit the ground. Not giving her time to recover, I hooked my arms beneath hers and bodily dragged her toward the house.

I cringed as glass shattered and metal shrieked behind us, like a hurricane was ripping through the front yard. I wanted to check that Lochlan and Kade were okay, but didn't dare. If I saw one or both of them injured, I might not stay focused on saving Isla.

When we made it to the stairs, I struggled to pull up her dead-weight. As we hit the top, August's glassy stare greeted us. Isla screamed, so shrilly that the noise behind us ceased. Every hair on my body stood on end. I didn't have to look to know that four pairs of eyes were now boring into the back of my head.

With a sinking feeling, I knew we weren't both going to make it. The front door was feet away, but it might as well have been a mile. Still, *one* of us could make it inside. And there wasn't a doubt in my mind who it should be. With one last heave, I shoved Isla across the porch.

Her body didn't soar like Everett's had, but it stumbled forward just far enough to land in a heap at the door's threshold. Someone grabbed a chunk of my hair and yanked a second later. As I fell backward down the stairs, Lochlan's bellowing roar cleaved the air.

But he was too far away to catch me.

I went down, down, down, striking the frozen ground so hard that stars splintered my vision. Before I could drag in a breath, a pair of unforgiving arms hauled me upright. They swung me around to face the yard and the world spun dangerously. Lochlan's tall form swam in and out of focus, close yet so far away. He moved closer, then stopped dead as a gloved hand wrapped around my throat.

"Don't make me do it, Loch," Everett said, his voice loud in my ringing ears. "You know I will."

I tried to swallow, but his hold was too tight. Panic filled me and I fought to clear my vision. When it did, Lochlan's expression was the first thing I saw. The fear had returned, and he wasn't hiding it this time.

"Let her go," he said quietly, his eyes locked on mine. *It's okay,* they seemed to say. *I will protect you.*

I wanted to believe him, I really did. But fates, he should have told me. He should have told me everything.

Everett released an irritated sigh. "This is for your own good. You'll thank me later." Without warning, his fingers bit into my throat, stealing the last of my air. I choked and grabbed onto his arm.

I could have died then. I should have.

I knew how fast Everett could snap a neck. Lochlan couldn't reach me in time, even with his vampire speed.

But then something happened.

Lochlan bellowed, "Kill her and you kill me!"

And Everett hesitated. Moments later, his grip loosened and fell away entirely.

Then . . . he let me go.

Hope surged through me and I stepped toward Lochlan.

Only to hear several explosive pops. Like gunshots.

Lochlan's body jerked violently.

"No!" Everett shouted, then grunted, falling against me. His deadweight bowled me over, flattening me to the ground.

A mixture of snow and mud soaked my shirt and filled my nose. I twisted my head sideways to gasp for air. Panting, I clawed to escape, desperation giving me the strength to wriggle out from beneath him. He didn't stop me as I staggered upright and frantically searched for Lochlan.

My hearing was muffled, my brain struggling to understand what had happened. When I found Lochlan in the same spot though, standing stiffly and staring sightlessly, everything else disappeared.

"Lochlan." I stumbled toward him, weak with relief that he was okay. We were both okay. Then he swayed. Gasping, I rushed to stop him from falling. I floundered under his weight, clutching at his back for balance. He grunted in pain and alarm spiked through me. "Lochlan, what—?"

"Silver . . . bullets."

I didn't understand. His words didn't make sense.

Then I felt it. The warmth. The stickiness.

"I'm sorry," he said, and something about the way he did drove fear through my heart. "I'm sorry for everything."

I leaned around him to inspect my hand and discovered it covered in blood.

An unbearable helplessness trembled through me, and I jerked my gaze up to his—only to find his black eyes dull, nearly lifeless. "Lochlan?"

"McKenna, I—" He went limp against me and I couldn't bear his weight anymore, crying out as he slipped from my grasp and hit the ground.

I threw myself beside him and lifted the back hem of his shirt. When I saw blood, I inched it higher, gasping in dismay when I found several weeping bullet holes in his back.

More popping sounds filled the air and I reacted instinctively, covering Lochlan's inert body with mine. When there was a lull, I searched Lochlan's face for signs of life. His eyes were closed, face deathly pale. My heart twisted in agony at the sight. I reached out to check for a pulse, then yanked my fingers away.

Crap, I wasn't wearing gloves!

"Lochlan? Lochlan, look at me. *Look at me!*" I yelled. It couldn't end like this. Not after everything. "I'm not letting you freaking die, do you hear me? Wake up. *Wake up.*"

Prying my eyes away to look for Kade, I blinked, stunned to find the sheriff's car parked on the lawn. He and his deputy were hunkered down beside it, guns drawn. As one, they peeked over the side and fired shots.

Kade suddenly appeared, streaking toward them.

Just as suddenly, a force threw him backward several yards. He crashed to the ground in a shower of snow and dirt.

What the crap? Nothing had touched him. Nothing had freaking *touched* him.

I looked to the sheriff again and blinked hard at the sight of his hands. They were lit up like two mini suns.

A weak groan nearby caught my attention and I focused on Everett's prone body. The shaft of two arrows were sticking out of his back.

None of what I was seeing made sense. How was this happening?

And then I heard it. My aunt's stern voice. "Get inside the house, Kenna."

I turned my head and there she was, gripping a . . . crossbow? A quiver of arrows poked over her shoulder. What the freaking fates was going on?

"He needs help, Aunt Tess," I said, swallowing when she glanced down at Lochlan with pure hatred.

"Get away from him, McKenna," she hissed, striding toward me. "He's a vicious monster." Before I could guess her intentions, she shoved me aside and raised a silver dagger. Then brought it down, aiming for Lochlan's heart.

"No!" I screamed and threw myself at him. The blade halted mere inches from my face.

"Have you lost your mind?" Aunt Tess shouted, dropping her weapons to grab my shoulders. When I struggled to remain where I was, she jerked back with a curse.

I made a terrible mistake then. I looked away to make sure

299

Lochlan was okay. Underestimating my aunt entirely.

So when she muttered, "You're giving me no choice," I didn't for one second see the blow coming. Pain splintered through my skull and I slumped against Lochlan, my ear pressed to his heart as the world faded to black.

CHAPTER 29

". . . can't thank you enough for accepting her. Once she understands, I'm sure she'll give you no trouble. It's her ignorance that has caused her to make poor decisions lately."

"We are happy to have her, Tess. But if she proves to be a danger to the other students—"

"She's a good girl and normally very responsible," the voice that I recognized as my aunt's quickly said. "I should have trained her years ago but thought keeping her in the dark would be best, all things considered."

"Of course," an unfamiliar woman replied. "Protecting a young Syphon from the Demonic Trinity must have been a trying task, one that Thornecrest Academy fully intends to take on. Your ward will be safe here."

Aunt Tess thanked her again, and after a few moments, a door clicked shut.

As silence fell, I struggled to open my eyes. They felt glued together and sluggish to respond. I raised a hand to rub them, except that it wouldn't move. Something was firmly holding down both my wrists. I frowned and tugged at the restraints, growing more agitated with each passing second.

"It's okay, Kenna," Aunt Tess said soothingly, but I flinched when her fingers brushed my hair back. "It's just a safety precaution. I'll remove them after you answer a few questions."

"What . . . happened?" I croaked, peeling my heavy lids open. "Where . . ."

Blinding brightness greeted me, and I blinked repeatedly to clear my vision. Besides my aunt's fiery red hair, everything in the room was stark white. And something was weird about the walls, like they'd been specially reinforced.

Oh fates, did she stick me in a *mental* institution? My heart galloped in frenzied bursts.

I was five days away from turning eighteen. *Five days.* I'd spent years counting down the months, hours, *minutes* until I could be free of the constant moving and lies. All to end up *here*, wherever here was, strapped to a bed.

I twisted my wrists, but the restraints held fast. "Let me go."

"I will. But first, we need to make certain your system hasn't been compromised. Are you experiencing any unusual urges? Heightened hearing and sight? An unbearable thirst, perhaps?"

"What? No. Let me go!" I struggled in earnest, wincing at the pounding ache in my skull.

Her lips pursed, but she reached over and unbuckled the leather bindings. The moment my wrists were free, I sprung off the bed. And promptly sprawled onto the floor.

The room spun, and I clutched my pounding head. Despite the pain, I fought to remember how I got here. And why I was wearing a loose white shirt and gray sweatpants. No shoes.

"I apologize for the disorientation. The drugs will leave your system soon."

I raised my eyes to Aunt Tess with a gasp. "Drugs? Wait a second, you *hit* me. You knocked me out!"

She had the decency to look guilty, at least. "I'm sorry for that.

I couldn't think of any other way to protect you. That vampire obviously had you under his thrall. But everything's okay now. You're safe. They can't get to you here."

I gripped my hair as my mind desperately tried to keep up. "I-I don't . . . Lochlan. Is he okay? Is Lochlan okay?"

Aunt Tess frowned heavily, then rose from her chair to pace the room. "He still has a hold on you, I see. I'm sorry, Kenna. I should have intervened sooner, but Bill assured me the leech wouldn't hurt you. That with your bracelet, he couldn't control you. He must have forced his way into your mind when your first bracelet broke. I should have tested it, made sure the magic-blocking spell hadn't faded over time. If I had, maybe we wouldn't be in this mess."

I watched her agitated movements, waiting for my brain to catch up. "Who's Bill?"

"Sheriff Andrews. Isla's father." She looked at me sharply. "If not for him, you'd probably be dead right now. I wasn't prepared for all three of them to show up at the house today. What were you thinking, Kenna, lying about your whereabouts so you could spend time with a vampire? Do you know how *hard* it was for me to keep silent? To let that vial creature pollute your mind with its lies? You should have told me. I raised you to be on your guard. To be *safe*."

Speechless. I was struck speechless, incapable of understanding who this woman was. How she knew *everything*. And apparently knew even more than I did.

She stopped and blew out a long-suffering sigh. Before I could utter a word, she said, "I should have told you sooner. Maybe if I had, we could have been open with each other and avoided this disaster. There's so much you don't know about the supernatural world, Kenna. It's dangerous, and I've dedicated my life to protecting the innocent from it. To protecting *you*. Those vampires only want to use you. They—"

"Need me to break their curse? Is that what you were going to say? Or were you going to keep me in the dark about that part?" I pressed my trembling fists against the cold floor as bitterness rolled through me. "Yeah, I know about the prophecy. I found the jewelry box in the basement, along with *pictures* of my parents. Were you going to tell me about how they got there? About how we moved to Rosewood and my childhood *home* of all places? About me being a *Syphon?*"

I snorted, curling my lip in disdain. "Yeah, the vampires want to use me, but the way I see it, you're no better than they are. You've kept secrets from day one, lying to me about who I *am*. I'm not human. I'm not an innocent who needs your protection. I'm a freaking witch who can stop a *war* from starting! How could you keep that from me?"

My throat burned from yelling and I shook all over, sick and angry over what she'd done to me. She'd *ruined* my life with her secrets and lies. I should have been prepared for this impossible task that no one but me could take on.

Aunt Tess had frozen, her eyes widening with each syllable I spoke. Finally. *Finally.* The gloves were off. The cards were on the table. The words we'd hurled at each other hung heavily between us. And now that they were out, I couldn't see how we'd ever recover from them. Maybe she didn't either, because her expression hardened and she stiffly said, "Did Lochlan tell you who he is? That he's one of the Demonic Trinity, one of the princes who *deserved* this curse?"

The blood drained from my face. She huffed a mirthless laugh.

"I didn't think so. What's worse, every Syphon he's hunted down over the past century has died by his or his brother's hands. He doesn't want you to save them, Kenna. He only wants to kill you. The sooner you accept that, the sooner you can put this obsession behind you and do what you were created to do. Destroy them all."

She left then. She left me to drown in the heartbreaking words. The door of the room snapped shut, sealing me inside to face my fate.

ACKNOWLEDGMENTS

I stumbled across paranormal romance about a decade ago, not realizing what I'd been missing out on. I then devoured all the books, tv shows, and movies I could in the genre.

And now, finally, it's my turn to add to it. I had so much fun writing this story. Having the freedom to write about things that bring joy to my life and then share that joy with others is such a wonderful feeling. I really hope this series brings a little happiness to your life!

I want to thank my beautiful beta readers—Kate Anderson, Melissa McMurry, and Shiza Khan—for your enthusiasm over this project. I so appreciate your feedback!

I also want to thank the Elite Bananas for your unwavering support as I delved into a new genre. Thank you for always being willing to read my books and love on my characters!

Thank you to the bookstagram community for loving on the cover and helping with the reveal. Your kind words mean the world to me!

Thank you to God for the gift of words. Writing stories has opened up a whole new world for me, and I'm so grateful for this experience.

And last but never least, thank you to my readers, new and old. Without you, this life experience wouldn't be possible. Words can't properly express how thrilled I am that you've taken a chance on my books!

BECKY MOYNIHAN is a bestselling, award-winning author of YA/NA Fantasy & Science Fiction. Her debut series is *The Elite Trials*, a YA dystopian romance. Her newest series, *A Touch of Vampire*, is a steamy paranormal vampire romance. She's also co-written the *Genesis Crystal Saga*, an urban fantasy romance series. She lives in North Carolina with her family. To learn more about Becky's books, visit her online at beckymoynihan.com.

Printed in Great Britain
by Amazon

28424963R00178